# A Spider Sat Beside Her

K.E. Lanning

# DEDICATION

This novel is dedicated to the Earth and to my father—the hero who always believed in me.

Humans measure time by their limited lifespans, but the Earth's clock ticks at a different pace. Mother Nature may sit for eons—then dance to the tune that physics decrees . . .

# CHAPTER 1

Lowry's lungs burned as she scrambled up the steep slope across broken rocks, pulling her tired horse up behind her. Wind screaming, they cleared the ridge. She scanned the horizon. Nothing moved but the wind. Her tongue chased the rough edges of grit on her teeth, and she spat onto the ground. She took a drink, swallowing the silt left in her mouth.

The view was spectacular—a brilliant sapphire sky dotted with white puffs of drifting clouds. Sunlight spilled across golden mountain peaks against the indigo shadows of the valleys, with a mirror image of this intense beauty reflected in the crystal-clear lake below.

Global warming had melted an ice cap that had been in place for more than ten thousand years, leaving the rich earth exposed once again on the continent of Antarctica. The landscape evoked an odd mix of memories of long hikes of discovery of the land and of herself, and her escape from a mercurial, drunkard father.

A gust whipped Lowry's hair across her face, stinging her skin. She glanced at the horizon one final time, slowly mounted the mare, and turned her back along the trail. The mare quickened her pace now that they were heading home. They turned the last corner, past a row of tiny windblown evergreens, to where a thin man with auburn hair sat on a rock waiting for her.

Lowry waved happily. "Uncle Nick!" When she reached him, she halted the mare.

Petting the horse, Nick said in a soft Scottish brogue, "I thought you might want a ride to the airport. Are you packed?"

A lump came to her throat. "Everything is ready. Except my heart."

Lowry untacked the mare and let her out into the pasture. They went inside the small stone house tucked into the side of a hill. After Lowry showered, she changed clothes and packed her last items.

Nick grabbed one of her bags and glanced at her. "I see you cut your hair."

"Yeah, I decided short would be easier on the space station."

"I won't be able to pull your braids anymore."

Lowry grinned and stuck her tongue out at him.

Nick wrapped his arm around her. "With your short hair, you look like your mother when she was your age."

Lowry smiled. "She was a wonderful human being. I miss her."

They walked toward the hover, where Lowry hesitated, gazing at the rolling fields of her childhood. She bit her lip, trying to hold back her tears. Nick hugged her to him, and then they walked arm in arm to the hover and loaded her bags.

Hovering through town, Lowry stared out the window at the little school she went to as a child. She tilted her head as they turned down the road toward the airport. "What's Dad doing today?"

"He's meeting with some folks from New York." He shot a glance at her. "I'm sorry he couldn't be here to see you off."

"I would have been surprised if he had." She ran her hand across her brow. "I don't know if I'm strong enough today to deal with him anyway."

He parked, and with bags in hand, they walked into the small airport. She checked her luggage, and they strolled toward the security gate. They passed groups of miners and a few families just arriving to Antarctica. She glanced at one young mother looking tired and lost as she tried to keep her brood together. Lowry silently wished them well. It was a tough life, especially for the mothers and their children.

When they reached the security checkpoint, Nick held her by the shoulders, gazing down into her eyes. "Lowry, I've always loved you like my own daughter and admired you as a person. You're a beautiful young woman who takes the bull by the horns despite all odds and wrestles it to the floor. I know you're hurting and probably a little scared right now, but you'll do great. Just don't let the bastards get you down." He ruffled her hair. "Go get 'em, Tiger!"

The steward announced the boarding call for her flight.

Lowry squeezed her uncle's arm. "Nick, thanks for being a father to me all these years."

"My pleasure and honor." He shrugged. "I'm sorry that my brother doesn't seem to have the aptitude for fatherhood."

"Some people rise to the occasion, some don't."

*    *    *

"Hurry up, you're the last passenger!" A man in an orange jumpsuit glared at Lowry.

She stumbled out of the Roxi robocab, dazed from her long journey from the bottom of the world. "Sorry, my flight had a major delay in Rio."

His face softened, and he grabbed the larger of her two bags. With a jerk of his head, he pivoted toward the hangar. "Come on, miss. The shuttle is ready to take off." He loped through a maze of space junk toward the end of the metal building.

Lowry shouldered her backpack and trailed after him, dodging a squadron of robots methodically moving equipment around the warehouse. Her ears hurt from the cacophony of clanks, whirrs and beeps echoing through the building. The nose of a jet rolled across her path, and she lost sight of him. She squeezed around the robot pushing the jet forward, catching sight of a flash of orange as the man disappeared through doors under a SHUTTLE GATE sign.

The glare of the sun reflected off the space station shuttle, blinding her as she reached the tarmac. She shielded her eyes, staring at the thin silver rocket with pint-sized wings and engines purring, waiting for its last passenger to the stars.

The man turned back, scowling. "Come *on*," he said, leaping up a flight of stairs to the open shuttle door. He handed the large bag to one of the flight crew, and with a quick wave of his hand, he shot past her to the bottom of the stairway. Heart thudding, she scrambled up the stairs and through the doorway.

A robo-attendant pointed to an empty seat in the shuttle and then secured the door behind her. Lowry lurched to her seat and stowed her backpack. Dizzy with exhaustion, she slumped into the seat and buckled the safety belt. The monitor above her head flashed a demand to put on her helmet, and as the buckle of the helmet snapped closed, a voice came over the speaker, announcing their flight would be taking off momentarily. They backed out of the berth and headed for the embanked runway.

A melodious voice came through the headphones: "Please prepare for excessive G-force."

The rocket exploded forward, arching upward into the blue sky at a blistering speed. The oppressive force shoved Lowry's fatigued body deep into the cushions, and she fought to breathe normally. She tilted her head to catch sight of glittering ice crystals rushing past the window, the blue sky fading to black.

The compression abated, and Lowry undid the plexi-shield in front of her face, breathing deeply. She glanced at the other passengers on the shuttle, but all seemed preoccupied. It would take several hours to get to the space station. Lowry pulled up the information the station head had sent her on the layout of the station.

Lowry took a sip from her water bottle and then looked down at her shaking hands. She whispered to herself, "Did you have to run this far?"

She had initially passed on the opportunity to be a research assistant for the space station's Landsat department when she married her loving spouse, but now, since her divorce, she had decided to finish her graduate studies in the stars. With her unique knowledge of Antarctica, her professor was thrilled when she told him she could now go.

It would be a two-year commitment, with the first several months spent collecting detailed images of the continent now that the terrain was bare. Then she would combine the new data with the existing geologic and geophysical data to produce maps of Antarctica's aquifers and surface geology for possible habitation.

The blue Earth shrank as they blasted through the stratosphere. Lowry craned her neck to catch a view of the North American continent—coastlines drowned by the Melt, with millions of people losing their homes and livelihoods, in less than a century.

She furrowed her brow, trying to remember what the old maps had looked like before the melting of the ice caps had occurred. *Hadn't there been a state called Florida?*

The sky turned to black and the cabin dimmed. Lowry rested her head on the seat and drifted into a restless sleep until the voice came back into her helmet.

"Ladies and gentlemen, we are approaching the International Space Station."

She jerked awake, peering out of the window for her first look at the new ISS. It had replaced the earlier and much smaller version several years ago. This huge space station was built for humans to stay in orbit for years with accommodations for a hundred people.

The ISS resembled a child's gyro toy spinning on a black surface. The design was elegantly simple: a slowly revolving wheel with four globes built into the ring, connecting four spokes extending from its central hub. Except for rows of tiny windows, arrays of sparkling gold solar panels covered the exterior, rotating with the sun to catch the maximum amount

feel the artificial gravity slowly pulling you down to the floor."
Lights blinked, and a whistle blew. "Hold on tight!"

With a quiet *whoosh*, they started, and Lowry smiled in
excitement. She caught flashes of the exterior through small
windows as they flew past. As they approached the ring, the
artificial gravity increased and pulled her feet to the floor.

When the pod stopped, the doors opened, and the group
walked out into a larger reception area. The people unfamiliar
with the station had escorts waiting to take them to their
quarters.

A young woman smiled as she approached Lowry, looking
up from the screen of her phone. "Hi, I'm Ayana—you're
Lowry?"

Lowry shrugged. "I think so, but after thirty hours of travel,
I can't be positive."

"Ouch, thirty hours—you *do* look exhausted." Ayana
grabbed the larger bag at Lowry's feet. "You probably want to
freshen up—I'll take you to your cabin." Ayana pointed out
the cafés, exercise room, and theater on the way to Lowry's
cabin. "There are a lot of activities on the new ISS for you to
enjoy, Lowry."

When they reached her cabin door, Ayana touched a few
buttons on her phone. Smiling, she gestured to the pad next to
the door. "I've set up your station identity into the system, and
once you touch the pad, you'll be recognized. Your fingerprints
will open any door your security level allows you to access."

Lowry gingerly placed her hand over the pad, and the door
slid open. Lowry exhaled as she entered the cabin. "Home,
sweet home."

Ayana smiled and dropped the bag on a chair. "It's small,
like a ship's cabin, but everything should function like you're
used to." She pointed to a gift basket on the cabinet. "There's
some goodies for you. We're really glad you're aboard, Lowry."

"Thanks, Ayana."

Ayana turned to leave but hesitated at the door. Arching her
brow, she looked at Lowry. "One word of warning: some
people have difficulty acclimating to space-station life, so feel

free to ask one of the nurses on Deck One if you have *any* issues."

"Sure, I'll check in before I jettison myself into space."

Lowry explored the tiny cabin with as much curiosity as her tired body could muster, opening cabinets and pressing on the mattress. She wandered into the bathroom and perused the stark but adequate facilities.

Then she stopped in front of the mirror and stared at herself. Her fingers traced the high cheekbones—features which were angular but sensual. A beautiful, strong woman stood before her, but her brown eyes revealed a deep sadness that she was determined to chase away. Healing herself was one reason she was aboard the ISS. Sighing, she turned away from her image and stumbled over to the bed. Her head fell into her hands, and her shoulders jerked as her tears flowed. She had given herself permission to grieve; not so much for her failed marriage as for the loss of her innocence.

*     *     *

Lowry strolled along a path in the deep woods of her grandparents' land in western Virginia. She meandered into a clearing in the forest and, with a pirouette, breathed in the moist, earthy air. Like a *corps de ballet*, elegant redbuds stretched their ebony branches, laced with delicate pink flowers, into the sun-filled meadow.

Lowry blinked against the brightening light until a stark white ceiling above her came into focus. Puzzled, she turned to gaze at a black velvet sky in the tiny window. The lovely meadow was just a dream—she was on the ISS, floating thousands of miles above the Earth. The automatic lights brightened further, and then her alarm rang out.

She called out, "Okay, I'm awake," to shut the alarm up. Throwing the covers back, she rolled out of the bed and stood up with another yawn. Her head was sore, and rubbing her temples, she shuffled to the coffee maker and pushed the start button. She moved into the bathroom and glanced into the mirror at her short brunette hair, which was now sticking straight up like a cock's comb. She chuckled and then noticed her puffy eyes. She wet a washcloth with cool water and patted her swollen eyelids, evidence of her midnight tears. Sighing, she shrugged; she was in the post-divorce phase: shell-shocked and vacillating between ecstasy and anxiety. Lowry's lips trembled, but then she sneered at her image.

She threw the cloth at the mirror. "I'm tired of crying."

When the coffee was ready, she sat on the bed, sipping the hot liquid. Caffeine streaming into her body, she began to feel better. Divorce was like a bad cold—nasty and debilitating, but you get over it.

Walking over to the window, she caught a glimpse of the Earth hovering over the ring of the station. Mesmerized by the view, she methodically ate a breakfast bar from the welcome basket. Her spirits rebounded with the thoughts of her new beginning on the ISS. After a quick shower, she dried her hair and then dressed in her ISS-assigned attire. Grimacing, she glanced one last time at the mirror. *At least the clothes were free.*

With another coffee in hand and heart beating a staccato of nerves, she wandered down the hall to her section, passing offices and work areas spewing out a cacophony of music, whirring, and electronic beeps. Lowry moved through the still, dry air, walking down the smoothly curved metallic corridor with no organic shapes nor colors to comfort her eyes. She shivered—like a lightning bug caught in a jar, she was trapped inside of a gigantic computer.

Lowry touched the keypad and then stepped into the Landsat section. A few people smiled at her as she entered, but most concentrated on their work. A man waved to her, and she approached him.

With a smile, he shook her hand. "Welcome aboard. I'm Jin Hoshino. The university let me know you had arrived. I hope you slept well?"

She shrugged.

"It takes a while to get your bio clock set to station time."

Lowry raised her coffee mug. "Today, I will definitely need

caffeine."

Jin led her to a tiny cubicle. "I think you'll find everything set up to the university specs, and the data will automatically download to the department's cloud account every night." He smiled. "I'll leave you to it, but let me know if you need anything else."

A smile flitted across her face. "Thanks, Jin." She sat down and turned on her computer. Exhausted, she blinked against the flashing lights and humming noises as the computer booted up. She sipped her coffee as the screen dissolved into a soft blue background.

A melodious voice spoke: "Welcome to the ISS, Lowry. My name is Bob, and I'll be your assistant on board."

Lowry smirked. "How do you spell Bob, Bob?"

"B–O—ah, I hear the smile in your voice—you're joking with me, Lowry. Thanks, that's a friendly gesture. I think we'll get along very well."

Laughing, Lowry replied, "I think so, too, Bob."

raised eyebrows.

"One of our relatives was a Tuskegee airman—military service is part of our family tradition."

A young woman waved to Zoë and wandered over to the table.

Zoë introduced Lowry. "Nura, meet Lowry Walker, a newbie to our tinker toy." She turned back to Lowry. "I forgot to ask; what department are you working in?"

"Landsat in Section One—I'm collecting data over Antarctica for future use, perhaps opening it to homesteading."

"Wow, I hadn't heard that. I work in Section Two, the security department." She turned to her friend Nura. "Section One . . . Nura, doesn't Sevy work in Section One?"

Nura arched an eyebrow. "At least Sevy says so."

"Would you mind asking if he could join us and meet Lowry?"

"If he's not gaming." Nura shrugged, sending an invitation for him to join the group.

Zoë turned to Lowry. "Sevy's into virtual reality."

Nura snorted. "For him, it's not virtual—it *is* his reality. Life is just fill-in around his VR sessions."

In a few minutes, a young man ambled into the bar, and Zoë waved to him. "Over here, Sevy."

Sevy cocked his head, pushing his glasses back up onto his face. His pace slowed as he neared the table.

Zoë gestured at Lowry. "This is Lowry Walker; she also works in Section One. Maybe you guys could go to lunch sometime?"

Sevy cleared his throat. "I think I saw you the other day, Lowry." He stared at the table. "I work down from you a bit— I'm the IT guy for the space station."

Lowry nodded. "That's right, Sevy. It's good to place a name to a face."

Zoë bent toward Lowry, whispering, "Sevy's a little shy at first, but once he warms up, he's okay." She gestured to a chair. "Sit down, Sevy. I'm buying a round for the table."

A smile flitted across Sevy's face but faded in an instant. His lips were pinched as he struggled to get the chair out and then sat down abruptly. His fingers drummed the tabletop as he stared at the computer screen inset into the surface.

"Where are you from, Sevy?" Lowry asked as the drinks arrived to the table.

"Monterrey, Mexico," he said, staring at the foam on his beer. "My family was originally from Tampico, Mexico, before it flooded."

"I live in Antarctica now that it's free of ice. We're just on the outskirts of the main mining station." Lowry absently rolled her finger around the rim of her glass. "When I was a young child, my mother and I lived in Austin, Texas, not too far from Monterrey."

Sevy's face lit up, and his eyes finally met her gaze. "I love Austin—they have that huge South by Southwest festival for music and interactive reality." He leaned forward. "I went there one year, and they had booths with all the new virtual reality and gaming software." Sevy gestured violently, almost knocking his beer over. "You could try out all the different vendors' games—it was crazy!"

"I never made it to that festival."

"And you *lived* there?"

"Yeah, Lowry, what's wrong with you?" Zoë looked askance at Lowry with a shit-eating grin.

Sevy's wrist computer beeped. He gulped the rest of his beer and excused himself. "Gotta go." His chair scraped the floor as he shoved it back. "See you tomorrow, Lowry!" He waved and then ran out of the bar.

"Once he's out of his shell, he's out of his shell—how do we put him back in?" Lowry grinned at Zoë.

Zoë raised an eyebrow. "Well, maybe you've found the key to his heart . . ."

"Yeah, but how big is his hard drive?"

\*       \*       \*

"Lowry, push through it," said Zoë, climbing effortlessly next to her on an elliptical machine.

Exercising was a requirement for all personnel on the space station. Lowry thought she was in good shape but struggled on the machine next to Zoë's, replying between breaths, "This is a tad more strenuous than my last climb on Everest."

"In the Marines, this is a walk in the park." Zoë chuckled.

Lowry grimaced. "Thanks for making me feel better."

"You're in better shape now, and you've been here, what, almost a month?"

Zoë's elliptical machine beeped the end of her time, and she stepped off the machine. She grabbed her towel, wiped her face, and then bent down into a deep stretch, touching the floor with the palms of her hands.

Lowry sucked in her breath as Zoë's exercise pants crept up her calf, exposing a prosthetic leg. She and Zoë had become friends on the ISS, but Zoë had never discussed her deployments. Lowry chewed her lip and then dived into the question on the tip of her tongue. "Did you see action, Zoë?"

Zoë glanced up at her. "Two tours in the last war." She pulled up the pant leg to reveal the dark brown form rising to just below her knee. "Lost my lower leg from a land mine. The road had been mined haphazardly, and the devices were clumped together, so detecting them was tricky. I had located one, but stepping away from that IED, I hit the one right next to it." She tapped on the hard plastic shank, the sound echoing in the workout room. "I still have phantom pain occasionally, but overall, it works great."

Lowry exhaled and stepped off her machine as her session ended. "I thought they had robots for mine removal."

"We had one, but it got taken out by an enemy drone." Zoë pulled her pant leg down over the prosthetic. "My commander told me that the road had to be cleared and our unit had to do it. Besides, he said, 'You're cheaper than the robot.'" She shrugged. "Luckily, the Marines have a good education program for their wounded veterans and trained me for cyber-security after my injury. The pay is great on the space station, so I took this job."

Zoë stared dully into the mirror facing them. "I used to wear short skirts and sandals, but not now." She smoothed back her tightly curled hair. "My counselor warned me that it's harder on women than men to lose a limb. We are visually held to a higher standard, and this 'flaw' affects your sense of worthiness as a woman."

Zoë picked up her bag. "Let's get some steam." They moved into the steam-room area and undressed.

"I'm amazed they have a steam-room," Lowry said.

"They found that humans need more humidity than the electronics of the station can withstand, so they included steam-rooms. Besides, the water just recycles through it."

Zoë touched the pad to start the steam, and they moved into the room. Steam billowed from the center of the floor. They stretched out on the benches with rolled up towels under their heads. The steam filled the room, and Lowry relaxed in the warmth. Then her eyes shot open as Zoë's voice broke into her consciousness.

"Men see my prosthetic, and somehow, I never get to the next date." Her voice trembled. "I go to dinner with a man and perhaps cross my legs or get out of the car. They see the prosthetic, and I can almost feel them flinch away from me." Zoë exhaled. "You can't imagine the pain of that moment. I know they don't mean to be that way, but women are expected to be beautiful—and perfect."

Through the rising steam, Lowry stared at the dim light above her head. "Why do we have to make life harder than it already is by waging insane wars?"

"My brother says the rich and powerful will always wage war. Too much money lining too many pockets."

"You're intelligent and a lovely young woman. At some point, you'll find someone who's not so shallow. I would think that military men would be empathetic?"

Zoë's brow furrowed. "Empathy is one thing; marrying someone who is a constant reminder of your own torment is another. Normalcy is sacred to soldiers coming home from

17

war." Zoë pursed her lips. "Maybe when I get off this spinning hula hoop, I'll find someone who loves me, prosthetic and all."

She turned, smiling at Lowry. "Enough about my dismal love life—I'm tired of hearing myself talk." Casting her hand dramatically into the air, she said, "I want to live vicariously, so tell me about yours . . . maybe you've already hooked up with Sevy?"

Lowry made a face. "I doubt you want to channel *my* love life. I'm recently divorced with the bruises to prove it. After the wedding, I filled out a rental agreement, accidentally typing 'marred' instead of 'married'—a prophetic slip." She propped herself up on her elbow and took a drag on her water bottle. "I came up here as a retreat from all that, I guess. Romance for me is in the ditch, and there's not much hope for rescue."

Zoë raised an eyebrow. "He wasn't the man of your dreams?"

"Sometimes dreams turn to nightmares."

Lowry lay back down and closed her eyes as the clouds of steam enveloped her body. She clenched her hands against the pain cutting into her heart. Turning away from Zoë, she wrapped her arms over her despair, struggling to not break down.

Whether in war or relationships, there is a seed deep in humanity—the strong dominating the weak—poisoning all it touches. Is power over another human worth more than love—or peace? Lowry breathed in the warm, moist air as a tear seeped from her eye, merging with the sweat on her face.

The Earth warmed. The ice caps melted and the rising oceans crept onto the land like a cat upon its prey. Storms swept tides farther inland, breaking down the low-lying coastal towns, and washing them away. Erosion sculpted the coastlines into a new world.

# A SPIDER SAT BESIDE HER

# CHAPTER 4

Lowry rubbed her eyes to clear her head. For weeks, she had been immersed in mapping the surface topography of Antarctica, now unveiled to the eyes of the world. Through the satellite images, she was the first person to experience the breathtaking beauty of the unexplored land of snow-capped mountains and glacially carved valleys away from the mining station where she grew up.

Lowry leaned back in her chair, reflecting on the technology that she used for her mapping. Within the environment of the Virtual Cave, she literally dug with her hands, walked with her feet, and even flew within the data to find the signatures of water reservoirs revealing themselves with variations of color and sound.

But she was a mere human—too much time buried in her data, desperately needing a break from her imaging project. She sipped her coffee, musing on the intricate systems of the space station, where efficiency was mandatory and humans were the weak link in the system. The monitor began to blink annoyingly as it waited for her to set up the next Landsat collection pass. With a sigh, she pressed her fingers against the side of her aching head. *Technology is the master, and we're the slaves.*

Her computer asked smoothly, "Lowry, we're approaching another pass over Antarctica; are you ready to start the next topographic scan?"

Lowry replied, "Shut up, Bob."

The computer went silent and began a screensaver of landscapes.

Lowry looked at the screen. "Bob, did you know that because of you, we've lost the human race? It's all your fault, Bob."

"I really wouldn't know about that, Lowry," Bob calmly replied.

Lowry set her coffee down, mumbling, "Computers—can't live with 'em, can't live without 'em."

She tapped in the parameters, coordinating the drone cameras positioned on the ground to begin synchronously videoing the terrain while the Landsat was recorded. Then she said, "Go ahead, Bob. I'm sorry I snapped at you; please start the scan."

"It's okay, Lowry; I understand."

*Sure, Bob.*

Lowry pulled her video goggles on, streaming images from one of the drones close enough to the mining station to have a wireless signal. The drone banked over a ridge and descended into a large valley, and like a bird in flight over the land, she soared over a large river with elegant branching streams feeding it—an exquisite dendritic drainage pattern. Patches of green laced through the land: flora taking hold in the soils of Antarctica. She touched her cheek. But where was the wind on her face?

The data collection ceased as the space station flew past Antarctica and over the open ocean. She pushed her goggles onto her forehead as they glided serenely over Africa and Europe; far above the drowned coastlines and humans fleeing the influx of an uncaring ocean.

A voice came from behind her. "Ready for lunch?" Sevy's face hung over the wall of her cubicle.

"I guess." She shrugged, pulling the goggles off her head.

Sevy rested his hand on top of the cubicle wall, and his wrist sported the latest e-ware watch. "That's cool headgear— virtual?"

"Not virtual—real videos streamed in real time to sync with the satellite images I'm recording over Antarctica. I just check to make sure they're recording properly." She massaged her temples and stood up, stretching her body. "My brain is fried anyway—let's go."

"Don't be so enthusiastic. Food's not that bad."

They walked down the corridor toward the food court through a gauntlet of pop music spewing from speakers. Lowry quickened her pace, but there was no hope of escape from the endless din permeating the space station.

Sevy's pet rog—a robotic dog—leapt down the hall like a cute puppy. Sevy snapped his fingers and said, "Poppy!" The rog immediately heeled to his side. Sevy leaned down, petting Poppy as they stopped at the cafeteria door.

Poppy's body was covered with a soft, silky material warm to the touch. Rogs were programmed to have no bad habits, no hair to shed, no need to eat nor defecate—ideal for the space station. But Lowry felt her skin crawl as the rog looked up at him with "affection." It was all a bit antiseptic to her.

They walked into the cafeteria, waving at colleagues as they perused the food selections. Lowry supposed the designers of the space station had attempted to make the cafeteria pleasing to the eye, but to her, it looked like a food court in a mall, down to the plastic pictures of food choices. She was assaulted by the blend of smells from the myriad of multicultural foods; they were appealing one at a time, but the mix was insidious.

As they got in line to get their lunch, Sevy bopped his head to the electronic dance music pulsing from the speakers in the cafeteria.

Losing her composure, Lowry snapped, "Stop it!"

Sevy made a face. "You don't like it? It's the latest song from Argos."

Lowry looked at him. "Doesn't all this get to you?"

"All what?"

"You don't feel trapped living inside of a computer? No nature, no wind?"

He snorted. "And be bitten by bugs? No, I like it—no muss,

d toward the Earth outside the wall
there, it's a daily turf battle for

s and sat at a table. Lowry stabbed a
her plate as she mechanically chewed it,
Sevy. "Do you ever stop to think about the
vy? Outside of war, disease, and hunger,
fun anymore."

kind of sick, aren't you?" He smiled. "I like that in

felt him studying her as she pushed her peas into a semi-

"Lowry," Sevy said, munching his veggie burger, "You just need a night on the town. A little adult beverage will calm you down. Come join our gamer club; we're going partying tonight."

She shook her head and glanced at the faces around her, aware that she was different from the rest. She wasn't averse to having fun, but the thought of spending the evening in a loud techno-bar wasn't on her list. Her coworkers went from the intense cubicle life to the electric cafeteria to techno-disco with apparent ease. Of course, massive amounts of alcohol seemed to be a large part of their lives. The demand for booze was so great there was a distillery on board—had to anesthetize those brains somehow.

"How long have you been up here, Sevy?"

"On my third year."

"Three years crammed onto this prison ship . . ."

"No yard to mow. I love it."

The huge monitor dominating one of the cafeteria walls streamed a news feed of Southeast Asian peasants rushing the border of China to escape rising seas. Lowry's appetite faded as the Chinese military slaughtered them in waves of gunfire, the sound of the rifle volleys buried under the chatter of the cafeteria.

A furry panda baby sprang onto the screen, and everyone cooed in delight as she appeared to play peek-a-boo through

the bamboo shoots. Sevy drummed his veggie straw
beat of the incessant music.

Then a hologram image of the new Amerada flag ful
front of them.

Sevy nodded toward the screen. "They did a nice job o
flag, with the white maple leaf on a red field instead of stars
a blue field."

"I heard that Canada and America had merged since the
Melt." Staring at the screen, Lowry studied the flag. In place of
the red and white stripes of the old American flag, this new
one had six blue and six white stripes. Ten stars were along
each blue stripe, representing all the states and the District of
Columbia.

The monitor faded to the holographic face of the new
President of Amerada, Christine Nilats. "My fellow
Ameradans," began the president.

Sevy turned back to his lunch, mumbling under his breath,
"Lord, do we have to be subjected to *her* while we're trying to
eat? I was hoping for cartoons."

Lowry shrugged and narrowed her eyes at the image of the
new president. "One of the Nilats, huh? She seems sketchy to
me."

"Best president who ever bought an election." He lifted an
eyebrow. "The Nilats family has billions; yes, you heard right—
*billions*."

"I doubt a billionaire would bother to buy an election on
Antarctica."

"You and I are just lucky she's not *our* president, though
Amerada's tentacles are wrapped around every aspect of the
space station." He speared a fry and pointed it at her with a
deadpan face. "We'd better not talk too loud. I've heard rumor
this is a two-way monitor."

"Maybe I should flip her off?"

"Yeah, that would be mature."

Scraping of chairs and music drowned out most of Nilats'
speech. The crowd of diners thinned as her speech came to an
end: "Be assured that the borders will be secure and the

economy strong again. Together, we'll make Amerada a great nation!"

The world news came back onto the screen as Sevy caught sight of Zoë. "Over here, Zoë!" He beckoned to her.

Zoë waved to them, picked up a to-go lunch bag, and walked toward their table. She crossed in front of the monitor, which was streaming a video of protesters in the streets of Bengaluru, India. Lowry inwardly shivered at the bizarre image of Zoë walking in front of the marching rioters, momentarily merging with the activists. Then the camera zoomed in on the desperate, larger-than-life faces, and the newscaster said in a clipped tone, "The leaders of the rioters say they are protesting lack of food and land confiscation by the rich and powerful."

Lowry stared at her empty plate, surrounded by the chatter of happy people.

*So peaceful up here, but back on Earth . . .* She gazed over the crowd of laughing coworkers, marveling at the desensitized people around her. For most of her life, Lowry had existed in an unforgiving landscape of rock and wind. This fragility of life demanded a connection with the living. The inhabitants of the ISS, like much of the world, survived the incessant fear assaulting their lives by cordoning it off from their conscious minds. Lowry sighed. Self-preservation—like a bear hibernating in the winter.

Lowry shook off her dismal thoughts as Zoë reached their table.

With a smile, Zoë held up her to-go bag. "I'm just grabbing a lunch to take back to my desk."

Lowry and Sevy rose and took their dishes to the conveyor belt. All three strolled toward the exit, and Sevy snapped his fingers for Poppy. Growling, the rog ran at him and dove onto his leg, humping like a sex-charged beast.

"Poppy, no!" Sevy shouted, trying to shake Poppy off his leg.

The other diners laughed and cheered as Sevy wrestled the rog off. Poppy pivoted her buttocks to Sevy with an explosive sound reminiscent of passing gas. She flipped a somersault in the air, landing with a bow to the audience, and then bolted out of the cafeteria.

Sevy grimaced. "Son of a bitches reprogrammed Poppy again." He turned back to Lowry with a smile. "You look tense, Lowry—sure you don't want to come out with us tonight?"

"No, thanks, I can't really take the noise level in the techno-club."

Sevy gestured to Lowry with his thumb, murmuring out of the side of his mouth to Zoë, "She's into the solace-of-nature gig."

Zoë placed her hand on Lowry's shoulder. "Lowry, if you need a friend, don't hesitate to come talk to me. I know a few people who had to cut short their term of duty because of ship fever."

"Thanks, Zoë," Lowry said. "I'll admit that it's tough to survive living day to day inside of a computer—the constant mechanical whirring, the onslaught of blinking lights, no breath of fresh air."

Sevy snapped his fingers, pointing at Lowry. "Say, if you're so hungry for the 'natural world,' why don't you go to the Garden?"

"I heard about the Garden, but I thought it was just for the food personnel and not for us working stiffs," Lowry replied.

Sevy glanced at Zoë, rolling his eyes. "Orientation has failed again; she doesn't know she has access to the Garden." He gestured with his arms. "Go out these doors, turn left, and follow the ring to Section Four. In front of you will be a series of locking glass doors keyed to your fingerprints." Grimacing, he continued, "They can't let those nasty creatures into the rest of the station. On the station's maiden voyage, some insects slipped past the sterilization process, much to the embarrassment of the ISS biologist." With a wink at Lowry, he turned to leave. "Beware of the eccentric gardener, Adam—he might seduce you with a fable."

no fuss." He cocked his head toward the Earth outside the wall of windows. "Besides, down there, it's a daily turf battle for jobs."

They got their lunches and sat at a table. Lowry stabbed a carrot, staring down at her plate as she mechanically chewed it, and then glanced at Sevy. "Do you ever stop to think about the human beast, Sevy? Outside of war, disease, and hunger, there's just no fun anymore."

"You're kind of sick, aren't you?" He smiled. "I like that in a gal."

She felt him studying her as she pushed her peas into a semicircle.

"Lowry," Sevy said, munching his veggie burger, "You just need a night on the town. A little adult beverage will calm you down. Come join our gamer club; we're going partying tonight."

She shook her head and glanced at the faces around her, aware that she was different from the rest. She wasn't averse to having fun, but the thought of spending the evening in a loud techno-bar wasn't on her list. Her coworkers went from the intense cubicle life to the electric cafeteria to techno-disco with apparent ease. Of course, massive amounts of alcohol seemed to be a large part of their lives. The demand for booze was so great there was a distillery on board—had to anesthetize those brains somehow.

"How long have you been up here, Sevy?"

"On my third year."

"Three years crammed onto this prison ship . . ."

"No yard to mow. I love it."

The huge monitor dominating one of the cafeteria walls streamed a news feed of Southeast Asian peasants rushing the border of China to escape rising seas. Lowry's appetite faded as the Chinese military slaughtered them in waves of gunfire, the sound of the rifle volleys buried under the chatter of the cafeteria.

A furry panda baby sprang onto the screen, and everyone cooed in delight as she appeared to play peek-a-boo through the bamboo shoots. Sevy drummed his veggie straws to the beat of the incessant music.

Then a hologram image of the new Amerada flag furled in front of them.

Sevy nodded toward the screen. "They did a nice job of the flag, with the white maple leaf on a red field instead of stars on a blue field."

"I heard that Canada and America had merged since the Melt." Staring at the screen, Lowry studied the flag. In place of the red and white stripes of the old American flag, this new one had six blue and six white stripes. Ten stars were along each blue stripe, representing all the states and the District of Columbia.

The monitor faded to the holographic face of the new President of Amerada, Christine Nilats. "My fellow Ameradans," began the president.

Sevy turned back to his lunch, mumbling under his breath, "Lord, do we have to be subjected to *her* while we're trying to eat? I was hoping for cartoons."

Lowry shrugged and narrowed her eyes at the image of the new president. "One of the Nilats, huh? She seems sketchy to me."

"Best president who ever bought an election." He lifted an eyebrow. "The Nilats family has billions; yes, you heard right—*billions*."

"I doubt a billionaire would bother to buy an election on Antarctica."

"You and I are just lucky she's not *our* president, though Amerada's tentacles are wrapped around every aspect of the space station." He speared a fry and pointed it at her with a deadpan face. "We'd better not talk too loud. I've heard rumor this is a two-way monitor."

"Maybe I should flip her off?"

"Yeah, that would be mature."

Scraping of chairs and music drowned out most of Nilats' speech. The crowd of diners thinned as her speech came to an end: "Be assured that the borders will be secure and the economy strong again. Together, we'll make Amerada a great nation!"

The world news came back onto the screen as Sevy caught sight of Zoë. "Over here, Zoë!" He beckoned to her.

Zoë waved to them, picked up a to-go lunch bag, and walked toward their table. She crossed in front of the monitor, which was streaming a video of protesters in the streets of Bengaluru, India. Lowry inwardly shivered at the bizarre image of Zoë walking in front of the marching rioters, momentarily merging with the activists. Then the camera zoomed in on the desperate, larger-than-life faces, and the newscaster said in a clipped tone, "The leaders of the rioters say they are protesting lack of food and land confiscation by the rich and powerful."

Lowry stared at her empty plate, surrounded by the chatter of happy people.

*So peaceful up here, but back on Earth . . .* She gazed over the crowd of laughing coworkers, marveling at the desensitized people around her. For most of her life, Lowry had existed in an unforgiving landscape of rock and wind. This fragility of life demanded a connection with the living. The inhabitants of the ISS, like much of the world, survived the incessant fear assaulting their lives by cordoning it off from their conscious minds. Lowry sighed. Self-preservation—like a bear hibernating in the winter.

Lowry shook off her dismal thoughts as Zoë reached their table.

With a smile, Zoë held up her to-go bag. "I'm just grabbing a lunch to take back to my desk."

Lowry and Sevy rose and took their dishes to the conveyor belt. All three strolled toward the exit, and Sevy snapped his fingers for Poppy. Growling, the rog ran at him and dove onto his leg, humping like a sex-charged beast.

"Poppy, no!" Sevy shouted, trying to shake Poppy off his leg.

The other diners laughed and cheered as Sevy wrestled the rog off. Poppy pivoted her buttocks to Sevy with an explosive sound reminiscent of passing gas. She flipped a somersault in the air, landing with a bow to the audience, and then bolted out of the cafeteria.

Sevy grimaced. "Son of a bitches reprogrammed Poppy again." He turned back to Lowry with a smile. "You look tense, Lowry—sure you don't want to come out with us tonight?"

"No, thanks, I can't really take the noise level in the techno-club."

Sevy gestured to Lowry with his thumb, murmuring out of the side of his mouth to Zoë, "She's into the solace-of-nature gig."

Zoë placed her hand on Lowry's shoulder. "Lowry, if you need a friend, don't hesitate to come talk to me. I know a few people who had to cut short their term of duty because of ship fever."

"Thanks, Zoë," Lowry said. "I'll admit that it's tough to survive living day to day inside of a computer—the constant mechanical whirring, the onslaught of blinking lights, no breath of fresh air."

Sevy snapped his fingers, pointing at Lowry. "Say, if you're so hungry for the 'natural world,' why don't you go to the Garden?"

"I heard about the Garden, but I thought it was just for the food personnel and not for us working stiffs," Lowry replied.

Sevy glanced at Zoë, rolling his eyes. "Orientation has failed again; she doesn't know she has access to the Garden." He gestured with his arms. "Go out these doors, turn left, and follow the ring to Section Four. In front of you will be a series of locking glass doors keyed to your fingerprints." Grimacing, he continued, "They can't let those nasty creatures into the rest of the station. On the station's maiden voyage, some insects slipped past the sterilization process, much to the embarrassment of the ISS biologist." With a wink at Lowry, he turned to leave. "Beware of the eccentric gardener, Adam—he might seduce you with a fable."

# CHAPTER 5

Lowry walked down the corridor to Section Four and stood in front of glass doors. She touched the fingerprint pad, and the first set of doors slid open. She slipped inside and opened another set of doors until the third set opened to reveal the Garden.

Like a bee drawn to a flower, she moved into an organic world hidden within the sterile existence of the station. She meandered down the rock path, breathing in the moist air filled with the scent of the earth. To her left, rising high above her head, were tall, aluminum-terraced gardens bursting with vegetables, potatoes, and fruits, stretched up along the curved windows toward the filtered sunlight streaming through the top of the dome. She drifted past a cacophony of life bursting with colors—red tomatoes, yellow squash, and purple eggplant.

Lowry smiled at the unruly vines of peas and the boisterous beans, all spilling over the terraced beds. She had grown up surrounded by the fabric of nature—a diversity of texture and natural shapes instead of the relentless straight lines of the space station. Twirling on her toes, she spun in place, inhaling the *élan vital*. To truly breathe, her soul needed nature.

Wandering down the path, she discovered a pocket garden and tiptoed into a refuge from the noise and inorganic ISS. She sat quietly on a large, faux-stone bench and felt the tension of the past weeks slide away. Sitting still, Lowry melted into the background, and the birds returned, singing and fighting, engrossed in their own parallel universe where a human was an occasional irritant. Maybe that was why some people disliked nature; they would have to acknowledge that they weren't masters of the world but rather a passing nuisance to most of the creatures of the Earth.

Lowry leaned down, brushing her hand through the tender blades of grass, and then, with a sigh, she lay down in the fold of the cool, soft meadow. Lowry stared up into the canopy of limbs as bees swarmed in the warm sunlight and rabbits dined on the tender grass under the branches. She closed her eyes, and a lecture by one of her favorite professors at college floated into her head. He was considered a bit of a wacko, and she loved him for it.

"We must *demand* balance in our lives before we, as a society, have a nervous breakdown. What happened to the promise that the computer age would make things easier? Now all we do is work for the computer, creating a virtual treadmill for ourselves, on the computer's timeframe—twenty-four hours a day, seven days a week, three hundred and sixty-five days a year, until the computer crashes, and we scurry around like worker ants on the queen.

"Is it no wonder we are exhausted when we get to spend the precious little time we have with our children? And it just keeps speeding up; *we* have to stop it; we as individuals have to control the computer age. Ah, the Life of Riley! But wait, didn't we tell you? You don't get that life until you buy the new Orwell game! Better hurry; they're going fast! All the other kids have them!"

In the warm sun, serenaded by nature, Lowry's eyes began to flutter, and she curled onto her side for a nap. A sound of humming startled her awake, and she saw an odd man pushing a hovercart around the corner. She observed him from her hideout as he raked debris from the flowerbeds near the path. He was quite small and wiry with brown skin and black hair.

He had small glasses that seemed ready to fall from his face as he dug around the plants. This must be the elusive Adam, the gardener.

Lowry sat up quietly as Adam picked up some dead leaves and placed them in his hovercart. He pushed on, and when he was next to her, she called to him softly, "Hello, Adam."

He looked up in surprise and then squinted at Lowry through the branches, examining her like an unfamiliar bird or insect. With a twitch of his nose, he sniffed in dismissal, like she was an interesting bug but nothing else, and proceeded to gather more leaves.

With furrowed brow, Lowry studied Adam, now determined to get a response from him. With a smile, she ran her fingers through her hair and said, "I think you have the best job on the ISS, Adam."

He looked up again, and his face softened at Lowry's accepting gaze. A slight smile grazed his face for an instant, and then he nodded. "Man cannot live by bread alone."

Lowry laughed. "Ain't that the truth."

His eyes shifted from side to side, seemingly wary that others may be eavesdropping on them. Without another word, he turned and shuffled down the path, pushing the hovercart until he disappeared around the corner.

Lowry was a person who collected experiences, and she felt an impulse to draw Adam out of his shell. He had an indeterminable accent, and she could not discern where he came from, but he was definitely the most interesting person she had met so far on the station.

*   *   *

About a month later, Lowry saw Adam again. He was planting bulbs with a small shovel, with his back toward her. She came up beside him and said quietly, "Hello again, Adam. Your garden is beautiful, as usual; I can tell that you work very hard."

Adam's shoulders started at her voice. Like a snake, he twisted his head around, peering at her as if he didn't remember their last meeting. Then he nodded but turned back to his task, driving his shovel into the ground and pushing the soil aside to form a hole for the next bulb. She stood there while he plucked a bulb out of his wagon and knelt to press it into the open hole.

He patted the soil around the bulb and then straightened up. Leaning on his shovel with a shy grin, he looked at her. "May I tell you the fable of the silkworm and spider, miss?"

Amused, Lowry nodded.

As if he were an actor appearing in a play, Adam took on another persona. He gazed up to the sky with his finger in the air, quoting: "Having received an order for twenty yards of silk from Princess Lioness, the silkworm sat down at her loom and worked away with zeal. A spider soon came around and asked to hire a web-room nearby. The silkworm acceded, and the spider commenced her task and worked so rapidly that in a short time, the web was finished.

"'Just look at it,' she said, 'and see how grand and delicate it is. You cannot but acknowledge that I'm a much better worker than you. See how quickly I perform my labors.'

"'Yes,' answered the silkworm, 'but hush up, for you bother me. Your labors are designed only as base traps and are destroyed whenever they are seen, and brushed away as useless dirt, while mine are stored away as ornaments of royalty.'"

Adam looked at Lowry and said with grand finish, "True art is thoughtful, delights, and endures."

Lowry's face lit up with delight at the sight of Adam bowing with his hand on the shovel like it was a king's scepter.

Clapping at his performance, she said, "That's beautiful, Adam!"

Embarrassed, he stared at the ground. Then he put his shovel in the hovercart and shuffled away.

With a twinkle in her eye, she shook her head, watching him disappear around the corner. From what everyone said about Adam, Lowry was probably one of the few people to speak to him.

\*     \*     \*

The Garden became a refuge for Lowry, enabling her to escape and decompress from techland. A microcosm of the Earth and her Eden in the stars, it recycled the garbage and sewage of the station and returned clean water and organic food to the inhabitants. Wastewater flowed into the Garden and then returned to the humans filtered and clean.

Through the glass dome arching overhead, sunlight was reflected into the Garden by huge mirrors, which rotated with the sun for maximum exposure. Picturesque sunrises and sunsets painted the sky during the beginning and end of the "day," and during the artificial "night," the mirrors folded down, revealing a brilliant tapestry of heavenly bodies.

Like an orchestra, the Garden was divided into sections, which together created an organic symphony of terraced vegetables, fruit and nut orchards, and a small farm animal area with coops for chickens and rabbits. The only part of the food chain missing was the large animal protein, grown in a lab area along the ring for lack of space to raise cattle and pigs.

In her off time, Lowry explored the grounds until she became a thread in its intricate fabric. Daily, she meandered down the trails, picnicking in each of the lovely pocket gardens, accompanied by butterflies dancing in the air. She was not the only tourist in the Garden; it was a popular place for joggers, and she learned which paths to avoid so she wouldn't be run over. There was talk of building a workout facility in the middle of the orchards, a glassed-in bubble of blaring music and grunting jocks. She shuddered. *No thank you, sir—I'll take my nature straight up.*

A myriad of life existed in every nook of the Garden, all with a specific purpose to keep the human masters alive and well. But the Garden was a tamed version of Earth, where the animals were docile and the rain and wind were programmed to occur only at certain times so as to not disturb nor wet the human masters. Lowry missed the wildness of Antarctica and the exhilaration of a great storm billowing on the horizon with the slashing wind and rain. In this man-made Garden, the ever-present dome loomed overhead, both protector and prison.

\*    \*    \*

Sevy trailed behind Zoë and Lowry through the sliding doors of the Garden. Poppy followed him in, keeping close to his heels. "It's been years since I've been in the Garden," Sevy said.

"Really?" Lowry laughed. "I come here all the time. I even help out during harvest and these monthly Garden events."

Sevy cocked his head toward the doors. "Shouldn't they close behind us?"

Lowry shook her head. "During these events, they leave them open for a bit while crowds of people are coming through." She pointed to fans on either side of the doorway. "Those fans discourage any flying insects and birds from making an escape."

They strolled past the freshwater lake, and Sevy pointed at a pair of mating swans swimming toward them with wrath in their eyes. Then the artificial wind shifted, and the mist from the spouting fountain enveloped them with wet spray. Laughing, they quickly retreated to the path beside the saltwater lake. A school of salmon, their silver bodies glistening in the sunlight, swam in one of the containment nets bobbing in the middle of the lake.

Zoë patted her stomach. "That's what I want for dinner—I love salmon."

Sevy pointed to the next net over. "I'm ordering Snapper Almandine, with those little baby potatoes on the side."

Lowry looked toward the shore where a robot was hauling up traps filled with wriggling crustaceans. "Lobster for me—drenched in butter."

They stretched out on the sandy beach and soaked up the sun, filtered and reflected through the dome above them.

After a few minutes, Lowry sat up and scooped up a handful of sand. She let the sand fall through her fingers. "Here we are sunbathing on a beach, hurtling around the Earth in a tin can."

Sevy put his hands behind his head and looked at her, arching his brow. "Tin can?" He stood up and brushed the sand off his pants. "This is a pretty sophisticated tin can—the best money can buy."

They wandered to the other side of the Garden, and Sevy pointed at an overgrown briar patch near the side of the Garden capsule. "What's all that?"

Lowry shrugged. "It's supposed to be a berry patch of raspberries, blackberries, and blueberries, but they are hugely overgrown. The botanist has been fussing at Adam to trim them back."

They neared the cornfield, with only the brown and dried corn stalks left after the harvest.

Lowry gestured at the maze cut into the tall stalks. "They used a computer program and robot tractors to cut the maze—it's really cool."

Zoë grinned. "Let's get lost!" she yelled and then bolted toward the narrow entry.

Sevy snapped his fingers for Poppy to keep up as they ran after Zoë. They raced to the entrance, shoving each other playfully as they reached the front of the maze. Laughing, they slowed to a walk as the tall dried corn plants encircled them.

Sevy pulled up a map on his watch as they approached the first turn and pointed to the right. "This way."

Lowry wagged her index finger at him. "You're cheating, Sevy. We're supposed to try and find our way without the map."

He shrugged and turned off the screen with a sigh.

Halfway down the side of the maze, they came to a fork. Zoë pursed her lips. "Maybe we head to the left?"

They slowed down as the path through the corn narrowed—the air was heavy and still. Laughing, Lowry and Zoë led the way forward, skipping through the corn.

Sevy dropped back, and then he called out nervously, "Wait, guys."

The wind machines kicked in and a breeze picked up. The towering stalks of corn rustled like dried paper.

"Come on, Sevy!" Zoë waved at him to catch up. "We think we're close to the center."

A buzzing insect flew past Sevy's face, and he jerked back. "Bees—I think I hear bees." He flung his arms around his head and then ran backwards, away from the buzzing sound. "Help! I'm getting out—I might be allergic to bee stings."

"Sevy, just stay still. They won't sting you," Lowry said.

Still swiping at imaginary insects, Sevy bolted out of the maze. Zoë and Lowry looked at each other and shrugged. They followed him back out to the entrance.

Sevy stood with his arms crossed, biting his lip and staring at the ground, his face flushed with embarrassment.

"I guess you can't get stung in virtual reality." Lowry shook her head. "Reality's a bitch, Sevy."

Zoë smirked. "Lowry, I think you just composed Sevy's motto."

With an angry glance, Sevy snapped, "People can die from bee stings—why do they have bees loose up here?"

Lowry raised her eyebrows and extended her hands out. "Without bees, there is no pollination and no crops, Sevy."

"Someone should create an artificial pollination system so we can get rid of all the nasty bugs."

The dry stalks of corn trembled, and Adam appeared from behind them with a peculiar grin on his face. "Miss Lowry, I have an Aesop's fable, if you and your friends want to hear it?"

Lowry nodded with a smile. "Yes, Adam, please," she said, ignoring the raised eyebrows of Zoë and the grimace on Sevy's face.

Adam pushed his glasses back on his face and moved in front of them as if the entrance of the maze were center stage.

He lifted his hand into the air and began to recite in a clear voice: "At a country fair, there was a buffoon who made all the people laugh by imitating the cries of various animals. He finished off by squeaking so like a pig that the spectators thought that he had a porker concealed about him.

"But a countryman who stood by said, 'Call that a pig's squeak! Nothing like it. You give me till tomorrow, and I will show you what it's like.'

"The audience laughed, but the next day, sure enough, the countryman appeared on the stage. Putting his head down, he squealed so hideously that the spectators hissed and threw stones at him to make him stop.

"'You fools!' he cried. 'See what you have been hissing.' And he held up a little pig whose ear he had been pinching to make him utter the squeals."

Adam smiled, and then his eye twitched as he glanced toward Sevy. "The moral is this: men often applaud an imitation and hiss the real thing."

Sevy clenched his jaw and shot an angry look at Adam. "Thanks, Adam, for the *fable*." He picked up Poppy and shot a look at Lowry. "Now you see the problem with reality? It's too real." He turned and stormed out of the Garden.

# CHAPTER 6

It was her three-month anniversary on the ISS. Lowry gazed out her window at the Earth hanging in the dark sky. A gorgeous jewel—but after the Melt, more sapphire than emerald.

She hummed a few bars of a song written and sung with the bitter note of a world with too many humans on too little land.

*The ice melted, the water rose, and the land went under.*
*The ice melted, the oceans flowed, and our lives went under.*

It struck her that the last time she had sung that song was at the beach when she was five years old, after the melting had begun in earnest.

\*   \*   \*

The heat shimmered above the shoreline. Lowry meandered down the beach, pressing her toes into the soft, wet sand. Seagulls shrieked, hovering over the shore.

"Watch the wave, Lowry!" her mother called to her.

The wave raced up the beach, and she squealed as it encircled her feet. Giggling, she scampered up the beach, dancing just beyond the foam. "Ha, ha, didn't get me!" she sang, taunting the wave.

Her mother ran and caught her around the waist. "The wave didn't get you, but I did!" They fell to the ground, and a larger wave engulfed them both. They sat up, laughing and gasping from the saltwater.

Her father's brother, Nick, helped them up and wrapped Lowry in a towel.

Lowry wiped her face. "Uncle Nick, are you helping us move to the new house?"

"Yes, sweetie, except your mother tells me that we're selling all of your stuff." Nick pulled her wet braids, and his green eyes sparkled in amusement.

Wagging her head, she stuck out her tongue at him and then sat down to dig in the sand.

"That's not a bad idea, Nick; then we could move into a much smaller home." Her mother stuck her tongue out at Lowry.

Lowry opened her mouth to protest but grinned when she realized her mother was teasing.

Margaret spread out the blanket while Nick set up the umbrella and beach chairs. She opened the lunch basket, calling to Lowry, "Come eat, sweetie."

After lunch, Lowry threw her bread crusts into the air, shouting in delight as the gulls snatched the bread in mid-air. She chased crabs crawling along the beach and then sat down to finish her sand castle.

Nick sighed as he gazed out at the Gulf waters. "It's just amazing how far inland the beach has moved since the start of the melting." He ran his fingers through his auburn hair and pointed into the far distance to a steeple of an old church, where the cross was visible between the swells. "Houston is almost completely underwater now, and the water is still moving west."

A deep sadness came into Margaret's brown eyes. "All the coastal cities lost under the waves. And the citrus groves in South Texas—drowned." She gazed out at the sparkling water.

"But it's odd that the Gulf is so blue and clear now."

Nick nodded. "The currents have changed, and the Mississippi mud isn't heading this way anymore. If it continues to flood the lowlands without the influx of silt, you might see a carbonate bank develop along the Texas Gulf Coast. Most people may not know, but there used to be carbonate reefs all along the Texas coast millions of years ago."

Lowry strained her ears to hear as her mother said hoarsely, "It's frightening to see the water creep up the street and families forced to pack up and move to dry land. Millions of people are fleeing the coasts, never to return."

Nick sighed. "Yes, and most of the great, historic seaports of the world, drowned like Atlantis."

Her mother looked up at him. "Nick, what's going to happen to us? Where will the water stop?

Lowry dug furiously in the sand.

"I don't know, Margaret. There's not enough data to predict how high the water will reach. The icecaps are still melting, and no one knows how far down they will go." He shook his head as he looked out to sea. "Icecaps that have been in place since humans first appeared on the earth, disappearing within a human lifespan. It's just unbelievable." He rubbed his face thoughtfully. "Maybe this is the end of the last ice age—in the geologic record, there are so many instances of massive swings of sea levels."

Margaret gazed out at the water. "But even if we are in a cycle of warming climate, couldn't air pollution and cutting of forests have exacerbated the warming, creating a tipping point?"

Nick bent down, catching a candy wrapper blowing across the sand, and angrily crushed it in his hand. "Humans excel at two things: having children and consuming resources. Did we, in our madness to procreate, overwhelm the stasis of the Earth?"

Her mother shook her head. "And it's sick the way that politics played a hand in this disaster." She sighed and continued sadly. "There is such a delicate balance of humans versus nature, and I'm afraid that nature has given us the answer to our own stupidity."

Lowry felt her mother's hand upon her head. She looked up at her mother's face, frowning at the worry in her eyes. "Mommy, are we going to be all right?"

Her mother's face softened as she smiled down at her. "Yes, baby, we'll be fine." Then she pointed out to sea. "Look, Lowry—the dolphins are dancing for us!"

Lowry jumped up. Nick came over and lifted her onto his shoulders so she could see the dolphins leap out of the water in front of them. Lowry giggled and clapped her hands in delight.

Nick stared ahead and asked her mother softly, "How's Duff?"

They did not look at each other. Margaret replied dully, "Fine. I haven't seen him lately."

They watched the dolphins move through the surf, their glistening bodies cutting through the waves like knives.

Nick cleared his throat. "I may see him before you do—I'm scheduled to go back to Antarctica soon. I believe he will be helping manage one of the seismic crews down there temporarily."

Margaret touched his arm. "I know we have you to thank for getting him that job."

Nick shrugged. "Perhaps he can find a more permanent position back in the States after that."

Lowry waved at the dolphins as they raced away down the shore, past an abandoned car with sparkling waves crashing over its hood. Though she loved her father, she knew it was best not to ask questions about him.

Nick squatted down, and Lowry hopped off his shoulders. She knelt in the sand, troweling a hole under her castle until she connected it to the other side. She put her hand through the tunnel and waved to herself.

Her mother gestured with her hand. "We have to finish packing tonight, so let's get going."

Nick and her mother packed everything and then headed

They drove off the deserted overpass. Her mother glanced back, smiling sweetly to Lowry. "Don't worry—you'll make lots of new friends when you start kindergarten this fall." Margaret shifted in her seat, staring intently out the windshield. She brushed her hand across her pinched face. "We'll have a wonderful life in Austin, you'll see."

# CHAPTER 7

Lowry's eyes shot open at the sound of ringing. Groggy, she sat up and fumbled to answer her phone.

Bob, her computer, said softly, "Lowry, I thought I'd check on you, we're approaching the next satellite imaging pass, and I noticed that you weren't in your office yet."

She scratched her head with a yawn. "Crap. I'm sorry—I overslept, Bob. I'll be there as soon as I can."

"Okay, no problem, Lowry. We'll be at location in thirty-two minutes."

"Thanks, Bob. I'll hurry!"

Lowry stumbled across the room and pushed Start on the coffee maker. She moved into the bathroom, flipped on the shower, and stubbed her toe as she stepped in. "Shit!"

Feverishly, she washed her hair and body and then jumped out, drying off with a quick swipe of the towel. She jerked open her closet, grabbed the first shirt she touched, and threw it over her head. Grabbing the hair dryer with one hand, she dried her hair while pulling on her pants with the other hand. She slipped on her shoes and then glanced into the mirror to make sure she was fully dressed. *Check—all body parts covered.*

She poured a cup of coffee and then rummaged in a drawer, fishing out an old granola bar for breakfast and jamming it into her pocket. With hair partially wet and coffee mug in hand, she trotted down the hall—she'd just make it before the parameters needed to be punched in and the satellite started recording.

As Lowry reached her office, she gulped some hot coffee and burned her tongue. Gritting her teeth, she sat down in front of her terminal. It was just going to be one of those days. Setting the mug down, she concentrated on setting up for data collection as the space station approached Antarctica on its orbit around the Earth. She hit the Go button, heaved a sigh, and collapsed back into her chair. She yawned as the data began to pour into her monitor with another swath of detailed recon work over the continent.

"Thanks for waking me up, Bob. I'm sorry I slept late."

"No problem, Lowry. We were able to get the data parameters in on time. I hope you slept well."

Lowry sipped her coffee, which was now at a drinkable temperature. She leaned back in her chair, watching the surface of the continent drift past as the space station soared overhead, and chewed the stale granola bar. The caffeine was kicking in when a flash of light came from her monitor, blinding her momentarily. She jerked upright, staring at her screen—perhaps a piece of space trash had bounced off the space station? A number, 1998, flashed onto her screen and then vanished. *What the hell?*

Bob said, "Lowry, I was able to capture a portion of the file before it disappeared."

She shoved her coffee mug onto the table. "Fantastic, Bob, but what was it, and where did it come from?"

"It was an OPALS laser message from Antarctica, and I have the ground coordinates, Lowry."

A map popped onto the screen, and a stickpin highlighted the location—an uninhabited area west of the main station in Antarctica. It crossed her mind that Uncle Nick might be sending her a message just in fun, but it seemed too far for him to bother trekking that distance for a lark.

Lowry sat back in her chair, rubbing her chin. "Bob, what's an OPALS message?"

"OPALS is an acronym for Optical Payload for Lasercom Science, or light-based communication via lasers. They're much faster than radio waves."

"Can you tell what the message says, at least the portion you captured?"

"Unfortunately, it's encrypted, and I don't have the software to—"

Bob's voice was cut off mid-sentence as the computer screen went blank. The lights overhead died. Lowry sucked in her breath. All the power in her office was out. A faraway warning siren began howling, and the emergency lights came on, glowing dimly. There was a cold pit in her stomach as she spun her chair around, listening in the eerie silence, but the only sound was her heart thumping. Even the ever-present whisper of air through the vents was curtailed.

She felt around for her phone and then stood up on shaky legs. Panicked voices of her coworkers filled the room. The power outage must be widespread. Everyone knew by the safety films that if the air supply went out, they only had about a day's worth of oxygen before the levels became critical.

Lowry came out of her cubby to join the restless group of her colleagues, faces pale with worry. "Who do we eat first?"

Bessie, one of the technicians whispered, "Maybe it's just a drill?"

"I'm going to the next sector to see if it's everywhere or just here."

"We're supposed to stay here, Lowry."

"Screw it. I'm going."

The light from her phone wavered as she picked her way through the cubbies toward the connecting airlock door. The finger pad didn't function without power, so Lowry tried the emergency handle, but with the loss of power, the airlock had automatically sealed itself shut. Peering through the glass, she could see people milling around like cattle under the eerie emergency lights. Turning away from the chilling scene, she leaned back on the door, breathing deeply to calm her nerves.

Lowry stumbled back through the oppressive silence of the

lifeless space station. She shrugged as she approached the huddle of coworkers. "Well, looks like the outage is everywhere."

"We're all going to die!" screeched Nam, one of the engineers. "I knew I shouldn't have come up here."

"That's not helpful. We need to calm down and think." Lowry rubbed her chin. "Does anyone know if there's any emergency oxygen? I thought each sector had spacesuits."

They spread out, searching for the suits. The workspace echoed with the sound of doors banging open and closed. It had been a scant fifteen minutes, but Lowry could already taste the staleness in the air.

"Over here—the suits are over here!" yelled Sevy, waving his arm.

They gathered in front of the open storage closet, and Sevy pointed to three spacesuits hanging in the back of the closet. Unfortunately, there were four people.

"Eeny, meeny, miny, moe?" said Sevy.

A distant hammering noise reverberated through the room. "What the hell is that?" Lowry asked.

"Maybe it's a rescue?" Nam said, smiling.

Together, they crept toward the sound. The banging got louder as they approached the door to the main hallway.

Sevy's face went pale as he gazed down at his phone. "I was able to connect with the video feed in the hall—look."

Bessie gasped, and the blood drained from her face. Four men and a woman were at the entrance of their sector, beating the door with a metal battering ram, their faces fixed and determined.

The booming echoed in Lowry's chest, matching the thunder of her heartbeat. She mumbled, "This doesn't look good . . ."

Like a drum, the pounding reverberated through the room, getting louder as the door began to fail. Dents appeared on the inside of the door, and quivering in fear, Bessie sank down and crawled under a table.

Lowry glanced at Sevy. "Why would they be trying to get

into *our* sector?"

Sevy snapped his fingers. "My god, they're after the spacesuits." He raced back to the closet.

Lowry turned and sprinted after him. The suits may be their only chance of survival—if they had any chance at all.

The pummeling thrust the lock askew, and the door crumpled away from the frame. The metal door groaned as they popped it open with a crowbar. The five dashed into the room, brandishing pieces of pipe and metal.

A large man led the group, swinging a metal pipe over his head. With a scowl on his face, he shouted, "Get out of our way!"

Nam froze in place, and they bowled him over, shoving him to the ground. One man screamed for him to stay on the floor, threatening him with a jagged piece of steel. The other four ran after Sevy and Lowry.

Sevy reached the closet and yanked the spacesuits out, throwing one of them at Lowry. With the other two suits, he bolted toward an airtight safe room that could be locked from the inside. "Come on!" he yelled over his shoulder.

Lowry threw the suit over her arm and glanced back at the swiftly approaching invaders. The hair on the back of her neck bristled as she dashed after Sevy. The safe room was close, but the pounding of footsteps was closer.

The leader wheezed to the smaller man, "You get the woman. I'll get the guy."

The smaller man leapt toward Lowry and caught the trailing leg of the spacesuit. With a heave, he yanked it backwards, spinning her to the floor. Lowry gasped as she hit the ground but clutched the helmet with all her strength. She twisted over, wrapping her body around the suit, and kicked out at the man grasping the legs of the suit.

The woman of the group joined the attack, her face livid with fury, and like someone demon-possessed, she jumped at Lowry's head. Screeching, she pulled Lowry's hair and scratched at her eyes, enabling the man to wrench the suit away.

Lowry shoved the woman back. "Get off, bitch."

Breathing hard, they faced each other.

The other man tossed the woman a crowbar. "Watch her. I'm going to help Vlad."

With a glare, the woman waved the crowbar at Lowry.

The larger man caught Sevy at the safe room door, grabbing him from behind, and then slammed him to the ground like he was wrestling a steer.

"Give me the suits, asshole!" he screamed.

He jerked one of the space suits out of Sevy's arms, drawing Sevy's face up toward himself. The big man coiled his arm back and struck Sevy in the jaw, knocking him back onto the floor. Sevy clutched the remaining suit, but the smaller man leapt onto Sevy's chest, punching his face until Sevy released the last spacesuit.

The large man dragged the final spacesuit away. "Good job. We got all of them."

The woman laughed, and then she bared her teeth and stomped Lowry's leg. Lowry grunted in pain, but with a swift upward punch, she caught the woman in the gut.

The woman groaned and bent over, clutching her stomach. Then she brandished the crowbar, yelling, "Bitch!" and sprang on Lowry, thrusting the flat side of the metal tool at her neck.

The leader shouted to the woman, "Get back over here. We've got all the suits."

Winded and breathing hard, Lowry sat up as they lugged the suits back to the rest of their group.

The large man strapped Sevy's hands with duct tape. "This is survival, buddy. No hard feelings," he mumbled. Then he yelled to Lowry, who had gotten to one knee, "Just stay there, lady, or we'll strap you too."

She glowered at them as they pulled on the suits. "Aren't you still missing a suit?" she yelled.

"I think you're right. I guess we'll have more fun in the next sector." The leader smirked as the armed troupe moved into the hallway through the mangled door.

Lowry touched her face, stinging from the scratches. She

stood up and stumbled over to Sevy. "Are you okay?"

"I've been better," he murmured through swollen lips. "Can you find some scissors or a utility knife?"

"Sure." Lowry went back to the utility closet, found a pair of scissors, and cut the duct tape from Sevy's wrists.

Sevy sat up, rubbing his wrists where the tape had been. His hands shook as he vacantly gazed at Lowry. "Believe it or not, I've never been in a fight before."

Exhausted, Lowry sat down and draped her arm around him. "The World Wrestling Entertainment recruited out of our school, so I got more practice than I wanted."

He turned and examined her face. "Looks like you got scratched up."

"Yeah, she was quite a hellcat."

Sevy exhaled deeply and stared intently at the floor. Lowry furrowed her brow, trying to discern if he was feeling okay. Without looking at her, he reached out and pulled her to him. A fleeting smile crossed his face as he gently kissed the scratches on her face. "Maybe that will make them feel better." He turned away but kept his arm around her shoulders. "I've wanted to do that for a long time, and since we might die soon, this might be my last chance."

Lowry grinned and patted him on the back. She shifted her position and felt a slight difference in her weight. Her heart sank. The thrusters that maintained the station's rotation must be off as well. They were slowing down. Sevy was right; if the space station was dead, so were they.

Bessie and Nam crawled to them, and they sat in a gloomy circle. Lowry looked from face to face, all etched in fear, as they bobbed in the lessening gravity. A humming sound drifted near, and they looked up to see a drone recording them.

Nam took off his shoe and chunked it at the drone, which smoothly avoided the projectile. "Get outta here!" He shook his fist at the drone. "It's like some kind of vulture hovering over us, waiting for us to die."

Sevy glanced up vacantly and then murmured, "It's documenting the emergency; they are programmed to record every aspect in order to prevent the next one."

Lowry stared at the drone. Odd that watching it calmly record the debacle on the space station brought home the realization of their dire situation. She bit her lip, clasping her hand over her mouth, endeavoring to keep herself from breaking down into uncontrollable sobs. *I'm not going to die crying like a child.* She had to pull herself together.

Sighing, she staggered up. "I'm going to see if I can find a walkie-talkie in the utility closet; maybe I can find out what is happening in the rest of the station."

In the diminishing gravity, she walked with an exaggerated stride over to the closet. The drone followed her, videoing as she searched through the drawers.

Lowry whispered, "Yes!" She clicked on the near-range communicator, but it was dead. She turned it over, opening the back. *Shit, no batteries. Some jerk must have stolen them.*

Lowry chunked the radio at the drone, but it neatly dodged her assault. She wandered back to the group. "No luck."

The drone continued its careful surveillance around the room, documenting the death of the ISS, and then disappeared out of the damaged door.

Nam sneered. "Bye, asshole."

Lowry gestured toward her cubicle. "I'm going to see if I can get a message to my family." She sat down at her desk and exhaled to steady her fingers as she texted a terse message to her father and uncle: *The power is out on the ISS, and we don't know what is happening, but it doesn't look good for us. Love you very much— hugs and kisses.* She had to try even though she didn't know if the message would get to them.

Lowry checked to see how much time had passed. It had been about an hour since the power outage had begun. She moved to the window, staring out at the black abyss. It was strange to see the space station dead; what had been alive with lights and sound minutes earlier was now just a hunk of junk rotating around the Earth. Unfortunately, this space trash still had people inside.

Lowry drifted off her feet and grabbed the bar around the

window to keep herself in place. She wished upon the first star that she would not die tonight, caressing the glass in front of the Earth's image floating over the motionless ring of the station. She swallowed hard. Diving headlong into its atmosphere was not on her bucket list.

The muffled talking of her colleagues sitting in the circle hushed when the lights came on. Like a miracle, Lowry felt air on the back of her neck, and she listened with bated breath to the computers as they all booted up—the once tiresome sounds of the space station now heralding their salvation. Smiling with relief, she breathed in the fresh air now pumping through the ducts.

Laughing, she pushed herself toward her coworkers. "The power's back on!"

Floating with legs crisscrossed, Bessie clung to the leg of a chair, crying uncontrollably.

Nam and Sevy jumped up, propelling themselves to the ceiling in the near-zero gravity.

"Yippee! We're going to live!" yelled Nam. He high-fived Sevy hovering near him, and the impact of their hands spun them away from each other.

The speaker overhead crackled, and a voice boomed out, "Please keep calm; power has been restored. Sorry about the outage, but please return to your offices or quarters—you will be given more information later as we research the problem."

Lowry drifted over and placed her hand on Bessie's shoulder. "Bessie, are you okay?"

Bessie looked up, nodding like a child.

With the spinning of the space station restored, the artificial gravity force began to pull them down to the floor. Lowry put her hand out. "Come on, Bessie; it's over. Let's go back to our offices." She put her arm around her, guiding her back to her cubicle, and then brought her some water.

Sevy bounded over to Lowry and whispered, "I'm still glad I got to kiss you."

Lowry laughed and grabbed his arm, whirling him around so she could inspect his face. "You need to go to the clinic and get examined—you'll have some nice bruises for show-and-tell."

He nodded and started walking past her, but he stopped as she asked, "What do you think will happen to that crazy group who broke down the door and stole the spacesuits?"

Sevy grimaced. "A one-way ticket home, at the least." He pointed at one of the cameras. "Fixed cameras are everywhere in the work areas, all on battery backup, so their 'performance' will have been recorded to a T."

Lowry returned to her office and sat down in the reassuring gravity as it returned to normal. She looked at the rebooted screen, remembering the strange transmission just before the outage had occurred. She logged in, and the blue screen glowed.

Bob said, "Lowry, that was strange."

She laughed at the relief of hearing Bob's voice. "Bob, you were able to capture a part of the file?"

"Yes, Lowry. Let me find it." In a second, he said, "I have it, but it's an encrypted file, and I don't have the capability to break the code. The only lines I can read are the first two lines in the file: the first says '1998,' and the second line indicates an executable file for the main power computer."

A chill came over her—this seemed more than just a coincidence. Her heart beat in staccato. *There are more ways to skin this cat.*

Lowry called Zoë. Her face appeared in the screen, etched in an odd mix of fear and relief.

Zoë asked, "What the hell happened?"

"I don't know. Zoë, are you up and running?"

"Yes, though scared enough to pee in my pants."

Lowry raised her eyebrows. "That would be awkward in zero gravity."

"Thanks for that visual, Lowry."

Lowry took a deep breath. "Zoë, I have a favor to ask—can I send you a file, at least a part of a file? Just before the power outage, I received a weird file via a laser transmitted from the ground as we passed over Antarctica. Bob was able to copy the first portion of the file before the original wiped itself off my computer, but it's encrypted, and we can't read it. I'm hoping you have a better program to break the code than the piece-of-shit computer I have—oh, sorry, Bob."

"No offense, Lowry; my encryption-breaking software is as you describe—a piece-of-shit."

Shrugging, she whispered to Zoë, "You have to keep this hush-hush for now until we figure this out."

"Uh, sure, Lowry. Send it to me, and I'll call you when I break it."

An hour later, Zoë called her. Lowry could hear the tension in her voice. "Lowry, you'd better come down here."

Lowry's heart thumped as she walked to Zoë's office. The grim look on Zoë's face scared her. She whispered hoarsely, "What is it? Tell me!"

Zoë pointed to the screen, where the file commands were converted into English. Lowry's eyes grew wide as she read the words on the screen. *Shut down all systems in ten seconds: power, air, artificial gravity.* The second command was: *Restore power in sixty minutes.*

Lowry's mouth dropped open as she turned to Zoë. "Sabotage."

Zoë nodded and then looked quizzically at her. "Lowry, how and why did *you* receive this message?"

Lowry shook her head. "I have no idea. I was collecting data over Antarctica when a flash hit my screen. At first, I thought the burst of light was space trash hitting the skin of the station, but then a filename popped up on the screen. Bob said it was an OPALS laser message from the surface."

Zoë said slowly, "Someone sent that file to temporarily shut down the space station as a protest or warning." She rubbed her jaw. "We have to tell the authorities about this."

Lowry nodded. "You're the one for that." Lowry squinted at the screen. "That message came from near the mining station. I'll contact my Uncle Nick. He's a volunteer police officer—perhaps he can find some evidence on the ground." She exhaled. "If the attack was from a terrorist group, they are probably already on the move."

Blue ice sheets collapsed, yielding to the laws of thermodynamics. The Arctic Ocean opened, and ships navigated the fabled Northwest Passage. A catastrophic shift came to the world's ocean currents, and the warm Brazil current flowed past Antarctica. The great movement of melting ice chiseled valleys on their journey to the sea, and the southern ice cap melted away within a human lifespan. Antarctica—bare and quiet in a world gone mad.

# A SPIDER SAT BESIDE HER

# CHAPTER 8

Nick's boots crunched in the loose gravel as he walked along a stream in the valley west of the mining camp. A melting glacier had carved the bedrock into a U-shaped gorge as it glided to the sea, but now the bare rock focused the sun down its steep sides, warming the air at its base. He stopped to take a drink and took off his jacket, tying it around his waist. He checked the GPS on his watch—Lowry's coordinates for the message transmission were just ahead. As he rested, he scanned the ground for any sign of footprints or a campfire.

One more swallow of water and a splash along the brim of his hat, and then he continued toward the transmission site. Nick shook his head, trying to figure out who would have ventured into this rough area to send a lethal message to the space station. It just didn't make sense, this message being transmitted by any of the miners on Antarctica. No doubt some of them who had immigrated were a rough lot, but most just wanted to make enough money to get drunk and then lose it in a card game.

Besides a few birds flying lazily in the sky, he was utterly alone at the bottom of the world, and his thoughts wandered as he walked along this desolate area. People always considered him a simple man, but in reality, he was a deeply complex human being. Still, he had found it easier to veil his inner thoughts, especially on a thinly populated outpost such as

Antarctica, where everyone knew everyone's business.

He followed the river downstream, and the valley sides began to open with boulders strewn about like children's blocks. Dammed by a ridge of earth, a small lake had formed with low brush growing along the edges. Flocks of various birds gathered around the open water. He smiled—the habitation success story on Antarctica was the explosion of the bird population.

He stopped, gazing at the arcuate shape of the mounded dirt and debris until his mouth fell open. This was the remains of what had been a glacier. Before him was a terminal moraine, marking the final descent of a great glacier, like a mammoth's final resting place, but now just a puddle of water.

Tears came to his eyes at the beauty and sadness of this interrupted embrace between earth and ice, a monument to all which had been lost in the floods of world—his legs shook— and to the unrequited love which had forced him to flee to Antarctica. He fell to his knees as the onslaught of memories crashed into his mind.

*     *     *

He had never believed in love at first sight until it struck him between the eyes. Who could resist falling in love with a beautiful, intelligent woman whose banter filled a room with laughter—and pierced his heart? She was another man's wife, but like a moth to a light, he could not resist her.

After a fight with her husband one night, she had escaped from the house to walk off her anger. She was lovely and vulnerable when he stumbled upon her in a garden drenched in moonlight. Like a dream, he had pulled her to him while their eyes locked together.

Sadness veiled her eyes, and he saw the redness of a slap on her white cheek. He caressed the mark on her skin and then kissed it gently. She closed her eyes, tilting her head back, and he kissed her warm lips. She yielded, and he pulled her to him, crushing his mouth into hers.

Breathless, he stepped back and stared into her eyes—astonished at the passion between them. His lips met hers again, and his fingers followed the curve of her neck until he touched the thin straps of her summer dress. He slipped the straps off her shoulders, and the dress fell away from her body.

She stared at him silently in her nakedness, her skin glowing in the moonlight like a marble sculpture. His hands trembled as he drew her into his arms, and they dropped to the cool grass. Between kisses, her hands peeled his clothes away, and their warm skin touched. On this summer night, with no guilt or thought, they made love as the moon sank behind the trees—an act of desperation where two souls converged at one time and place.

Their needs temporarily sated, they held each other and fell into an exhausted sleep under the branches of an old oak. The first rays of the sun stole through the leaves, waking them to a new day. He pulled her to him, and they made love again. Afterward, she held his face between her hands and kissed him deeply, but a tear rolled down her face as she said, "I can't do this." Staring into his eyes, she caressed his cheek and then grabbed her dress, fleeing in the pale light of dawn. The affair ended with his heart broken, and he left for Antarctica, knowing that one night was all he could have with her.

In the desolation of Antarctica, he had never found another woman to love and share his life with, especially with the poor pickings in the mining camps, where women were either married or prostitutes. He did not judge the latter, and many became wives to lonely miners, but he simply had not connected with anyone at the outpost. And so he had spent his adult life focused on geologic expeditions and coordinating negotiations between the owners of the mining company and the miners.

\*     \*     \*

Nick knelt in the loose gravel, vaguely staring out at the mounded rim of the terminal moraine, and then brushed his hair away from his moist eyes. He had come to the bottom of the world, so far from his past—until it sucker-punched him in the gut. He drank from his canteen and staggered up, unsteady from the emotional storm that had overcome him. He breathed in the dry air, shoving his memories back into the hole where he had locked them way. He stumbled across the rocky debris of the moraine, his thoughts as scattered as the stones.

Exhaling deeply, he shook the cobwebs away, focusing his mind as he strolled along the outer edge of the moraine. The scientist in him took control. He was in awe of the power of flowing ice to bulldoze this mass of earth into a giant ridge of soil and rocks. Nick took GPS readings and a few images so a geologic team could return to this location and map the moraine in detail.

Nick left the moraine area, walking along the stream flowing downhill from the dammed-up lake, assuming that the perpetrators would have stayed near water. There was a roughed-up look to the sand ahead, and he slowed his pace. He reached the spot, leaning down to get a closer look at the ground. Someone had purposely brushed the sand here, hiding tracks as they walked along. He jerked up at the shrieks of seagulls flying over his head. The ocean must be near.

His heart thumped as he stood over a darkened area in the sand. *A campsite?* He glanced around, listening for footsteps or movement in the brush, but there was nothing except the sporadic sounds of birds. He knelt and carefully dug into the sand where the campfire had been. He started as the wind rustled the bushes behind him, and he swallowed hard as he looked around. He hoped that whoever had been here was actually gone. A lost geologist in the wilds of Antarctica would be back-page stuff, one of those chin-scratching mysteries that no one solves and nobody really wants to.

He turned back and dug away into the soft sand, flinching as his fingers touched a sharp object. He carefully brushed away the sand grains, uncovering what was left of the cooked and eaten carcass of a bird, probably a grouse by the size of the body. Then he saw beneath the bones what appeared to be some type of dart. He picked it up and studied it carefully. It looked like it was carved from bone or wood, but the tip had been broken, and it had a singed cotton-like material—a type of seed pod—on the end.

His forehead furrowed as he realized that this looked like an Amazonian dart, the kind used with a blowgun. *Why would native tribesmen travel from South America to attack the space station?* He put the dart down and continued to dig until he pulled up some blackened wood coals. He removed his gloves and felt them—they were still a little warm. They weren't far ahead of him.

He glanced again over his shoulder and then held the dart up, taking a series of 3D photos of it before he carefully placed it in a pocket of his knapsack. Nick took detailed panoramic shots of the area. Nature would soon destroy fragile evidence, and it was imperative to gather all he could.

Nick found the low evergreen tree from which the trail-scrubbing branch had been cut and checked the ground closely at the base of the tree. The ground was brushed here, and he followed the light markings of the needles, videoing the trail as it led toward the coast.

Soon he heard the ocean and the din of seabirds; the shore was just ahead. Aware that the perpetrators may still be in the vicinity, he stowed his phone and crept quietly forward to the beach. He pushed his way through the brush on the edge of the beach, stumbling on the discarded cut branch and falling face first with a grunt onto the exposed beach. He pushed himself up on his elbows and gasped at the fresh footprints in the sand in front of him. With thumping heart, he cautiously peered up and down the beach to make sure he was alone.

Nick slowly rose, brushing himself off with shaking hands. He edged onto the beach, watching for any movement ahead, and followed the footprints down the shoreline. He came to the stream that flowed from the lake, and the tracks became clearer in the wet sand. He glanced around and then squatted down to study the footprints. There appeared to be two men, both with small feet—one barefoot and the other in hiking boots.

He took photos of the tracks as he followed them along the brush at the edge of the beach. He stopped where the footprints became chaotic and realized that next to the prints, there were gouges in the sand. The gouges led into the low brush at the edge of the beach, and Nick pulled back a branch; the score of a boat extended under the bushes. *This is where they must have hidden a small canoe.*

He took more photos and then followed the footsteps and mark of the boat as they dragged it toward the sea. The tracks disappeared at the edge of the surf.

Shielding his eyes, he scanned the horizon. Birds wheeled overhead, their cries lost within the crashing waves on an empty beach. Whoever they were had gotten clean away.

# CHAPTER 9

Two days after the shutdown of the space station, Lowry heard a knock on the wall of her cubicle. Irritated with the volume of gossipmongers she had been dealing with since the power outage, she growled over her shoulder, "Hold your horses!"

She finished setting up her parameters, pushed a couple of buttons, and then asked the computer, "Are we good, Bob?"

"All set, Lowry."

Lowry exhaled and turned around to see who was interrupting her work. She blinked at the sight of a drop-dead-gorgeous man standing in front of her cubby—dressed to kill in an expensive pinstriped suit and crisp white shirt, perfectly accentuated with a classic silk tie.

His pursed his lips, studying her with penetrating blues eyes. Then a smile flashed onto his chiseled face, revealing his beautiful white teeth. "Lowry Walker?"

Lowry cleared her throat and chuckled with embarrassment. She'd been staring at him as if he were an apparition. "Sorry, I've been inundated with tourists lately."

He continued in a low voice. "I'm sure you have—that's one of the reasons I'm here." He pulled his phone out of his pocket, and a hologram of his identification popped up. "Let me introduce myself: I'm Edward Douglas, one of the lawyers from the US Justice Department investigating the space-station shutdown, and please, call me Edward." He grinned, gesturing toward the hallway with his hand. "Why don't we take a walk?"

Self-consciously, she brushed back her hair and stood up. *He's good-looking, but don't make a fool of yourself.* She straightened her back and strolled past him into the hall. At first, she wasn't sure where to go, but she found herself heading to the Garden. They entered through the heavy glass doors, and Lowry grinned at the surprised look on Edward's face when they moved into an Eden of lush vegetation and roosting chickens.

"I got the hint that you wanted to get away from eavesdropping ears."

"Yes. This will be perfect." Edward gazed at the menagerie of plants and animals. "This is really quite amazing."

They walked along the path, and Lowry explained the importance of the Garden to the space station. "It's the lifeblood of the ISS. Without it, we could not survive." Lowry led him to a quiet alcove off the pathway to the orchards.

Edward motioned her to sit on a bench, and then he sat next to her, clearing his throat as he set his phone to record. He smiled and said, "What I need from you is a statement of exactly what happened the day of the station shutdown from start to finish."

Lowry cocked her head. "Before we begin, can you tell me why this is so hush-hush?"

"We're still investigating and gathering information through our interviews, so I can't tell you much. But we are very aware that the space station might still be vulnerable."

Lowry recounted the events of the shutdown, and after she finished her story, she turned toward him. "So what is the next step? Do you have any possible suspects?"

"This is one of the first major e-terrorism cases in the history of humans—believe me, it may be a while before we figure this out." Edward looked at her intensely. "We must be on our guard at all times, and we have to expect another assault, Lowry."

Edward drummed his fingers on his knee and looked at

her intently. "Lowry, I must ask you to not discuss this with anyone. This is deadly serious."

She curled her lip, annoyed at his patronizing tone. "No kidding, Sherlock. I understand the situation."

He chuckled, but then his smile faded. "We've been interviewing everyone involved, including your computer assistant, Bob. And one question still is unanswered: Lowry, why is it that *you* received this transmission?"

Lowry frowned. "I don't think it was just coincidence. My dissertation is to collect surface imagery data over Antarctica, and we were in the midst of recording a swath. The attackers must have figured out a way to transmit the OPALS message from the surface under the path of the high-definition camera." She shrugged. "This project has been widely publicized for several years, so plenty of time to prepare, but what I don't understand is how they were able to transmit a file through the satellite and then get it into the main computer."

"Why would they choose to send the OPALS message from Antarctica?"

"The space station wouldn't receive a laser message from everywhere, and the ISS's data-gathering satellites were trained onto a fairly narrow region for the Antarctic mapping project." She gestured with her hands. "And who would think to look for terrorists on the remotest spot on the Earth? And how would you trace them back to anywhere?"

He nodded. "Then you contacted your uncle at the mining station after the space-station power came back on?"

"Yes, after we figured out it was an actual attack on the space station, I contacted him. There aren't very many people on Antarctica, so besides being a geologist, he's also a member of the volunteer police and fire department, so he has authority to investigate criminal activities."

"I see. Do you know what he has found, if anything?"

"No, I haven't heard from him since I sent him the coordinates of the OPALS transmission site." Lowry brow furrowed. "I'm frankly a bit worried—it's not like him to not get back to me."

Edward shrugged. "Until we nab a suspect, communications are restricted to and from the ISS, but I'm sure he's fine. The mining station on Antarctica is crawling with investigators from around the world. He's probably being peppered with a lot of questions." He looked down at the transcript on his phone. "Well, I can't think of anything else at the moment, but I'll be back and forth to the space station for the next several weeks, and I'm sure there will be other questions as the investigation goes on."

He leaned back on the bench and grinned at the chatter of a squirrel. He exhaled and asked, "So how is it living on a space station?"

"Perhaps you wouldn't mind turning off the recording mode."

"Oh, yeah."

\* \* \*

Two weeks later, Lowry saw Edward again. She turned toward a knock on her cubicle wall and sucked in her breath; it was Edward, standing there with his captivating smile.

"Can I persuade you to walk with me again?" he asked.

Her heart skipped a beat—or three. Biting the inside of her lip, she forced her face into a smile while she inhaled deeply to calm her heart. Lowry was slightly annoyed with herself. She was quite taken with him, and the maddening part of it? Edward knew it. Clenching her fist, she blurted out, a bit louder than she meant to, "Certainly."

With a twinkle in his eyes, he asked, "Another garden stroll?"

"Sounds good to me." She rose from her desk, and her heart fluttered as she passed near him.

Edward turned with her, and they stepped out into the corridor. Lowry hesitated for a moment, and then, for fun, she led him around to the opposite entrance to the Garden from their last visit. He chatted about a college buddy as they strolled down the corridor until the heavy glass doors swooshed close.

"The Garden looks different today."

"I decided to show you another side of it."

They meandered along the garden path, and Edward was less formal than their first meeting, pointing out different flowers and laughing at the antics of the rabbits.

Finally, curiosity won out, and she asked, "So what's up? Why did you want to go for a walk?"

He took her arm, pivoting her around to face him. With a charming grin, he said, "I just wanted to take a walk with the prettiest girl in the stars."

"Bullshit."

He chuckled. "Seriously."

Lowry raised an eyebrow. "Isn't flirting some kind of conflict of interest or something?"

"Nah. I'm only a junior attorney anyway."

The artificial breeze of the Garden kicked in, and Lowry breathed in the scent of the flowers carried on the gentle wind. But the playful wind mussed Edward's hair, and his grin withered. He turned his head, smoothing it back into place.

Puzzled at his change in demeanor, Lowry studied his profile. Her smile faded as she noticed the taut cords of his neck. Edward perfected his appearance and then turned back to her, flashing his signature grin, but he remained silent.

Lowry tilted her head. "Are you okay? You seem stressed."

He blinked, but his eyes didn't meet hers. "I'm fine." Shrugging, he continued. "Well, maybe a little stressed—it's hardly begun, and already this trial is exhausting." With a faint sigh, he gazed vacantly out into the orchards nearby.

A troop of chickens marched by, filling the awkward silence between them with their clucking and scratching. After they had passed, Lowry fumbled for something to say, asking, "What's happening with the investigation?"

With a grimace, Edward shook his head. "Frankly, I don't want to discuss it." He closed his eyes and rubbed the back of his neck. "I'd like to forget about the ISS case for a bit. I've been living it for weeks now."

Lowry smiled and placed her hand on his arm. "No problem, Edward, I understand."

A rustling noise came from the row of blueberry bushes lining the path. Edward and Lowry jerked around, staring at the trembling branches of one of the bushes until Adam pushed his way through the hedge. With a branch sticking in his disheveled hair, he guided a hovercart, filled with garden tools, onto the path. He paused for a moment to adjust his glasses, which had slipped down his nose, back into place, and then he began to steer the hovercart along the path toward them.

Edward stepped backward, muttering, "What the hell?" under his breath.

Lowry whispered back, "Oh, he's the gardener. I don't know his real name, but everyone calls him Adam. He's a rather odd man who talks in fables and rhymes. He's perfectly harmless."

Adam stopped and grabbed a rake. With his nose twitching, he came toward them, brandishing the rake in front of him like a medieval weapon. As if they were invisible, he stopped and calmly raked the leaves on the side of the path near their feet.

"Hi, Adam—" Lowry began to say.

Edward glanced sideways at her and then slipped his arm under hers, gently pulling her along the path away from Adam. "We'd better keep walking, Lowry." When they were out of earshot, he said, "You didn't tell me the ISS housed a funny farm."

Lowry shot him a sideways look. "Perhaps Adam's a bit different, but he's a very hard worker."

Edward pursed his lips. "I'm surprised they let a nut like that up here."

"They try to have representatives from around the globe."

"I guess he's from Kookysvania?"

"Mr. Comedian, don't quit your day job—you ain't that funny," Lowry replied with a sneer. Then she shrugged. "I've asked Adam where he's from, but he just grins and points to the overgrown berry patch."

"Ah, he's Br'er Rabbit!" Edward chortled.

A rabble of butterflies crossed in front of them, and they paused for a moment, admiring the iridescent pageant. Lowry gestured toward the passing swarm. "And that, my friend, is why a swarm of butterflies is called a kaleidoscope."

They walked along the trail and came to a stream. Edward held her hand as they stepped from rock to rock to the other bank. Once they reached the other side, Edward paused, still holding her hand. With a smile, he slowly turned back to gaze at the gurgling brook. "How lovely."

"And just think that only a few hours ago, that was servicing someone's bathroom."

Narrowing his eyes, he looked at her. "Thanks for bursting my happy thoughts."

"You're welcome."

He gave her hand a little squeeze. "I wasn't just referring to the stream."

With a raised eyebrow, she sneered, "You're a big tease, Edward," and then turned away to hide her smile.

They walked toward the freshwater lake, and from time to time, Edward placed his hand gently on Lowry's back. With each touch, she drew in her breath.

When they reached the shore, they sat down on a bench, quietly watching the swans sail across the surface.

Edward cleared his throat, and Lowry turned toward him. He exhaled and tilted his head toward her. "Lowry, there is another reason I needed to talk to you. I know you're not going to like this, but you might be called as a witness in the trial."

Her mouth dropped open, and she turned to him sharply. "What? I thought my deposition was going to be enough."

Edward shrugged. "Your giving testimony during the trial is not in stone as yet. But the prosecution wants to have a preliminary meeting with you in case you go on the stand." He gazed at her. "You are an important witness, my dear, as the only link between the ISS to the terrorist group allegedly involved in the attack. The prosecution team has arranged a meeting in conference room B, Section Two, to go over your possible testimony. You need to be there at ten o'clock sharp."

Lowry stared across the water at the pair of swans. They momentarily linked their necks together, only to break apart with a flurry of squawks, and the black swan chased the white one, disturbing the smooth surface of the lake with their wake. *Was this new bombshell the reason Edward had been so cagey earlier? And his flirtation dance—was all of this some sort of push-pull tactic to keep her off balance?*

Edward touched her arm. "Don't worry, Lowry. I'll be there, too."

Lowry pursed her lips, squinting her eyes at him. "Yeah, but which side of the table will you be on?"

*   *   *

The next morning, she walked down the hall to the meeting and paused at the conference-room door for a deep breath to settle her nerves before she entered the room.

She slid inside the door, and Edward rose to greet her. Once he was facing away from the rest of the group, he gave her a sly wink. With a nod, he said in a formal voice, "Thank you for coming, Ms. Walker."

He motioned her to approach the table, gesturing toward a heavyset, middle-aged man sitting like a lord at a banquet. "May I introduce you to Mr. Gerwin, who is the Assistant District Attorney for the United States and is leading this investigation of the ISS attack?"

Gerwin's head was cocked to the side as he stroked his mustache with beads of sweat dotting his brow, ignoring Lowry while he read a document on his tablet. Lowry stood there awkwardly before he finally spoke, still not bothering to look up from his screen.

"Ms. Walker, I believe?"

"Yes."

Raising his head, he scrutinized her with a squint in his eye. "Ms. Walker, I have read over your deposition, and if I understand it correctly, you somehow received a strange laser file, supposedly by accident? Is this correct?"

"Whether it was accidental or intentional, I suppose, is still in question. What happened is that we were moving over Antarctica in the midst of surface imagery data collection, when the file hit my computer—apparently beamed through the Landsat satellite dish."

"Ah, yes, I see." Gerwin ran his sweaty hands across his mouth. "I believe you had said that you contacted your uncle, Nick Walker, just after the sabotage occurred?"

Lowry nodded. "Yes."

"Can you tell me his occupation and why you felt he was the one to investigate this?"

"He's a geologist and came to work for the mining company on Antarctica years ago, before all of the ice had melted. He collects samples from outcrops to analyze the geologic history of the continent, so he knows the area." With her palm toward him, she gestured with her hand. "You have to understand that the outpost on Antarctica has a very small staff, and he is also a volunteer for the fire and police department."

Gerwin stood up and leaned toward her, resting his hands on the table. The conference room became quiet as his eyes narrowed under furrowed brows. Lowry edged back in her chair away from Gerwin's penetrating stare.

His lip slowly curled up like an angry dog's before it bites, and he snapped, "And would he have any reason to sabotage the space station?"

Lowry stared at his twisted face and froze for a second in disbelief, astonished at the insinuation that her uncle might be involved. The absurdity of the question sunk in, and in her shock, she threw her head back and burst out laughing.

Gerwin slammed his hand down on the table, the sound ricocheting around the room. Lowry bit her lip to stop laughing but helplessly snickered, holding onto the arms of her chair.

"This is no laughing matter," Gerwin snarled. "Someone

tried to destroy this space station and nearly a hundred lives. We are going to get to the bottom of this!"

Lowry stared at him. Her face flushed, and a switch within her clicked from hilarity to umbrage. *Look asshole, it's best not to wave a red cape at a newly divorced woman—gut-punching a lawyer would make my day.*

She stood up and bent toward him with her hands clenched in fury. "Just because you don't know who did it, don't hang Nick up as a scapegoat! He's one of the finest men I know!" Lowry got into the groove of her rant, relishing the look on Gerwin's pale face as he tilted away from her. "And aren't you forgetting a critical element? How about motive? *Why* would Nick try to destroy the space station? His only niece is aboard, and there is no benefit to him if I lose my life." With teeth bared, she thrust her index finger at him like a dagger. "You would be torn apart in about three seconds by the defense and destroy any remnant of credibility you may have. Is that what you want? Or do you want to try to figure out who really did this?"

Lowry sat down, staring at Gerwin, who blinked in shock at the ferocity of her attack. *I guess that will teach you not to poke me.*

Gerwin pursed his lips and sniffed. "All right. Well, I had to ask the question." Then he sat down and ignored her, swiping a few pages on his tablet.

The door to the conference room opened abruptly, and a young man stuck his head into the room but shrank back at the angry demeanor of the group.

Gerwin growled, "What is it?"

The young man held up his finger. "Uh, I was told to give you a message as soon as possible—I hope I'm not interrupting?"

Gerwin impatiently waved him in. "Give it to me."

The young man crept toward the table and whispered in Gerwin's ear. Gerwin nodded, dismissing him with a wave of his hand. He retreated from the room.

Gerwin narrowed his eyes, stroking his short beard. "That

will be all for now, Ms. Walker. But we need you back here at, say, nine tomorrow morning for a follow-up session." He beckoned Edward with his finger and spoke in a low whisper to him.

Lowry exhaled and stood up, still internally vibrating from the confrontation with Mr. Nice Guy. Clenching her jaw, she left the conference room and walked quickly down the hallway—at least it was over for now. She heard the door open, and Edward ran after her.

When he caught up to her, he stopped and reached out to grab her arm. "I'm sorry about that, Lowry. He's a real jerk."

Lowry grimaced. "No shit."

Edward chuckled. "But you gave it to him with both barrels." He grabbed her around the waist. "I loved the way you dominated that son of a bitch!"

She pushed his hand away. "Only an idiot would think Nick or myself had anything to do with this attack. It just doesn't make sense—neither of us would have any motive to shut down the space station."

"Sense isn't the name of the game—speed is. He's under the gun to get this case solved." He looked both ways down the hall and whispered, "We've just gotten word that we have a suspect in custody—an Inuit rebel leader from the Eskimo territories. Ever since the Melt, the Inuit tribes have been holding protests over the population invasion from the south into their territories. And with him in jail, we just don't know what the tribe might do; they may retaliate."

Bewildered, she shook her head. "Eskimos? How strange—this is sort of déjà vu of the American Indian struggles of a past century, but I guess they are frustrated since from what I've heard, the United States tacitly 'supports' the invasion. But of course, knocking out power to a space station isn't the way to do it."

"Isn't it?" Edward said, raising his brows. "It would put them on the world stage."

"From the top of the world to the bottom would be a ways for them to travel to send a virus to the space station."

"Are you sure an OPALS message can't be sent to the space station via the other satellite dishes on the station?"

Lowry furrowed her brow. Tapping her chin, she replied, "They would have to know the angle and the location of them, which would be much more difficult than the broad data collection mode I was doing, which was aimed straight at the ground."

"They are the one group we know who has a motive." He glanced back toward the conference room. Turning back to her, he brushed his lips against her ear. "Look, Lowry, I have to get back in there, but let's meet later in the garden."

Her ear tingled with the touch of his warm lips. She nodded weakly.

With an irresistible smile, he tugged on a strand of her hair. "Great, it's a date. Five o'clock in the little pocket garden where we first talked."

She watched him disappear through the door and then shook her head to clear her thoughts. Like a fly, her thoughts kept returning to the same scent—Edward.

Lowry went back to her room and, once inside, gripped the arm of a chair as if to hold onto her heart. Edward was intelligent, charming, and good-looking . . . and totally aware of it.

*But he laughs at my jokes.* She ran her fingers through her hair, hating to admit that she was attracted to him. Her ex-husband Frank had been such an ass that Edward's smooth brand of sexuality was a breath of fresh air.

Lowry shivered as her mind went back to her "marital bliss" in the States. In her abject embarrassment, if nothing else, she had kept Uncle Nick and her father only vaguely informed of her short but disastrous marriage to Frank.

She had come of age in the small-town atmosphere of the mining station on Antarctica. Everyone knew everyone's weaknesses. Nothing was hidden. She had only fleetingly dated a couple of boys, so she had been innocent in love until college. Lowry was intellectually strong but had sucked miserably in her first serious relationship.

*Frank.* What an education that had been. They had met her freshman year; he was an upper classman, and she had just arrived from Antarctica—a wide-eyed, emotionally immature girl. Frank was good-looking, athletic, humorous and sweet for the most part, but a hidden vein of low self-esteem raised its head in a few outbursts of anger and jealousy. Through college, they dated but lived apart, with no pressure points to expose the depth of his rage. After he graduated, he asked her to marry him. Like many couples at graduation, marriage seemed to be the next step in life. But . . . she didn't truly know him.

She completed her geophysics degree, and they set a date for the wedding, but as the day approached, the angry scenes became frequent. *Oh, everything will be all right; he'll change after we get married—he's just a little nervous.* On her wedding night, reality hit her—this was all a mistake. She felt revulsion at his touch, and after they made love, she felt an emptiness inside. Listening to his breath rise and fall as he slept beside her, she wondered about annulment.

It had gone downhill from there. She began the graduate program for geophysics, and they moved to a small apartment . . . and her hellhole for the next year.

Gone was the tenderness and the fun side of Frank. All that was left was an extraordinary temper, which exploded at the slightest pretense. His initial approach had been mental abuse, but the day came, as they drove home in the car, when it turned physical. He hit her on the arm, and for several minutes, she couldn't feel two of the fingers on her left hand. A large, dark bruise appeared, a warning sign of what might be ahead for her.

Then, like a miracle, Frank was transferred overseas for several months, and a great weight lifted from her as his plane left the tarmac, like the end of a storm. As the days passed without him, she regained her former personality and realized that she had to get away from him.

He wrote her letters swearing he had changed and wasn't the same man she had married. It was almost if he sensed that she was mentally cutting the bonds. He asked her to come and visit, and though torn about what to do, she did go to him. Marriage meant enough to her to at least try to see if he had truly changed. And oddly enough, she was curious about her own feelings toward him.

When she landed at the terminal, he came into view, smiling and waving. An electric shock went through her. She still hated and feared him. That night, as they lay in bed, he asked her if there was any hope.

She had blurted out, "No." Both were stunned by her words.

After her admission, Lowry wrapped herself in a cold barrier to keep her emotions from spilling out, dazed from the emotional battles. Luckily, there were other people in the flat to provide protection from any physical blows.

Lowry left the next day on an early morning flight. She remembered the surreal ride to the airport, the cab racing through the streets as the fog lifted in the sunlight, and her relief that she had finally told him that she intended to leave him.

But it was only just the beginning of the next phase of the war after he returned from overseas. Her fear of him lingered as his rage brewed just beneath the surface. One evening, Frank snapped, slapping himself until he was red in the face. "Is this what you want of me?" he screamed, his eyes bulging madly.

Like a doe hiding from the hunter, she sat frozen on the barstool where he had plunked her down to watch his self-flagellation. He moved toward her, and she screamed at him, "Leave me alone!" She backed him off with the ferocity of her verbal assault, but she feared it was only a matter of time until it was her turn to be slapped around.

Terrified and with no hope of reconciliation, she now secretly planned her escape from him. She found an apartment and left work early one day to move herself. With a friend, she moved out all her possessions, careful to not take anything that might be perceived as "theirs." She found a lawyer and started the divorce proceedings just a little over a year from the day of their wedding.

Had she married Frank because she was more afraid of losing his love than of his anger? Or, perhaps, had her father's violent temper made Frank's anger feel almost natural? She shook her head. Had she inadvertently wed her greatest fears as she grappled with the unresolved issues of her family?

Lowry sighed. Love and marriage were not something that just "worked out"; they were a real game of Russian roulette where there were probably more bullets than anyone cared to admit. Love is a many-splintered thing.

# CHAPTER 10

Lowry rummaged in her drawers for something pretty to wear. She held up a summer top and matching skirt that she had thrown in her bag at the last minute. She slipped the light blouse over her head and drew on the skirt. Her hands trembled as she smoothed the soft fabric over her body. Gazing into the mirror, her heart pounded at the prospect of love—it had been a long time since her mind had buzzed with romance.

Her divorce started the healing process, but there was still a hollow spot where love had been. The drought between lovers left her vulnerable to Edward's seduction. Almost sensing her thirst, he would linger his hand on her arm or "accidentally" touch her hand—gently awakening her desire.

Glancing at the clock, she exhaled and brushed her hair one last time. She left her cabin and walked toward the tube for her rendezvous in the Garden. She waited in front of the pod doors, and when they opened, Sevy and Zoë stepped out.

Zoë smiled and whistled. "Wow, you clean up nice. Got a hot date?"

Sevy looked at her dully. "She's probably going out with that Edward dude."

*Shit.* "Um, well, yes, I'm meeting him—we're going over some more of the details of the shut-down."

"He only interviewed me once." Sevy pursed his lips. "I

guess he's not interested in my *details*."

Zoë squinted at Sevy and then asked Lowry, "I finally talked Sevy into coming to lunch. How about joining us?"

"Um, I'm not sure how long the meeting with Edward is going to last."

Sevy cocked his head at Zoë. "See, Zoë? She doesn't want to come either." He turned toward Lowry. "I have a bad feeling about Edward. He's just too perfect."

Lowry shrugged and started past him as the next pod arrived. "Too perfect might be just what I need."

Frowning, Sevy said, "I guess I can't compete with that." He turned and walked down the hall.

Zoë called after him, "Sevy, wait."

He just waved behind his head without turning around.

Shaking her head, Zoë grabbed Lowry's arm. "I want to talk to you a minute."

Lowry studied the grave look on Zoë's face and then leaned back against the wall. "What's wrong, Zoë?

"It doesn't seem like you've noticed, but our friend Sevy has been suffering from something akin to PTSD ever since the attack on the station."

"I knew I hadn't seen him as much, but with the depositions . . ."

Zoë snapped, "Depositions, my ass—more likely Edward." Her face softened, and she touched Lowry's arm. "Sorry, it just hits close to home. I've seen this in too many friends and colleagues—some of whom chose to end their lives. I'm not saying that Sevy is suicidal, but our friend is withdrawing from us. We need to reach out to him."

Lowry chewed her lip, remembering her last conversation with Sevy, when he had admitted to gaming obsessively as a teenager.

He had stared ahead and said dully, "My mother worked nights and my father was . . . distant. I had no real friends at the time."

She knew of loneliness but couldn't imagine a life with no friends to form bonds with, cry with, laugh with—another human to share the burden of life. People have an instinctual need for companionship and will seek out whatever avenue is available, whether real or not.

She exhaled. "Zoë, you're right—I've been insensitive and self-absorbed." She smiled at Zoë. "Let's get Sevy back out of his shell."

\*     \*     \*

Her heart fluttered as the final glass doors opened to the Garden. She brushed her hair back with her fingers and, deep in thought, walked down the path to the pocket garden where Edward was waiting.

In many ways, Sevy was right; Edward was perfectly dressed, perfectly coifed, perfectly handsome. Not the usual man she was attracted to. She had little experience with relationships; the pickings at the mining station had been slim at best, consisting of rough-and-tumble young men in jeans and flannels. At college, between her ignorance of who she was and who Frank was, she found herself caught in a destructive relationship with an insecure brute.

Nearing the meeting place, she slowed her steps and then stopped, staring ahead like a squirrel deciding whether to cross the road or not. She exhaled, crossed her fingers for luck, and tiptoed across the artificial stones leading into the alcove. Pushing back the low-hanging branches of the weeping cherry tree, she stepped into the hidden garden.

*No Edward.* In the shadows, she stood motionless—an odd mix of disappointment and relief swept over her.

Hands covered her eyes, and the scent of Edward's subtle cologne drifted into her nose. Then his lips nuzzled the back of her neck. "Edward!" she gasped, goosebumps racing along her skin. Edward twirled her around with a smile. "It's been ages since I saw you last," he whispered, stroking her cheek with the back of his fingers.

"Aren't we supposed to discuss the—"

Edward put his finger over her lips. "Not now." He tilted

his head to the side, caressing her hair. "You have beautiful hair. I've wanted to touch it for weeks."

She felt dizzy, and he grasped her hand, drawing her to a bench in the secluded spot. He nibbled her ear and then slowly moved down to her shoulder. Rattled, Lowry tilted her head away, but Edward reached up with a gentle touch, turning her face to him. Gazing into her eyes, he slowly kissed her hesitant lips.

He wrapped one arm around her waist and the other under her legs and lifted her into his arms. He pushed under the branches of the weeping cherry tree and laid her down on the soft grass. Kneeling beside her, he kissed her cheek and then stretched out along her body, placing his hand on her stomach.

Lowry tilted her head back, staring into the veil of dangling boughs full of cherry blossoms, the sweet scent of the flowers enveloping them. She touched her face with her hand. Her body cried out for the dance of love, but was her mind ready?

Breathless, Lowry lifted her hand. "Edward, I'm not sure about this."

Edward gave her no chance to think. "Shhh, baby." He leaned over her, kissing her hard and deep. His lips soft and sensuous, he pummeled her mouth with an onslaught of kisses, shattering her resistance. His hands caressed her skin and then stroked her belly through the thin material of her clothes.

Her desire had been confined too long. Like a starving dog, she was hungry for love. Her body awakened to his touch, her skin tingling as he swept his hands over her breasts. Lowry reached out and pulled his mouth to hers. In between kisses, he smoothly peeled her clothes away, stroking her nude body into a frenzy.

Edward shed his clothes as he covered her with kisses. He satisfied her needs, and then she arched up to him, and they made passionate love under the cherry tree.

Afterward, he rolled beside her, breathing hard, and wrapped his arm around her, hugging her close to his chest.

"Lowry, you are wonderful."

Lowry lay her head on his shoulder, spent and unable to move. "Oh, Edward . . ."

Edward's breath became quiet and even. She glanced up at his relaxed face and realized he had fallen asleep. In the soft light, Lowry gazed at her lover's features, unsure of what their next steps would be, if any.

She gently kissed his shoulder and then shifted from under his arm without waking him. Shivering, she found her clothes swaying in the branches. Lowry pulled on her clothes, watching Edward's chest rise and fall as he slept. She combed through her tousled hair with her fingers and then knelt and kissed the tip of his nose.

He twitched and opened his eyes. "Oh, did I fall asleep?"

"Yes, Edward," she said softly, cupping his face in her hand.

"Hey, no fair—you're dressed." He smiled and reached up, yanking on her skirt.

Pulling her skirt back into place, she laughed and shook her head. "I have to go to back to work, Edward."

He sighed. "You're no fun." He crawled over to his clothes and pulled on his pants. He stood up and then jumped toward her, lassoing her with his shirt. He drew her into his arms and whispered in her ear. "What are you doing later?"

Lowry didn't reply, just abstractly stroked the hair on his chest. She raised her head, gazing into his eyes, but was unsure of what she would find. Was Edward just a transient lover, or something more?

Edward rubbed his nose against hers and then nuzzled her cheek. "Are you sure you have to go to work?"

"I'm afraid so." Shyly, she placed her hands around his neck. She closed her eyes, and with a small sigh, her head fell back and her lips parted.

He grinned at the invitation and dove down onto her lips, reddened from use. "You don't seem so sure now."

His kisses were slow and deep, and their passions began to burn again until Lowry placed her hands on his chest and pushed him back. She sighed and then lifted her eyebrows, pursing her lips. "Yes, Edward, I really need to get back."

Edward shrugged. "Game over." He ruffled her hair and then pulled on his shirt. He plucked a cherry blossom off the tree and tucked it behind her ear, playfully tugging a lock of her hair. They shared one last embrace in their lovers' hideaway, and then, arm in arm, they left the Garden.

# CHAPTER 11

Nick shifted in his seat for what felt like the hundredth time. He had been asked to meet with the US federal agents investigating the space station shutdown. When he had arrived, he'd been shown, like a suspect, into one of the small interrogation rooms at the police station. He'd been sitting there for over an hour, and they had yet to come to question him.

He stared down at the table, thinking back to his recent visit to one of the South American miners who had come to Antarctica. Already acclimated to a cold climate, many of the miners working on Antarctica had immigrated from Patagonia. Recently, he had heard that there was one miner who had come from Colombia, so he had decided to ask him some questions about the dart and see if he could shed some light on its origin.

\*     \*     \*

Nick knocked on the door of one of the miners he knew, Yagan Calderon, from the Patagonian region in Chile. Yagan came to the door with a cautious smile and gestured him to enter. Yagan was a tall man, descended from the Patagonian "giants," and though he was polite, Nick knew him to be a man of few words.

When Nick asked him about the Colombian miner, he

glanced at Nick with a puzzled look, admitting that he knew him, but not well. In a guarded tone, he asked Nick why he wanted to see him. Nick held up the dart and told him that he'd found it about three hours west of the station and asked if it could be from an Amazonian tribe. Yagan studied the dart, but Nick sensed his reticence to play the informer on the Colombian. Yagan shrugged, saying he wasn't sure about the dart, but offered to take him to the Colombian's room in the next building.

They walked over to the one-story cement building. Yagan found the room and knocked on the door. There was no answer, and Nick tried the knob. The door was unlocked, so he pushed it open and peered in. He furrowed his brow at the condition of the room, which resembled a college dorm room at the end of the year—drawers and closet door thrown open with nothing inside, trash and torn clothing on the floor. It was obvious the Colombian had packed in haste and left.

Yagan stuck his head in and glanced around, but he drew back at the disarray. He looked at Nick, saying that whatever was happening was none of his business, that he couldn't afford to get involved. With a wave, he retreated down the hall and left.

Gazing at the mess before him, Nick rubbed his chin and slipped on some gloves to not contaminate any evidence. He edged into the room, and the back of his neck itched with the creepy feeling that this was a crime scene, but was it connected to the attack on the ISS?

He combed the drawers, closet, and desk, searching for clues to connect this Colombian miner to the space station attack, but the only thing left was debris. Sighing, he turned to leave but then saw a wad of paper under the leg of the cot. He knelt and lifted up the leg, pulling out a small manila envelope that had been folded up as if to level the bed. He sat on the cot and unfastened the brass clip, holding his face away from the opening of the envelope in case there was some noxious substance inside. He peered inside at a yellowed newspaper clipping. Nick's eyebrows shot up. *I haven't seen a real newspaper in ages.*

Cautiously, Nick drew the clipping out and unfolded it onto the cot, smoothing it flat on the mattress. The paper was in English and detailed an account of a Colombian tribe that had threatened to commit mass suicide if a petroleum project commenced on their tribal lands. He looked at the date and noticed it was from the year 1998. He gasped—that was a hundred years ago—a historic anniversary. With shaking hands, he slipped the newspaper clipping back into the envelope. Could there be a connection between the tribe in the old article and the current shutdown of the ISS?

*   *   *

The sound of voices brought Nick back to the present, and he heard the *clip, clip* of regulation footwear echoing down the corridor. The footsteps stopped in front of the interrogation room where he was sitting. Swallowing hard, he stared at the door.

Nick's heart beat faster as the door swung open, revealing a large man in a dark suit, dark tie, and starched white shirt.

The man strode into the room, saying brusquely, "Mr. Walker, thank you for coming in today." He shook Nick's hand. "My name is Agent Brown." Three agents followed him into the room. They spread out around the room, surrounding Nick as they sat at the table.

This invasion of federal agents had unnerved everyone on Antarctica, Nick included. On Antarctica, no one wore suits, so the feds stood out like sore thumbs. They combed every property throughout the mining community like a mutt searching for his bone. Everyone felt guilty. Even the dogs avoided them.

The agents sat stiffly around a table, staring at him with blank faces. Nick shifted in his hard chair, studying each of them in turn, trying to discern why he seemed to be a target of their investigation rather than on their side.

Abruptly, Brown said, "Mr. Walker, we hear you have

found some evidence."

Nick replied, "Yes, my niece informed me that something serious had happened . . ."

A gash resembling a smile flashed over Brown's mouth, but the hardness of his stare remained. "Let's just get to what you found, sir."

Nick felt his temper rise as he returned Brown's gaze. Instead of telling him to fuck off, he chewed the inside of his mouth. Brown blinked and asked again in a softer tone, "Mr. Walker, can you please tell us what you found?"

With a curt nod, Nick said, "I went to the site where Lowry said the transmission to the space station had been initiated—about three hours west of here. I discovered where they had camped, though the campsite and their tracks had been concealed." He cleared his throat and leaned forward. "I found their campfire and dug down into it to see if the coals were cold or warm. They were warm, so I knew they had been there recently. And I found a carcass of a bird and what appeared to be a broken dart."

Brown nodded. "Okay, anything else?"

"Nothing else at the campsite, but I followed the remnants of their trail to the beach. Once there, they didn't bother to conceal their tracks, and there appeared to be two sets of footprints. Farther along the shoreline, I saw drag marks from a small boat, which had been hidden in the brush. The marks continued to the water's edge, and this, I assume, is how they escaped, probably to a larger vessel out at sea."

Nick glanced at the men around the table. "Lowry mentioned possible video evidence on drone cameras linked to the Landsat data collection. There should have been one flying over that swath at the time of the message. Have you checked those?"

Brown pursed his lips. "Did she see the video from the drone recording over the 'campsite' you found?"

"No, Lowry can only stream video from the drones closest to an internet signal, which is the set nearest to the mining station. The rest of them record to a chip, and then the video is recovered when the drones land."

"We'll check those." He nodded to one of the agents, who got up and left the room.

Brown rocked back in his chair, stroking his cleanly shaven face. Squinting his eyes, he asked, "So what is your theory as to who perpetrated this attack on the space station?"

Nick shifted in his chair again, drumming his fingers on the table. "I have done some initial research on the dart, and it points to a tribe of Indians in Colombia." He shook his head, gesturing with his hands. "I know it sounds strange, but there was a Colombian working down here who bugged out after the attack. In his room, I found an article about a Colombian tribe who threatened a mass suicide a hundred years ago when an oil company planned to explore on their land for oil. Apparently, to the people of the tribe, this drilling and extraction of oil would constitute draining the 'lifeblood' of the Earth."

Nick tapped the tabletop. "While I researched this particular incident from 1998, I discovered that a new power plant is scheduled to be built near their homelands and has the same tribe in an uproar."

A pregnant silence filled the room as the agents stared at him, the expressions on their faces ranging from skepticism to hilarity.

Brown glared at him with his mouth twisted like a pretzel. With his hand next to his mouth, he whispered harshly, "I'll tell you a secret—a primitive tribe of Colombian Indians is *not* on our list of suspects."

The agents around the table guffawed, and the young agent at the end of the table asked, "Why the hell would an Amazon tribe of Colombians attack the space station?"

Sneering, the agent sitting on the other side of Nick joined the game. "Maybe their next attempt would be to have their warriors rain darts on Paris." Grinning, he shook his head. "It would be disastrous. All those flat tires would shut down the entire city."

Brown waved his hand sharply to cut the jests. His face

looked as hard as cement, and his eyes were locked onto Nick's as he clenched and unclenched his hand. Suddenly, he slammed his fist onto the table, the report reverberating like a shot around the small chamber.

"Mr. Walker, you may think this is some kind of game, but it's not." He leaned forward, and with his lips pinched, he said, "We are working hard to find the real perpetrators, and this group may try again. We're on a clock, my friend. If you have anything to add, we need to have it—*now*."

Nick looked around the table as a deathly quiet settled over the room. If they thought he was crazy, why didn't they just kick him out? Nick blinked at the stalwart face of the lead agent, matching stare for stare.

"So, do *you* have an idea of who sent the virus?" he asked.

"I'm not at liberty to share with you the thoughts of the Federal Government of Amerada as to who we think attacked the ISS." Brown's voice became deathly cold. "I will just say to you, turn over the evidence so we can complete our investigation."

Nick breathed in, scrutinizing the grim faces of the agents. Something was not right—he felt it in his bones. He hesitated, unconsciously laying his hand on his knapsack that held the dart.

Brown's lips curled into a snarl. "If you do not give us the evidence, Mr. Walker, we have the authority to throw you in jail. Is that what you want?"

The agent to his left grabbed the knapsack away from him. Nick started up, but the other agent on his right shoved him back into his chair. The agent handed the bag to Brown, who unzipped and dumped the contents onto the table. The agent next to Nick kept his hand firmly on Nick's shoulder, preventing any interference while they rifled through his gear. One of the agents found the pocket where Nick had stowed the dart, ripped it open, pulled out the dart, and handed it to Brown. Then the agent turned the bag inside out, searching for any other evidence.

Brown held up the dart and turned it around, sniffing

disdainfully. "Of course, we don't even know where this thing came from, do we? After all, the site was tampered with prior to any federal agents investigating the area."

Nick furrowed his brow and snapped, "I'm on the volunteer police force here in Antarctica and trained in criminal investigation."

He snorted. "And do you have a police costume too? I guess it comes in handy at Halloween."

Nick's lip twitched as they scowled at each other.

One of the other agents handed Brown a plastic bag, and he dropped the dart into the bag and sealed it. He snapped open his briefcase, put the evidence inside, and locked the case. A smile flitted across his face as he gestured for them to return the knapsack. He turned back to Nick and dismissed him with wave of his hand. "You can go for now, but don't leave the base station without notifying us."

Nick rose, shoving his chair away from the table with a screech, and jerked back his knapsack. Clenching his jaw, he snatched his gear strewn across the table and stuffed everything inside. Without a word, he turned and walked out the door. As he left the building, he thought to himself, *At least they don't know about the photographs.* He hurried to his office.

Nick closed the door to his office, shaking his head as he mulled over the tense interrogation he had just left. No doubt, it was an oddball connection between a Colombian tribe and the attack on the space station, but the agents seemed determined to reject any of the evidence.

He transferred the image of the dart to a tiny hard drive and then packaged it with a few wisps of the cotton-like seedpod material, which he had plucked out of the Velcro of his knapsack. DNA analysis would reveal the exact plant they originated from. He smiled to himself; it was doubtful that the feds would bother to inspect the antiquated physical mail service. He would send them via snail mail to a colleague of his who was a professor of South American Indian tribes. She would be able to tell him if this was from that particular Colombian tribe who was protesting, and real evidence, or whether all of this was just a bizarre sideshow.

Nick picked up the envelope and shook it at the sky. *I don't know what the hell is going on, but Lowry, my girl, you'd better watch yourself.*

# CHAPTER 12

"Corner pocket—upper quadrant."

"You'll never make that shot, Lowry," said Sevy, shaking his head.

"Just watch me." Lowry bent over, aimed, and shot the seven-ball straight into the hole with a whoosh. The mellow voice of Cube Pool confirmed the shot. "Seven ball in the pocket."

"Bitch," Zoë grumbled.

The vacuum pump sucked the ball back to the holding space. Lowry undid the hooks, pulled herself around the cube, positioned herself, and clicked in for the next shot. She aimed carefully and called the next ball. "Side pocket—mid-quadrant."

"You don't have to call every shot, Lowry—you're just showing off," Sevy mumbled.

Zoë sighed, leaning on her stick. "Wake me up when you've finished running the cube."

Lowry's shot went in, but it had too much force and bounced out of the hole. "Arghh."

"Such a shame." Zoë pulled herself into a position at the bottom of the cube and clicked herself into the frame. She positioned her stick and aimed with a determined squint.

Sevy put his hand to his throat, making choking noises to distract her.

"Shut up." Zoë's arm shot forward, but she twisted in her harness—the stick struck the ball on the side, and it careened into the laser net, wildly missing the hole. She flipped Sevy the bird. "A salute to General Asshole."

"My shot." Sevy squinted as he studied the cube, and then he launched himself to the top, clicked in, aimed, and barreled the ball into the lower corner pocket. "Yes!" He moved around, aimed, but missed his next shot. Glaring at the ball floating aimlessly, his shoulders slumped. "I'm starting to hate this game."

Lowry narrowed her eyes at the last ball, positioned herself, and then called out, "Eight-ball, center pocket—upper quadrant." She aimed carefully, and with a light touch on the shot, she put the winning ball away. She twirled her stick, chuckling. "Want to rack up and lose again?"

"Even with all of my gaming, I've never gotten the hang of zero gravity cube pool. I just can't figure why you're so good."

"Misspent youth."

Two other players floated into the pool room. "Hey, guys, I think our time has started."

"Thank God," murmured Sevy.

Sevy, Zoë, and Lowry unharnessed and pulled themselves into one of the pods leaving for the outer ring. Once inside, they grabbed the loops, and after a low whistle, the pod started down the tube. When they arrived at the outer ring, the artificial gravity had brought them to the floor, and they walked down the corridor to one of the rec-room bars.

Lowry smirked. "I won, so you guys owe me a drink."

Zoë made a face at her. "Gladly—I heard they have a special on cyanide slushies."

They ordered a round and then sat on a couch while the robo-bartender mixed their cocktails.

Zoë said to Sevy, "You haven't been coming out to the club lately, Sevy. Did someone make you mad?"

Sevy shook his head, scrutinizing his phone. "No, I just haven't felt like partying lately."

Zoë shot a look at Lowry with a cock of her head. Turning back to Sevy, she needled him. "You should come out next time," she said, wagging her finger at him.

Lowry joined the chase to get Sevy out of his cocoon. "I'll come with you guys this time." She grinned. "I'll just wear earplugs."

He shrugged. The robo-bartender brought a tray with their drinks and set them on the table with a bowl of popcorn.

"This Mai-Tai is good," Zoë murmured. Then she winked as Lowry glanced at her watch. "Big date tonight?"

"Um, yes, I'm meeting Edward in a bit," Lowry mumbled, sipping her rum and Coke.

Zoë lifted an eyebrow. "I've heard rumors that he's a real ladies' man."

"Just because he's good-looking doesn't make him promiscuous."

"It makes it easier to be. I'm thinking about cutting in line."

"Lowry thinks he's perfect," said Sevy with a sarcastic wigwag of his head.

Lowry made a face. "You're just pissed because I just beat the snot out of you."

Sevy downed his Scotch and lifted his finger as if ordering more drinks. "Let's have a round of denial for everyone!"

"Shut up!" yelled Lowry and Zoë, throwing pillows at him until he retaliated, and the three started a pillow fight. One of the pillows flew awry, hitting the robo-bartender's tray filled with drinks for another table and knocking the tray and drinks all over the floor. They stopped in mid-fight, leaping to pick up the tray and glasses rolling across the floor, but the robot spun around frantically cleaning up the mess, saying over and over, "No worries, no worries, no worries."

Lowry mimicked the robot by throwing up her hands and turning in a circle. "No worries, no worries!"

Laughing and breathless, they picked up the pillows and fell back onto the couch. The robo-bartender gave them a wide berth as he took replacement drinks to his customers.

"Sorry, buddy!" Zoë called out to him, chuckling as he sped past them.

Sevy exhaled, checking his watch. With a smile, he stood up and waved goodbye. "It's been fun, but I'm heading out."

"You have a hot date, too?" Zoë laughed.

"A new girl arrived on the ISS, and she's all mine." Sevy grinned.

Lowry smiled at the happy look on his face. "Excellent, Sevy." She held up her hand. "Wait, Sevy, maybe you both could come to the beach party at the lake; they're changing the weather in the Garden from spring to summer this weekend— it'll be fun!"

Sevy chuckled. "She's one of those gals who doesn't like the water, Lowry." He saluted and walked toward the exit with a bounce in his step.

Lowry watched him leave with a quizzical look. "I didn't hear there were newbies to torture."

Zoë turned to Lowry, her brow furrowed. "I've been trying to get him out, but he's always busy." She exhaled. "I've heard he won't go to counseling, but at least he seems happier." She sucked up the last of Mai-Tai with a loud slurping sound. "I'm surprised he has a girlfriend with as much time as he spends gaming in Holoville."

*   *   *

Lowry waited in the Garden for Edward. Honey bees bounced from flower to flower in front of her, like the thoughts pinging around in her head.

She was startled out of her daydream by Adam shuffling toward her. "Oh, hello, Adam." With a smile, she asked, "How do your gardens grow?"

His face lit up. "With silver bells and cockle shells and pretty maids all in a row."

Edward came around the corner, smoothing his hair into place, but stopped abruptly at the sight of Adam next to Lowry.

Adam glanced at Edward with no expression on his face.

He turned back to Lowry, smiling and bobbing his head. "Miss, may I tell you the fable of the dancing monkeys?"

Lowry beamed. "Please do." She ignored the foul look on Edward's face and waved him over. "Come on; Adam is going to tell us a fable."

With a sour smile, Edward sneered, "Lovely." Then he sauntered past Adam to Lowry's side.

Facing them, Adam's demeanor changed into that of a dramatic actor on the stage as he recited: "A prince had some monkeys trained to dance. Being naturally great mimics of men's actions, they showed themselves most apt pupils, and when arrayed in their rich clothes and masks, they danced as well as any of the courtiers.

"The spectacle was often repeated with great applause, until on one occasion, a courtier, bent on mischief, took from his pocket a handful of nuts and threw them upon the stage. At the sight of the nuts, the monkeys forgot their dancing and became—as indeed they were—monkeys instead of actors. Pulling off their masks and tearing their robes, they fought with one another for the nuts. The dancing spectacle thus came to an end amidst the laughter and ridicule of the audience." With a slight nod of his head, Adam ended his performance.

Lowry clapped her hands. "Wonderful, Adam!"

Edward narrowed his eyes and his lips quivered into a snarl. "And pray tell, what is the moral, my good man Adam?"

Adam looked straight at Edward and replied softly, "Not everything you see is what it appears to be."

Lowry watched in amusement as Edward stared daggers into Adam's face. Edward jerked his head, motioning with his hand. "I noticed some weeds in the next garden over, boy."

Adam's eyes twinkled for an instant, and with a brief bow to Lowry, he headed down the path.

Edward plopped himself down on the bench with a sideways glance at Lowry.

Lowry looked at him, surprised at his sharp response to Adam. "What was all that about?"

"What are you talking about? Oh, Adam? Who knows.

That guy is a loony."

Lowry shook her head, chuckling in a puzzled way. "He's odd, but I don't think he's crazy."

He turned to her sharply. "You should stay away from that guy. I'm not kidding."

With pursed lips, Lowry said, "Edward, just to let you know, I don't take orders well."

On a dime, charming Edward returned, his beautiful smile on full display. "Okay, okay, do what you want. God knows I'm in too good of a mood to let Adam ruin my day."

Edward sat back and breathed deeply, with a satisfied smile on his face. "This case is the best thing that ever happened to me, Lowry. I'll be able to write my own ticket when I get back to the States."

Lowry felt dazed at his admission. She and her uncle were being crucified, and all he could think of was his career.

He turned toward her, with a sheepish grin, then took her hand. "Sorry, Lowry, I know this has been hard on you, but you've got to admit, it's a once-in-a-lifetime opportunity for me!"

She turned to him and spat out, "I don't have to admit jack shit."

He laughed. "You are such a pistol!" He grabbed her and kissed her, and at first she hesitated, but then she kissed him back.

He whispered in her ear, "Let's go somewhere more private—that Adam nut might be a voyeur."

He got up and offered his hand to her, drawing her up from the bench. He stroked her hair, and then, with his arm in hers, they walked back down the path. Adam weeded in the bushes as they passed through the Garden doors.

Edward held her hand as they strolled down the corridor. He swung her toward him, putting his arms around her in the middle of the hall. He drew her into his arms, whispering, "Are you my girl?"

Lowry smiled shyly, biting her lip, and then she looked into his eyes and nodded.

Edward laughed and, with a possessive arm, piloted her toward his quarters. They rounded the bend, and Poppy stood facing away from them with her head cocked to the side.

As they passed, Edward kicked out at the rog, and Poppy jumped away to avoid his foot.

"What are you doing, Edward?" Lowry snapped. "It may not be alive, but nevertheless, it's not nice to bully her."

Sevy walked into the hall, snapped his fingers, and said, "Poppy, heel, and stay away from that jerk." Sevy flashed a hateful look at Edward as he and Poppy passed them.

Edward glanced back, and Lowry felt his arm jerk up behind her back. "I think that guy's jealous of me." He smirked.

"Did you just give him the bird?"

"How perceptive of you, my love." He nuzzled her neck with his lips.

"Sevy's actually a nice guy."

"He's a nerd."

"Yes, but a nice nerd."

They passed one of the cafés, and a wall monitor streamed a newscast of a ship's crew evacuating people in a newly flooded area of Italy. The emergency levee built at the start of the Melt had been breached by the sea, and water streamed across an eroded gap in the earthen dam, drowning one of the most ancient regions of Europe. The camera panned across dozens of families gathered on the top of their homes, their faces in shock—forced to abandon land that had been in their families for generations. Lowry stopped to watch, shaking her head. "Sea level is still rising—those poor people."

Edward shrugged and then encircled her waist, pushing her down the corridor to his quarters. He opened the door, and with one of his hands touching the small of her back and the other gesturing for her to proceed, she stepped into his cabin. Without a word, he followed her in, and the door clicked shut behind them.

"Welcome to my humble abode." With a smile, he pulled her toward him. Edward put his hands on her shoulders and drew her to him, nuzzling her gently on the neck. He ran his fingers through her hair and pulled her head back gently with strands of her hair, kissing her deeply.

In between kisses, Edward said softly, "I'm beginning to really like you Antarcticans." He rubbed his face against her cheek. "It must be a hard life down there."

Lowry felt herself becoming aroused. "It can be cold and lonely."

Edward pivoted her around and pushed her gently to the bed. He sat down, placed his hands on her hips and slowly pulled her into his lap. He ran his finger down her neck and rotated her onto the mattress, caressing her hair. "Tell me how you and your family came to be there."

Lowry was succumbing to him; it had been a long time since she had felt loved. He stroked her hair, and she found it hard to think clearly. "It all started with my Uncle Nick. He is a geologist and was offered a job out of grad school to be on the first expedition to map the continent, which of course was exciting, but he hesitated with such a huge commitment."

"I can imagine." He caressed her cheek with the back of his fingers and then nibbled on her ear.

"But life can get complicated, and from what my mother told me, he had fallen in love with a married woman, so rather than be shot, he opted for Antarctica."

He kissed her eyebrows. "Talk about a lifestyle change. I wouldn't have a clue how to survive."

She chuckled. "I'm afraid, dear Edward, they didn't have blow dryers down there at that time. But the mining company had a good training program, and they sent him to live with the Eskimos for a couple of weeks to learn survival techniques."

"Really? That's interesting." Edward's eyes opened wide. "Good friends to have." He traced his finger around her ear. "Obviously, he adapted to Antarctica." Mussing her hair, he whispered, "What about you?"

"I refused to move until they had blow dryers."

Edward kissed her gently, and then he stretched across her, clasped her hair, and kissed her roughly. He pressed his

ˌers, and she could barely breathe as he
ˌs away.

ˌached up and unbuttoned his shirt. He jerked the
ˌd threw it on the floor, followed swiftly by his pants.
ˌy lay down on top of her naked body, and they made
but this time, Edward seemed hurried—once the
ˌquest was fait accompli, was his interest abating?

Afterwards, he rolled to the side, sighing as he stroked her thigh. "You are so lovely." Shifting onto his back, he exhaled and closed his eyes with a little smile.

Lowry lay her hand on his chest and asked, "What about you, Edward? Did you attend some fancy prep school, and then onto a prestigious law school?"

A twinge rippled across Edward's face and he turned away from her. Blinking at his reaction, her hand lingered on his arm as silence filled the room.

Edward cleared his throat. "No prep school for me. My dad left us when I was about six years old. My mom couldn't pay the mortgage, and the bank kicked us out." Then, with a sigh, he continued softly, "We were homeless for months, moving from shelter to shelter, until one of the agencies found an apartment that my mom could afford."

Lowry felt his muscles tense under her fingers.

With a voice as thin as a whip, he said, "My mom worked twelve-hour days, but I studied hard and got a scholarship out of high school, and then a full ride at Yale Law."

Edward turned back to her with a smile. "I met Attorney General Halder my senior year at Yale, and he hired me to work at the Department of Justice. I've never looked back because, you see, Lowry, the day we moved into that little apartment, I decided that I'd never be poor again."

Lowry pursed her lips. "It's not a crime to be poor, Edward."

He stared up at the ceiling with his smile frozen in place. "Isn't it?"

His phone whistled. He grabbed it off the side table and stared at the screen. The pain of his past slipped away from his face, and he returned to the confident Edward she knew— thought she knew.

"I'm afraid I have to go to another meeting, my sweet." He kissed her tenderly and sat up. He retrieved his clothes and went into the bathroom.

She shivered and pulled the sheet over her nude body. Edward's past was not what she had imagined, and she was surprised to hear that he had bootstrapped his way upward.

Lowry listened to Edward hum, grooming himself in front of the mirror. Staring at the ceiling, she shook her head. Somehow, there was a puzzle piece missing. She glanced around his room and noticed a tablet next to the bed streaming photos of him at exotic resorts or leaning on expensive cars, usually accompanied by a beautiful woman. Lying there, staring at photo after photo flashing by, Lowry felt a cold dose of reality. She didn't know Edward at all.

Lowry jerked the sheet away and sat on the side of the bed, staring at the floor. Edward's extreme façade of perfection contrasted with an honest man who had climbed from the gutter to be an up-and-coming lawyer at the DOJ. Had he risen above his childhood plight, or was there a more sinister path he had taken to hide the wounds of his past?

She grabbed her clothes, and with her hands shaking, she threw them on. *Who is the real Edward?*

If he was not who she thought he was, could her "love" of Edward be a rebound from her relationship with Frank? She exhaled and, with furrowed brow, sank into a chair near the bed. Did she just swap flat beer for a highbrow martini with a rotten olive?

When Edward returned to the bedroom, he had a grin on his face, but his smile faded as he noticed her change in mood. He came over to where she sat and knelt in front of her.

"What's wrong, baby?" he asked, reaching out for her hand. Turning her hand over, he kissed her palm and then held it to his cheek. "Am I being an insensitive male, leaving you at a tender moment?"

Bewildered by her emotions, she said nothing but swept

her hair back with her free hand.

Narrowing his eyes, Edward folded his arms. "I knew I shouldn't have told you my background." His jaw tightened as he stared at her.

Lowry blinked as she returned his piercing gaze. She had had no hint of anger issues with Edward, but fresh out of a violent relationship, perhaps discretion was the better part of valor.

Pursing her lips, Lowry shook her head. "It has nothing to do with your past, Edward." She pointed to the photo slide show. "I just feel a little odd joining your parade of women."

A smile broke over Edward's face. "Ah, you don't need to be jealous, my love." He held her hand to his cheek, studying her face, but she stared at the floor. "I'll come by your room in two hours, and we'll have dinner and continue our, uh, conversation, okay?"

She met his eyes briefly and then murmured, "All right." Safer for him to think she was merely jealous instead of having serious doubts about him as a person.

"Good, see you at seven." He smoothed her hair and kissed her nose tenderly, seeming to know he needed to shore up his defenses.

Lowry followed him out of his quarters and stumbled back to her room. She ran a hot bath, rubbing her temples as she stared at the flowing water. When the bath was full, she relaxed in the warm water and tried to sort her thoughts in the quiet.

To "make love" implied that one loved the other participant, but somehow, with reality shining a new light on Edward, she just wasn't sure this was the case. She dunked her head under the water to block the sour note ringing in her ears.

She pulled herself out of the water and dried herself off slowly. She looked in the mirror. Her skin was fresh, and her body nicely muscled. She was desirable but also vulnerable. She dried her hair and finished dressing, but she could not shake her disquiet.

\*      \*      \*

Lowry started when the doorbell chimed at seven o'clock. She knew it was Edward but called out, "Who is it?"

Edward said, "Sweetheart, didn't we have a dinner date?"

She hesitated but went to the door and opened it. "Come in, Edward."

Edward walked through the door and pulled her into his arms with a seductive look. His lips brushed her ear. "Maybe we should order in instead?"

Lowry stared out into the corridor, murmuring, "No, I'm starving. Let's go." She glanced up at Edward's puzzled face but grabbed his arm, and they walked out of the cabin toward the café.

They sat at an intimate table in the Observation Room. Edward ordered a carafe of red wine from the robo-waiter. "I'm surprised they have a decent list up here."

The robo-waiter brought the carafe and poured two glasses of wine.

Edward twirled and sniffed the wine, took some in his mouth, gurgled, and then swallowed with a nod.

Distractedly, Lowry gazed out of the window at the stunning vision of Earth—the planet she had retreated from to heal from life and yet . . .

Lowry choked on her first sip of wine.

"You don't like it?" asked Edward. "It's a good vintage."

"No, it's good. It just went down the wrong way."

The dinner came, and Edward dominated the conversation with light chitchat about his first days at the DOJ. Lowry smiled and nodded as necessary but spoke little. Digesting her emotions was proving more difficult than digesting the meal.

With the arrival of the after-dinner drinks, Edward glanced at her and cleared his throat. He reached out and covered her hand with his. "Um, Lowry, I hate to be the one to break the news to you, but we just heard that the defense has called you as a witness, so I'm afraid that you will need to be at the trial in D.C."

Staring at him, Lowry's mouth dropped open. "What? When?"

Edward picked up his drink and downed it, and then looked at her. "You'll be leaving next Tuesday on the ten a.m. flight to D.C."

They walked back to her room, and Lowry's mind was in disarray. When Edward started to follow her in, she turned, put her hand on his chest, and said, "Edward, I'm sorry, but I think I'm going to have to call it a day. I'm frankly exhausted, and with this news that I have to testify, my mind is in a jumble." She could tell he was not pleased.

With lips pinched together, he snapped, "Look, Lowry, this might be our last night together." Bending down to kiss her, his voice softened. "Our afternoon delight was just a tease."

Lowry drew back from his lips, and replied softly, "Perhaps so, Edward, but I'm in a muddle right now." She gave him a quick kiss on the cheek and ducked into her room.

*Was Edward a shimmering image of love—or just a mirage?*

# CHAPTER 13

The next week, Lowry poked her head into Zoë's cubicle. In an annoyed voice, she asked, "I've been looking all over—do you know where Sevy is?"

"I don't know, but I'd take a bet he's in Holoville again."

"Dammit! He promised to help me with mapping the Wilkes area today, and I have to leave in the morning." Lowry lowered her voice. "I'm getting worried about him and this Holoville virtual thing; if he's doing it during working hours, he must really be addicted to it."

Zoë snorted. "He's addicted, all right—he spends hours in Holoville after work and, from what I hear, most of the night." She sighed and her voice dropped to a whisper, "Rumor is, he might even be sleeping down there."

"Since when could reality ever compete with fantasy?" Lowry shook her head. "I guess everyone has some type of addiction, but when it starts to affect other people, it's got to stop."

Lowry walked down to Section 3 toward Holoville, thinking about the kids, particularly boys, who were addicted to gaming and cyber-worlds. It was hard to believe that their parents, who would never let their kids take drugs, would abdicate their responsibilities and allow their children to spend hours in a virtual world, etching images of sex, crime, and violence into their brains. How could a kid learn about life and relationships if all they knew of "life" was through avatars and violent video games instead of youth activities and something crazy called family life?

Lowry hesitated at the entrance to Holoville, taking a deep breath before she entered the fantasy world of goggles and light swords. Slowly, she opened the door and stepped inside. When her eyes adjusted to the dimness, she edged her way into the room, trying to find Sevy's virtual cubby.

She grunted as she bumped into something hard and rubbed her leg with a grimace. The flashlight on her phone revealed a virtual assault weapon sitting on a chair, its barrel posed for maximum damage on some poor fool's shin. She shifted it onto a table and heard a voice murmuring in another room. Lowry kept on her phone's flashlight, following the sound toward a darkened chamber. There were the faint sounds of music and a muffled voice as she stepped into the room. She beamed the flashlight toward the sounds and then sucked in her breath—someone was dancing in the middle of the room, their body completely covered in a Virtual Suit.

"Sevy?" she called out softly as she crept into the room.

No one answered. Music drifted out of the helmet, and she recoiled backward to avoid the bizarre dancing figure as it careened toward her. The figure came to a stop, and she moved in front of it, peering into the masked helmet. A muffled laugh came from behind the mask, and a hand reached out, caressing something in front of his face.

He said softly, "My sweetness." And Lowry knew it was Sevy.

Lowry shivered, watching this bizarre dance of love before her, realizing with dread and pity that Sevy had fallen in love with a Virtual Woman. She took a deep breath and then tapped Sevy's outstretched hand, and she couldn't help smiling as he flinched. He straightened up and slowly pulled the helmet off his head.

Lowry waved at him like they were kids in high school. "Hi, Sevy, what's new?"

Sevy looked dazed for a moment as his mind returned from his virtual world. Then he pulled the virtual googles off his face and stared at her for a moment, his face flushing with embarrassment.

"Why are you following me around? What I do in my time off is my business!"

"Sevy, you're right that your time off is your business, but unfortunately, this is not your time off. You were supposed to be helping me with the Wilkes project this morning."

Sevy's brow furrowed. "What time is it?"

"It is ten o'clock in the morning—time to rise, shine, and deal with reality." Lowry's face softened as she touched his arm. "Sevy, I hate to be the one to tell you, but this virtual love relationship is a very bad idea."

"What do you care?" He turned away from Lowry. "No one else wants me."

"Don't blame this on me. I never led you on."

"I know." He looked down at the floor. "Lowry, I truly love her." Then he smiled. "She's wonderful and so beautiful."

Lowry exhaled, throwing up her hands. "Of course she's perfect; you made her up from all the fantasies in your mind."

Sevy looked at Lowry and grabbed her shoulders. "I love her, and I won't let her go."

Lowry stared at him. "Sevy, there is nothing to let go of!" She flung off his hands and paced in front of him. "Get a grip! What, are you going to have a virtual marriage and have virtual kids?" She gasped as Sevy's face lit up with the idea.

She felt a cold pit in her stomach. It was entirely possible. No babies crying in the night, no diapers—just gurgling sweet babies to play with, handing them off to a virtual nanny when you were tired of them.

*That should put a damper on the birth rate.*

Angrily, she pointed to the door. "What about your responsibilities? Do you know I found poor Poppy wandering up and down the corridor outside the Garden searching for you? I had to take her back to your quarters before she got lost."

He blinked. "I guess I forgot about Poppy." He looked thoughtful. "Hey, maybe I could reprogram her, and she could be in here with me!"

Facing him, Lowry threw up her hands. "Look, I don't know if you get it or not, but you're going to get fired if you don't stop this obsession. Then you won't have your little love nest to come to at all."

Sevy turned pale. "I guess you're right." He grabbed her arm. "Look, don't tell anyone about this. I swear I'll straighten this out and work like I did before."

She shrugged. *Is that an improvement?*

"I will tell you, Sevy, I'm not the only one who knows about this, so you'd better go cold turkey on this whole mess for a while." She felt sick as she turned toward the door, signaling him to follow her. "Come on, and let's get this project on track before we are *both* fired. I have to leave in the morning to testify at the trial."

Walking out of the darkened virtual space with Sevy shuffling behind her through the dim light, Lowry trembled as if she were leaving a tomb. She glanced back to make sure he was following her—the misery on his face was revealed with the brightening light as they neared the exit. She couldn't help but feel sorry for him; he wasn't a bad person, just misguided and lonely, like most people are at some point in their lives. With her sad history of broken relationships, who wouldn't want a fantasy relationship—in some sense, isn't love a fable?

They walked past the cubbies; Sevy stopped and slowly stripped off the Virtual Suit and laid it over his chair. His face pale, he caressed the lifeless metallic fabric as if his Virtual Lover had perished in some virtual disaster, never to be seen again.

Sevy exhaled and mumbled hoarsely, "I'll try to break it off, Lowry."

He turned away and stumbled toward the door, and then he stopped like a mule refusing to move. Lowry turned around, the red light from the exit sign revealing his face as it morphed from sorrow into a face of desperate rage. His jaw clenched, he leapt in front of her, pointing to the door of Holoville. "You have your Garden, and I have my virtual world. Everyone creates their own reality—who decides which one is true?" His mouth twisted in anger as he crossed his arms and leaned into her face. "Who made you master of *my* world?"

She narrowed her eyes and, with a quick motion, pinched his arm. "In the real world, stuff gets bruised, bit, and stung. The Garden grows and dies, and though it exists in space, it's *alive.*"

He rubbed his arm where she pinched him. "My bruises in virtual space may not be blue, but they still hurt in my mind."

Lowry shook her head. "Sevy, you're good at playing games, so let's play one." Pointing at him, she asked, "What would happen to you if somehow you became trapped in a virtual world and could not return?"

Sevy shrugged. "I would get tired and fall sleep, and then I'd wake up and start again."

"No, Sevy, you would *die*, because you are a biologic creature—you need water, air, food . . . and love. That is why your addiction to a virtual world will lead you nowhere except into a dark empty hole." She waved back into the darkness behind them. "For players like you, this is no different than being hooked on drugs."

Sevy's lips were tight, and he refused to meet her gaze. "I wish I was an android."

"That's ridiculous—you are a human being." She grabbed him by the shoulder and shook him. "You can't push a button and make bad things go away; you have to fight through the agonies life throws at you." Lowry clenched her teeth. "If you take the easy road of fantasy, you will never push yourself to the breaking point and find the cracks in your psyche." She stared vacantly beyond him. "After you're shattered, you pick up the shards of your humanity and rebuild them into the person you were meant to be, warts and all."

# CHAPTER 14

Nick half-heartedly waved at his brother's big grin as Duff walked into the café. He had asked Duff to meet at a diner on the outskirts of town—less chance of being overheard. Nick concentrated on drinking his coffee to avoid seeing Duff's phony smiles to a few of the patrons as he worked his way to Nick's table. Duff approached the table, and noticing a hard edge to his eyes, Nick almost regretted the meeting.

They were brothers in name only. Even as children growing up in Scotland, Duff and he had never gotten along. Years ago, desperate for work, Duff had contacted him, and Nick had found him a temporary job on a crew exploring the subsurface of the new continent, assuming he would return to the States when the project was completed. But Duff enjoyed the rough and ready life of the mining station, staying when a political post became available, and didn't seem fazed that his wife and daughter were still back in the States. But after the tragic death of Margaret, Duff decided that Lowry should come live with him in Antarctica.

Lowry's arrival was unexpected joy for Nick, who had been unaware as to the depth of his loneliness. With his newfound political career, Duff had little time for the child, so Nick found himself "adopting" Lowry, pouring his love into the child as she grew up. She was a bright child and full of life; she took to nature with both hands, and they had spent time hiking and riding together, exploring the new land of Antarctica.

Duff pulled out a chair and sat, his politician grin still plastered on his face. "What's up, brother?"

Nick fiddled with the saltshaker. "You're aware that Lowry sent me the coordinates of the laser transmission?"

Duff nodded, but his smile faded into the scrim of his still face.

"After I found the camp of the suspects, I contacted the local police chief, but he said the US had taken over the investigation." Nick grimaced. "Then I was interrogated by the feds on the attack of the space station as if *I* was a suspect." He glanced at Duff and whispered, "Not only that, I found some evidence, and they've confiscated it."

"It's evidence for the case. Of course they took it," Duff replied with a frown.

"Perhaps, but it's the way they did it—and why are the US agents involved and not the UN?"

"Apparently, the US agents have expertise, so the UN asked them to lead the investigation."

"The feds haven't said anything to you?"

Duff snorted. "I'm just the regional commissioner—why would they talk to me?" He drummed the tabletop. "The only communication I had with them was to get the videos from the drones."

"Lowry mentioned the drones, and I told that to the feds. Did they tell you whether the perpetrators were on the video?"

"After they returned the chips, they told my office there was nothing on the videos."

"Yeah, now there's nothing on them." Nick rubbed his chin. "I'm worried that Lowry may have inadvertently gotten involved in something."

Duff twisted his mouth, staring at Nick. "Both of you need to quit playing detective and leave this alone. This has nothing to do with us, Nick." A scar of a smile flicked onto his face. "Life teaches us to endure—something I learned on Daddy's knee."

Nick shot a glance at Duff and then stared at the top of the table. The disquiet of the past slammed into his head with flashes of their father's drunken rages. Duff was the eldest and had taken the brunt of the beatings while their mother shielded little Nick in her arms. Duff rarely missed an opportunity to stir up the dark past of the family. The sounds of screams and blows still meandered into Nick's dreams.

Swallowing hard to push the memories down, Nick absently swept crumbs from the table with his hand. He exhaled, narrowing his eyes at Duff. "Let the past lie and stick to the present."

"'Let the past lie.' That's a truth if there ever was one," Duff growled.

Two men sat at a table next to them.

Nick's voice dropped. "All I'm saying is that this investigation doesn't smell right."

"You're as bad as Lowry, believing conspiracy theories." Duff replied in a matching tone, pointing his finger at Nick. "I'm up for reelection, so I really don't want to get involved in this mess." Then his face brightened. "But the good news is, my opponent can't get any coverage—the local news is dominated by the investigation."

With pursed lips, Nick raised an eyebrow. "Yeah, that is good news." He darted a look around the café, which was now becoming crowded. "Let's take a walk."

They strolled out to the park nearby and sat on a bench. Nick turned to Duff. "I read that the US Attorney has brought charges on the ISS attack against an Inuit leader who happens to be negotiating treaty renewals with Amerada. With the treaties in limbo, the Eskimos are angry that thousands of people from the south have been squatting on their lands." He rubbed his chin. "My gut tells me these charges may be a part of a land grab." Nick stared vacantly in the clear blue waters of the bay. "The world's chess board has been overturned after the Melt—power is shifting as fast as the sea level."

Duff shrugged. "I try to keep my head down and stick to my own business, but I'll admit there seems to be something

115

devious happening behind the scenes." He pretended to turn knobs and pull cranks. "Remember the old line, 'Don't pay any attention to the man behind the curtains.'"

"What I can't understand is how they would get away with it legally."

Duff guffawed. "The good old days of the United States being a pillar of justice were washed away with the floods. Chaos creates a vacuum, which will get filled, either by—God forbid—that rare, honest politician, or most often, a political charlatan only out for power. And I should know." He cocked his head. "In this brave new world of the United States of Amerada, the leaders assembled an airtight oligarchy—all nicely labeled with 'Democracy' airbrushed on the outside."

# CHAPTER 15

Lowry's hands trembled as she closed her suitcase. Any other opportunity to leave the confines of the space station would be welcome, except to be a witness at this trial. She looked at the clock. Perhaps time enough for a quick walk in the Garden before the dreaded trip to New York?

She sprang through the doors to her Eden, trying to shake her nervousness. Her steps slowed as she strolled along the path, inhaling the air steeped in the organic scent of earth. She moved past the towering rack of produce and smiled at rows of ripe melons facing the center of the Garden, resembling crowds at a stadium.

A flock of chickens wandered across the trail, and Lowry grinned at a procession of clucking fowl scratching and pecking their way through the Garden. After the hens passed, she ambled down the trail past the freshwater lake. Bees buzzed in and out of the tulips near the bank, and the swans glided across the still water. Under the warm sun, the tension of the last several days slipped away.

As she neared the orchards, the smell of ripening fruit filled the air. At the edge of the apple trees, she hesitated, puzzled at the sight of Adam hidden behind the branches of an apple tree, gaping at something in the distance.

She walked up behind him, softly calling his name. "Adam?"

He jumped at her voice but then turned to her with a peculiar look on his face, pointing in the direction in which he had been so intently gazing. She moved to where he had been standing and peered through the limbs of the tree.

In front of them stood a huge apple tree, heavily laden with apples, branches stretched toward the ground—shadowing two naked bodies writhing beneath them. Lowry's mind was in a tangle of guilt for observing their erotic act, but she could not turn away, staring from her hiding place at a white male with his arms wrapped around a black female arching up to him. The dappled light through the leaves played upon the contrast between the dark and light of their skins as they combined like an exquisite variegated flower.

In the throes of passion, they were unaware of being observed. A programmed breeze drifted past them, lifting the veil of tree limbs from the lovers. The branches parted, and the sunlight penetrated the shadows, revealing the man's face—Edward. Lowry gasped, taking a step forward, and then her eye caught a metallic sheen on the leg of the woman.

Lowry blinked in disbelief at the double betrayal under the apple tree—Edward was making love to her friend Zoë. The blood drained from Lowry's face as she turned away from the carnal scene, placing her hand over her mouth. She stood still, staring vacantly at the ground, with the sensation that her heart was tumbling to her feet, wrenching her insides on its way down, like a ball pinging its way down a pinball machine.

Then her shock was swept away by a rush of fury, and she glanced up at Adam with her hands clenched and her face twisted in rage. He shrugged and crooked his head toward the lovers—then handed her an apple.

Lowry's eyes brightened as she grabbed the apple and quickly gathered more from the ground. She leapt from behind the branches, running toward the entangled couple and hurling the apples into the midst of their ecstasy.

The first lob hit Edward on his perfectly sculpted back.

"What the hell?" he yelled, jerking his head around in time to meet the next shot in the forehead. "Shit!"

The lovers peeled apart like cold water had been thrown on them. Edward fell backward into the trunk of the tree, his skin scraping against the rough bark, while Zoë twisted away from Lowry, hiding her nakedness.

Lowry aimed one at the back of Zoë's head and then stopped in mid-arc, palming the apple. Staring at her, she exhaled and shook her head. "I thought we were friends, Zoë?"

Zoë held her arms across her breasts and turned back to face her. At the sight of Lowry, her mouth dropped open.

"Lowry!" Then she sat up, crying as she gathered up her clothes, and said, "I'm so sorry, Lowry—I don't know how this happened." Sobbing, she scrambled away, disappearing through the underbrush.

Edward jumped up and faced Lowry, his arms outstretched. "Look, baby, what can I say . . ."

Lowry gazed down at the apple she had in her hand and bounced it up and down, determining her target.

"Now, honey," Edward said, backing up until the sharp branches of the apple tree poked into his naked skin. Grunting, he thrust his hands backward.

Like a pitcher at the mound, Lowry quickly threw the last apple at Edward—a strike to his exposed groin.

He fell to the ground, writhing and clasping his shrunken manhood. Edward screamed hoarsely, "Goddammit, Lowry!"

Lowry yelled back, "You son of a bitch!" She looked around for another apple but stopped at the piteous look on his face.

"Lowry, stop!" Edward croaked out, groaning in pain.

In a daze, she turned and fled down the path, furious with her supposed friend Zoë, her supposed boyfriend Edward, and herself for being a sucker. Tears streaming down her face, she ran blindly until she stumbled over a rock and fell to the ground. Lowry pushed onto her knees, growling as she ripped the grass and threw the shreds into the air. Then she pounded the ground with her fists, shaking her head like a bull ready to charge.

"Goddamn assholes!"

119

Lowry stared down at the ravaged patch of grass and sat down to catch her breath.

*Soulmate, bullshit.* Breathing hard, she fumed at the thought of novels spewing garbage about finding "the love of your life" when the reality of it is that most of the time, the male of the species will basically do and say anything to procreate. *Isn't that what all the biology textbooks tell us?* Do we imagine that we humans are different just because we want it to be so?

Lowry became aware of a pair of legs next to her. Embarrassed, she wiped her eyes and glanced up into Adam's concerned face looking down at her.

"Are you all right, miss?"

She turned away, still grasping blades of grass in her hand. Like a child, she murmured, "No."

He knelt and took her hand until Lowry looked back at him, her lips quivering. Then Adam smiled innocently. "Yes, Edward is quite a man, Miss Lowry—I have seen him many times in the Garden."

She narrowed her eyes. "Many times?"

Adam nodded. "Yes, many times. He likes the ladies, you see."

Lowry ground her teeth and hissed, "So Zoë was not the only one."

Adam helped her up and brushed the dirt and grass off her clothes. He smiled and continued matter-of-factly, "Oh no, Miss Lowry, he likes the ladies, you see."

She was dumbfounded for a second, and then her anger smoldered up once again, and she looked around for something else to tear up. She saw the worry in Adam's face that she might destroy more of his plants, and she giggled. Then she couldn't stop laughing—her legs gave out, and she sank to the ground, lying on the carpet of grass and holding her sides as her body shook, laughing at the absurdity of it all.

Her sides ached when she finally was able to stop chuckling. "What an idiot I have been!" She leaned back into the grass and became vaguely aware that Adam had left.

Ancient coastlines vanished under the rising sea, flooding the historic seaports of the world. Death and destruction rippled around the world: Calcutta, Shanghai, Miami, New York City, Los Angeles, Venice, Bangkok, Tokyo, and the Netherlands, all drowned.

"My baby—help her, save her!"

# A SPIDER SAT BESIDE HER

# CHAPTER 16

Lowry felt drained as she stepped onto the shuttle, still shaken up from her "peaceful" morning stroll in the Garden. With a sigh, she slumped into the seat and buckled herself in while disappointment and anger clanged around her mind. To ease her nervousness, she flicked open a magazine on her tablet but found herself staring at the words, unable to make any sense of them.

The last of the passengers found their seats. Edward was among them. She snapped the tablet shut as he glanced around, looking for her. Avoiding his eyes, she leaned back in the seat and pretended to be asleep. She couldn't deal with another confrontation with him—one in a day was plenty. Breathing deeply, she tried to relax while the crew went through the departure procedures.

The shuttle popped away from the ISS and began the descent to terra firma. Lowry drummed her fingers on the armrest, only vaguely aware of the stunning image of the Earth outside of her window. A passenger behind her commented on a typhoon on its way toward Japan, and she gazed down at the swirling mass of white clouds. Beautiful at this height, but deadly if you were in its path.

Lowry chewed the inside of her mouth; here she was, headed to the capital of Amerada to give her testimony at the

"Trial of the Century," as it was now being called. She had hoped her deposition would be enough, but, perhaps in desperation, the defense team had insisted that she be called as a witness and have the jury directly hear her story. She had been the inadvertent recipient of the virus and was the only connection between the perpetrators and the attack on the station. Lowry rubbed her temple, trying to ease a blossoming migraine. She wasn't even sure whose side she was on—if either one.

After the shuttle landed, Lowry waited until Edward disembarked before exiting the craft. She strolled through the terminal, exhaling with relief that he was nowhere in sight.

Grabbing a cab from the airport to the hotel, she headed into the "new" Washington D.C. The Robocab scooted down the road, and Lowry gazed out of the window, amazed at the construction crews running amok like ants rebuilding a nest after a flood. Realtors were making fortunes building new high rises and moving tenants away from the rising oceans. Capitalism at its finest.

When the extent of the sea level rise was clear, Congress had carved out new boundaries for the District of Columbia west of the old Washington D.C. limits, and with herculean effort and billions of dollars, they had moved the White House, the Capitol building, and most of the historic buildings westward to higher ground. The Washington monument had been elevated and now stood like the Statue of Liberty, surrounded by the sea and assaulted daily by tour boats packed with sightseers.

Lowry arrived at her hotel and walked to the front desk to check in.

The clerk handed her the key card for her room and then said, "Oh wait, Ms. Walker, I almost forgot; I have a message for you." He handed her a small envelope with her name on the outside.

She glanced at her name on the envelope and blinked; it looked like Uncle Nick's scrawled handwriting. She put it in her pocket. "Thanks very much."

Picking up her bag, she walked into an open elevator and pushed the button for the floor of her room. As the elevator started up, she pulled the note from her pocket, and her heart beat a staccato as she opened it.

*Meet me at Mary's Café near the Washington National Cathedral at two p.m. today. Nick.*

A seductive voice came over the speakers. "I believe this is your floor." The door to the elevator was open.

"Yes, thanks, just a moment."

Lowry grabbed her bag, hurried off the elevator, and then stopped and looked at the note. She reread it, glancing from side to side as if someone were watching her. She tore it up and dropped it into the trash can next to the elevator. Her keycard guided her to her room and opened the door for her, and she heaved a sigh as the door shut behind her. She dropped her bag on the dresser and sat on the bed to think.

Through all of this turmoil, she hadn't heard from Nick in weeks, and now he was in Washington, D.C.? Edward had mentioned Nick had been questioned during the preliminary investigation, but had he been called for further interrogation or as a witness, just as she had been? It was odd and unlike Nick to not let her know that he was going to be here.

*What was going on?*

She sighed and went to the window, high above the city, and stared out at the shoreline. Underneath the waves were tops of buildings—the few that hadn't been knocked down by the floods or bulldozers. In portions of the historic district of D.C. that were not completely drowned, water taxis cruised down the submerged boulevards, which became a new Venice after the Melt.

Lowry glanced at her watch—it was a quarter to two. She ordered a cab and then went down to the street and got into the Robocab. "Mary's Café near the Washington Cathedral, please."

Soon, she saw the sign for Mary's Café, and the Robocab stopped. She waved her Mcard across the reader in the door.

A melodious voice said, *"Thanks, and have a nice day."*

Pulling on her jacket, she walked up the sidewalk, and her heart leapt at the sight of Uncle Nick in the window of the café. Tears came to her eyes as she realized how much she had missed seeing someone she cared about and who she knew loved her. He beamed at her and gestured for her to come in. He jumped up when she reached the table, hugging her fiercely.

He pushed her back and gazed at her. "It's so good to see you, Lowry! It's been months!"

Lowry chewed her lip, looking at the tension on his face. "How are you doing, Nicky?"

His face clouded as he looked away. "I've been better."

"I know what you mean," Lowry said with a sigh. She scooted into the booth and commented, "This looks like a really old place."

"Yes, it's an old-style diner." He shot a glance at her. "A good place for a quiet conversation."

The waitress came and took their order.

After she left, Lowry leaned forward and whispered, "What's going on, Nick?"

He kept his face placid, but in a worried tone, he asked, "Lowry, have you gotten any of my messages?

She shook her head. "No, apparently there was a quarantine of messages in or out of the ISS."

"I figured something like that may be the reason you didn't respond." Nick turned on the old-timey radio in the booth and then leaned forward with a tight smile. In a thin voice, he murmured, "Conspiracy."

She blinked as she absorbed his response. He was acting like they were being watched. Matching his calm face, she asked quietly, "What do you mean? And were you called as a witness?"

He shook his head. "Not called as a witness, but they asked me to give an encore presentation of my deposition directly to the Attorney General." Their meals arrived, and he pursed his lips and shook his head slightly.

Lowry nodded; the rest of the story would have to wait.

During lunch, they chatted about friends at the mining

station and how her animals were faring without her. After they finished eating, Uncle Nick stood up and shouldered his backpack, cocking his head toward the park. They left the café and walked silently along the sidewalk until they came to an empty park bench. He gestured to the bench, and they sat down.

Nick stared straight ahead, speaking out of the side of his mouth, "I went to the spot where the OPALS file was transmitted, and I found a campsite. I dug into the campfire and found some evidence buried on top of the coals." Nick rubbed his chin and stooped forward. "Lowry, I found a piece of evidence that points to a Colombian tribe that may be protesting a power company that is forcing their way onto the tribal lands."

He glanced around and then dug into his pocket and pulled out his phone. He held it up and tapped the screen, and up popped a hologram image. Lowry stared at the image, trying to grasp what she was looking at. It resembled a dart, with delicate, white, cotton-like material on one end and what was left of a point on the other.

Squinting at the shimmering hologram, she turned to Nick. "What is it?"

"It's a dart that is used with a blowgun in the Amazonian jungles, and I found it thrown into the campfire along with the carcass of a grouse. The dart must have been broken and then discarded by the suspected saboteurs of the space station. The investigators took the actual dart from me, but I had taken detailed photos of it at the campsite."

Lowry took the phone in her hands and twirled the image of the dart around as Nick continued. "All evidence points to this being a dart from a South American tribe. I also had wisps of the seedpod material still in the zipper of my backpack. I sent the hologram and the plant material to a colleague of mine who is an expert in South American tribes—she confirmed that it was made by Colombian natives. She also told me that these Amazonian tribes are usually a nonviolent people, and any aggression, such as this attack on the ISS, would be very uncharacteristic." Nick shrugged. "Perhaps the shutdown of the space station was done by some extreme individuals and not condoned by the leaders."

Nick leaned toward her, tapping his finger on her arm. "The kicker is, a miner from Colombia bugged out just hours after the transmission of the message. I searched his room and found a newspaper clipping of a tribe in Colombia who had threatened a mass suicide back in 1998 to protest oil extraction in the region. And that same tribe is protesting the construction of the new power plant in their tribal lands."

Lowry knitted her brow for a second. "What was the date?"

He told her. "What's wrong?"

Her eyes widened, and she turned to Nick. "The number 1998 flashed on my screen just before the power went out on the ISS."

He leaned back and scratched his head. "Well, blow me down. It sounds like they were making a statement, though it's odd they haven't claimed responsibility for it."

"If it was only a few radicals, perhaps the leaders of the tribe found out and stopped them from claiming the deed, so as to not give the government an excuse to condemn the whole group."

Nick slumped back onto the bench with his shoulders bowed as if the weight of the world was on them. Lowry glanced at Nick. *Is that gray creeping into his auburn hair?*

He stared at the ground, and his mouth twisted. Reaching out, she rested her hand on his arm, waiting for the second shoe he was on the verge of dropping.

Nick exhaled and then cocked his head toward her, clearing his throat. "Lowry, my meeting with the Attorney General was eye-opening, to say the least. During my deposition, Halder laughed when I told him my theory as to the perpetrators." His voice dropped into a whisper. "I think the investigators are covering up any link between the Colombian tribe and the shut-down. They are determined to pin the space-station incident on the Inuit tribes."

He fell silent as a couple with a baby in a stroller walked by. Leaning toward her, he continued, "I hate to say this, but I have a feeling that the Ameradan government has an ulterior motive to discredit them in order to force a turnover of land rights. The Melt has allowed access to virgin lands and raw materials, including massive diamond mines, and the corporate oligarchies are salivating." He shook his head. "And millions of displaced people want to move north, away from the submerged coastal lands. They're hungry for territory."

Lowry swallowed hard. "You think the US is simply using this incident on the space station to their advantage and is hiding the evidence that points to the real culprits?"

Nick pushed his hair back and sighed. "Yes. And if it's true, I'm afraid that we're in the midst of a political maelstrom, and unless we blow the way the government wants us to blow, we'll be in the teeth of it." He spoke in a strained voice—a chilling tone that Lowry had never heard from him before, "Halder has no concept of honor or justice." Nick bit his lip, staring into the distance. "He's a man with cold, dead eyes, a lover of power and without compassion. A dangerous combination." He turned to her, staring into her eyes. "I want you to fully understand who you're dealing with."

Lowry stared into Nick's anxious eyes, realizing his worry was for her. Unconsciously, she drew her hand away from his arm and tapped her teeth with a closed fist. Her voice shook as she whispered, "So you believe the feds will do anything to hide the real evidence?"

Nick nodded slowly. "I think they realized they had a brilliant opportunity to take out the Inuit protesters by accusing them of the crime and thereby tying up their land rights issue in court, possibly for years, while the trickle of settlers into their territories goes on. And I'm certain this would send a not-so-subtle message to all of the other Eskimo tribes that, if they protest the invasion, they'll be subject to the wrath of the federal government."

Lowry chewed her lip, letting Nick's words sink in. Nothing like a lovely political vise to get trapped in. Exhaling, she asked Nick, "What do you think I should do? If there is sketchy evidence accusing the Inuits or the Colombians, either case might be a coin toss. And if you're right, the DOJ only wants the Inuit side up."

Nick pursed his lips. "The defense wants you as a witness for their side, to bolster the case that the sabotage file could not have been from the Inuits." He shrugged. "With the clamp on the Colombian evidence, I doubt they know about other possible suspects."

"I'm supposed to see the defense lawyer after my meeting with Halder."

Nick took her hand and pressed it gently. "You don't have to tell her about the Colombian possibility. There is very little evidence, and what there is would be considered circumstantial."

Lowry leaned back, gazing out at the manicured grounds until her eye was drawn to a large flagpole in the center of the park, where the new Ameradan flag snapped in the breeze. A group of laughing children played chase at the base of the flag, surrounded by their parents—all innocent of the ominous symbol flying over their heads.

A barking dog chasing a chipmunk ran past them, followed by a frantic woman. "Tursan, come back!"

Nick watched the dog and woman disappear in the trees and then whispered, "Lowry, I don't want to frighten you any more than what you already are, but I don't think it's safe for you to go back to the space-station; maybe the interruption of power was just a test. There could be more radicals in the tribe who aren't going to behave." He shook his head. "I have a gut feeling that there may be more to come."

Lowry's mind was too jumbled to add another layer of panic. She looked at him with a shrug. "Perhaps the warning was all they wanted, and anyway, the station has blocked external transmissions coming in." She shook her head. "The feds have hinted that you and I are also under suspicion—if I don't go back, don't you think their case against us might be bolstered?" She drummed her fingers on the arm of the bench.

"They'll hang us with the same noose as the Inuits."

He sighed. "Yes, I understand that only too well, but honestly, they may hang us anyway."

Several joggers passed them as the sun neared the horizon. Nick cleared his throat and checked the time. "I wish I wasn't leaving you to face the lions, but I have to skedaddle to catch my flight."

Lowry heaved a sigh, touching his arm. "So soon? What about your luggage?"

Nick patted his backpack. "I travel light." He packed his phone away and fidgeted with the pockets of the pack. With a nervous cough, he shot a glance at her. "Lowry, I don't mean to pile it on, but your father is also in D.C. and wants to meet with you."

Lowry held her stomach as Mary's Diner Classic took a turn for the worse. She blurted out, "Oh, god, just what I need!" She shook her head. "But why is he here?"

"Halder is a perceptive bastard and correctly assessed Duff's talents in the art of passive aggression." He cocked his head at her. "Halder's pulling out all stops to persuade you to toe the line."

Lowry exhaled, rolling her eyes. "Just when this was starting to feel like a real vacation, now I get to look forward to a rousing family game of 'Find the Guilty.'"

Nick chuckled. "Or one of Duff's personal favorites: 'Project your sins upon others and see what sticks.'" Shrugging, he said with a grin, "Believe it or not, your father loves you." He stared out vacantly and then swallowed hard. "The past affects everything in his world—and trust me, it wasn't pretty."

They fell silent, wrapped in their own thoughts. A kuk-kuk-kuk sound made Lowry look up, and she saw a squirrel chase another along a huge limb of the giant oak above them.

Nick wrapped his arm around her shoulders and pulled her to him. "Lowry, there are times in our lives when we must stand up for truth no matter how painful it is. Truth can be painted many colors to disguise it, but someday, God's own rain washes it clean." He stared at the ground, kicking dust up into the air with the toe of his boot. "But until the rains come, Lowry girl, we can't become blind to what is right."

The squirrels switched aggressors, scrambling back down the tree and across the grass in front of them. A half-smile briefly crossed Lowry's face. She breathed in, steadying herself for the confrontations ahead.

*No matter what happens, by god, they'll at least know they've been in a fight.*

# CHAPTER 17

Lowry drummed her fingers on the table, glancing again toward the entrance of the lounge. By the time she had returned to the hotel from her meeting with Nick, her father had left a message, asking to meet with her. She had decided that it would be best to meet him at a neutral location, and since she knew a bar would be a natural place for him, she had asked him to meet her in the hotel lounge that evening.

She sat there sipping her wine, trying to relax but readying herself for the fight ahead—cat-and-mouse was an old game between them. Her father loved her as best he could, but hidden in the folds of his psyche was a nasty streak, and like a stiletto, it popped out at inconvenient times, cruelly slicing with his words. Lowry had learned to study him for signs of attack like one watches a mean dog.

She clenched her jaw. It wasn't that long ago that her father had struck her for the last time—a form of stress relief for him. Instead of a second shot of whiskey, how about a smack in the face for the rebellious kid? And even now, the weather was about the depth of their discussions if she didn't want an argument.

Lowry absently tapped her lips.

Her father was intelligent but petulant, never seeming to forget a perceived slight, no matter how minor. Friends would politely say he had never "realized his potential." He had found his true calling when an obscure political position in Antarctica became vacant and he grabbed it. He took to politics like a religion. With his manipulative personality, he had risen in the ranks and weaseled his way into the provisional governor's post. It was far from being a powerful position since his constituents were primarily miners and prostitutes, but he was as content as he had ever been.

She swallowed hard at his appearance at the door. He was a handsome man: tall and thin with a full head of dark hair except for the gray at the temples, which he bragged made him look more patrician and, happily, more electable.

He nodded as she weakly waved to him. Ever conscious of others' perceptions of him, he strode over to her table with his broad, politician's smile, and she rose to exchange "pleasantries."

With a brisk hug, he said in his faint Scottish burr, "Good to see you, Lowry, my girl!" Then he told the approaching waiter, "Scotch and soda, please."

He sat down. The sharp glint in his eyes belied his good humor. Lowry steeled herself for a fight.

Duff's smile faded, and a tense silence fell between them.

He cleared his throat and said with a brittle edge to his voice, "I hear that you're testifying on this crazy intrigue involving the space station?"

"Yes, I've gotten sucked into this charade."

He pursed his lips, tapping the table with his finger. "You know, Lowry, I'm up for reelection and don't really need any negative publicity right now."

She gritted her teeth. As usual, it was all about him, not how she was being torn inside out or how this sham of a court case was playing out.

Duff continued in a hushed tone, "Nick told me that he thinks it's another group entirely and not these terrorist Eskimos, but honestly, who cares? The government is going to win no matter what, and even if they're innocent on this deal, they're probably guilty of something else."

Lowry blinked in disbelief, trying not to react to his bald statement. The sad part of it all was that it was probably what most folks thought. If some people got their civil rights bent inconveniently, oh well—maybe they'd feel bad fifty years hence and have celebrations on the beauty of what Eskimo life used to be like. But now, they just wanted the land.

Duff's face brightened with a big smile for the waiter, who set his drink on the table. He turned back to Lowry, the shadow falling over his face again. "Look, Lowry, just do what the Attorney General says, and then it's over."

Knitting her brow, she replied fiercely, "That is something I won't do. If I allow them to use me as a tool against innocent people, then I'm as bad as they are. Can't you understand that what the government is doing to the Eskimos, they could easily do to the rest of us next year or even tomorrow?"

Her father glanced around and then said, "People are starting to stare. Let's go out onto the terrace."

They moved outside and then, like boxers in a ring, slowly turned to face each other.

His eyes glistened as he stared at her for a moment, and then he threw the first punch. "Lowry, you've failed at your marriage, but don't bring everyone else down with you."

She sucked her breath in at this gut blow. *He is just so loving.*

A white anger burned inside her, fueled by the years of malevolence he had served up to her. As if shaking off the final accoutrements of childhood, in the instant she faced her father on the terrace, she shed the collar he had placed around her neck after her mother's death.

Lowry straightened her spine as she turned to him like a cannon training its sights and met his piercing look.

Her lip curled, and with an almost bizarre joy, she hissed, "My relationships, whether failed or not, are none of your business. You may technically be my father, but honestly, you're no parent to me, and from now on, you will not speak to me disrespectfully, or I'm walking out."

The revelation of her hatred of him surprised even her, but there was no stopping now. "I'll not sanction your aggressive behavior toward me by allowing it to happen." She pointed her finger at his chest, snarling, "Do you understand me?"

She saw the shock in his face. Lowry had never stood up to him to this degree. Usually, she tried to smooth things over, but never again would he dominate her. With her arms folded in defiance, she stood still, refusing to back away. She bit the inside of her lip to keep from smiling as she watched him digest her serving of insurrection. *Would you like that with or without spit in your eye?*

He grunted, shook his head peevishly, and then walked to the railing, refusing to look at her. She stood her ground as he clutched the rail with fury, his head thrown back dramatically, staring off into the darkness like a spoiled child refused a toy.

Slowly, his shoulders relaxed, and he turned back toward her, his mouth taut. "Well, aren't we just full of ourselves?" His lip twitched into a sneer. "You were always a brat."

"Takes one to know one."

He snorted with a grudging smile on his face, and the tension between them eased. But she couldn't let her guard down since he hadn't gotten his way. She may have drawn the first blood, but the war was not over.

He paced in front of her, but she stood still, watching him maneuver for a better position to attack from. He stopped, and his face softened as he held out his hand toward her. "Look, Lowry, believe it or not, fighting the Ameradan government is not healthy for you either. Can't you see that?" Her father moved close, placing his hands on her shoulders. "You're young, and this type of thing could throw your future away."

Lowry raised an eyebrow at his sudden metamorphosis into a caring father.

She snapped, "I didn't go after this fight—it came to me—but I'm not going to lie for anyone. And if I lie in court, I could be prosecuted for perjury, which would definitely affect my future."

He stepped away from her, with his lips curled into a snarl. "But you have no real proof. Just crazy, circumstantial evidence that some primitive tribe in Colombia had anything to do with this. Nor does Nick. You could be slandering a totally innocent group of people."

"I know, but my gut tells me that something doesn't smell right, and I'm not participating in this farce. I'll tell the court what I know, but not what I *don't* know about the Inuit on trial."

He wagged his finger at her. "Well, I'm not going down the tubes with you; it's your party. Just don't say that I didn't warn you—you're playing with some heavy hitters."

"Don't worry; tomorrow I'll tell the Attorney General that you tried to persuade me to trot out the party line, so you're safe." Lowry threw her hands up in the air. "It's hard to believe they're getting away with this—isn't there a saying that you can't fool all of the people all the time?"

"That was before social media." He gazed at her with a sigh. Lowry blinked at a flicker of real concern in his eyes. His shoulders sagged, and he said in a soft voice, "Whatever you do, Lowry, please be careful. I may not be the best father in the world, but I do love you."

A sad smile crossed her lips. Her father wasn't a bad man, just a weak one adrift in a sea of vices.

"I know you love me." She returned his gaze. "But I have to do what's right—not for Nick, nor against you, Dad."

Her father shook his head and then exhaled. "Why can't you just be mediocre like the rest of us?"

"For some reason, I'd rather die than be mediocre."

"Well, these folks we're dealing with might accommodate you."

# CHAPTER 18

Lowry lay awake that night in the hotel, unable to fall asleep with the remnants of the day churning in her mind. She shifted under the sheets and then, with a sigh, gave in to her sleeplessness and stared up at the ceiling. Nothing like being a pawn in a farcical trial that had sucked her family, and all of its interminable baggage, into its vortex.

The blinking light of the smoke detector on the wall mocked her as she fluffed up her pillow again. She listened to the traffic in the busy street below her room, and the noise of a wreck wafted up to her, followed by the voices of the drivers yelling at each other in the darkness. It reminded her of a night years ago, when she was sixteen, and the fight between Lowry, her father, and Nick—and the last time her father had struck her.

\*   \*   \*

Lowry quietly opened the back door to the farmhouse outside of the mining town in Antarctica and crept into the house. She eased the door closed, and with her head spinning, dizzy from the effects of too much bourbon and coke, she sank onto the bench near the door. Unsteadily, she kicked off her boots and, clutching the arm of the bench, shoved the boots underneath it. Lurching into a standing position, she propelled herself toward her room, using the wall as a much-needed crutch.

Halfway down the hall, she fell over her giant Saint Bernard, Ollie, who was patiently waiting for her in the hallway.

The dog yelped, and Lowry whispered, "Ollie, *shh!*"

Ollie licked Lowry's face as she lay on the cold stone floor, waiting for the walls to stop swirling. She staggered up and resumed shuffling to her room but hesitated as the hall reached the living room, where her father sat illuminated by a dim lamp. Her bedroom was farther down the hall, just past no man's land. Could she make it across without him noticing?

"Lowry?"

*Shit.* "Uh, yes, Dad?"

"Come here."

She approached him slowly, trying to stand up straight, but sober enough to realize that he might be farther down the drunk lane than she was. *Yep, a glass of scotch in his hand with a half-empty bottle sitting next to him.* "Yes, Dad?"

Duff swirled the scotch in his glass. "One of the mine managers just called and said someone saw our hover hit a fence near town." He glanced up at her. "Is that true?"

Exhaling, she muttered, "Yes, I'm sorry," staring at the floor.

Duff got up, strode over, and stood in front of her, his bloodshot eyes staring into hers. "And you were going to sneak around me and go to your room without saying a thing?"

Lowry shrugged. "I was going to show you tomorrow. I thought you were asleep in the chair."

Duff's lip curled. "*Liar!*" He sniffed the air. "*And* you've been drinking—*perfect.*"

Lowry swallowed hard. Usually, he was a mellow drinker, but the combination of alcohol and any type of stress was a recipe for disaster. She tried to keep her voice steady. "Um, yes, I did have a drink at the party." She bit her lip and mumbled, "And I'm really sorry about the hover, Dad. I'll pay for any damage."

"You bet you will." Duff's mouth twisted as he paced the floor. "I'm already having to deal with the miners' strike led by my own *brother*." He shook his head. "And now my daughter gets drunk and wrecks the hover." He faced her. "And then you creep in, thinking that I wouldn't find out about the hover, didn't you?" His eyes bulged in a drunken fury.

Lowry kept her face still and calm, but her lip quivered.

Her father threw up his hands. "Nick decides to defy and embarrass me in front of my friends and constituents. Almost all of the miners go on strike, disappearing into the hinterlands for *weeks*. And the mining company is all over *my* back about it."

Her father shifted back and forth on his feet, rubbing his hand on his forehead. Then, like lightning drawn to metal, he pivoted back with his arm outstretched and slapped her full in the face.

Lowry slammed onto the couch, her face throbbing with pain. She screamed up at him, "Dad, stop!" as she held her cheek.

Rage twisted Duff's face as he lunged at her, grabbing her arm, and jerked her back up to face him. He grasped her shoulders and screamed, spittle showering her face, "I don't need more stress right now—can't you see that?"

"Leave me alone!" Lowry shouted, swaying on her feet. "Stop shaking me. I feel sick." She held her hand over her mouth, swallowing the bile percolating from her stomach.

Disgusted, he released his grip and turned away from her, his drunken madness assuaged.

The front door banged open, and they froze in place at the sound of footsteps.

Nick bounded into the room, his face pinched with anger, and went straight at Duff. "I saw you through the window. You hit her, you cowardly *bastard!*"

Nick dived into him and knocked him into the side table, Duff's glass hurtling through the window with a crash. Then Nick hauled him back up and punched him squarely in the face. With a grunt, Duff fell to the floor, but sprang back up and popped his elbow into Nick's stomach. Nick groaned and dropped to his knees. Smiling through bloody teeth, Duff started to punch Nick in the face, but Nick leapt forward, knocking Duff's legs out from under him. Duff fell back onto the reading chair, hitting the seat with his back.

"Son of a bitch, Nick!"

Huffing, Nick leaned over his brother, jabbing his finger in his face. "You piece of shit . . ."

Duff kicked him in the groin, and Nick fell back on the rug. Duff grabbed the lamp and leapt on top of him, swinging it at Nick's head.

Lowry jumped at them, shoving her hand between the lamp and Nick's head. "*Stop fighting!*"

Her father halted his swing in mid-arc and shot a glance at her, but he turned back to Nick with a scowl on his face. Breathing hard, the brothers stepped away, staring at each other in the dim light.

With clenched teeth, Duff put the lamp down, and the wavering lampshade cast flickering shadows across the room. "That's my favorite lamp. I wouldn't want to break it on *your* noggin." He cocked his head at Lowry. "It's her fault; she got drunk and wrecked the hover."

Lowry shook her head. "It's not wrecked. It was really minor. The road turned, but I didn't." She looked down, confused by the vacillating light from the lamp—either she or the room was swaying. "But I did get drunk."

Nick turned back to Duff, with a snarl on his face. "Even if she *did* get drunk and wreck it, that's no excuse for slapping her or any other woman. If you *ever* touch Lowry again, I swear to God, I'll beat you senseless—*do you understand me?*"

Duff glared at him, and they stood facing each other until Duff shrugged and turned away, picking up the side table and setting it back in place. He rubbed his jaw, opening his mouth to make sure it still worked. Then he gestured with his head at the broken pane and snapped at Nick, "You going to pay for that window?"

"With pleasure." Nick brushed his hair back out of his face. Exhaling, he turned away from Duff and walked over to Lowry. He turned her face to the light, examining the red mark on her cheek. "Are you okay, hon?"

Lowry trembled as a tear made its way down her face. "I'm okay."

Duff glanced at them, frowning as he shoved a handkerchief into the window to block the wind.

Nick brushed her tear away and hugged her. He kissed her forehead and then walked her toward the kitchen. "Better get some ice on that, and then get to bed." He turned back to Duff, his lips tight. "I need to talk with your dad about the strike."

Lowry went into the kitchen and opened the freezer door. She strained to hear their words over the clink of the ice cubes as she filled the ice pack. Holding the cold bag to her injured cheek, she skirted toward the door, listening to their argument.

Nick growled, "First thing I want to talk about is *you*—I know we grew up in a bad situation, but Duff, can't you put it behind you for Lowry's sake?"

"Put it behind me?" Duff guffawed. "The only way I can 'put it behind me' is with a shot of whiskey." He paused, and his voice became harsh. "Don't ever lecture me again, Nick. You don't understand half of what I went through."

Nick replied, "I will promise you this: if you ever strike Lowry again, you won't get a lecture from me. You'll get a beating from me that will bring back fond memories of our loving father."

The living room fell into silence, but Lowry knew the discussion was not over. She dug in a kitchen drawer, found an ibuprofen, and swallowed it with a glass of water.

*That'll help my hangover in the morning, too.* She shifted the cold pack back onto her face and quietly crept back to her listening post.

Nick said, "What I came over here for was to discuss the strike—we have a real issue, and we need you to be part of the solution. Duff, as you know, the mining company is illegally bringing in paroled convicts to work the mines, taking positions normally filled by paid workers. There's a veiled threat to reduce wages, and the regular miners know they can't compete with slave labor. They've protested for weeks with no response from the management." His boots pounded as he paced the floor. "Instances of theft and drug dealing have been documented, but what finally prompted a full-blown strike by the miners was that one of their wives was raped by a convict."

"That wasn't proven."

"Wasn't proven by the manager of the mine, who didn't *try* to bring him to justice." It was quiet for a moment, and then Nick continued. "You have to talk to the UN and put pressure on the mining company to get rid of these convicts."

"*Me?*" Duff replied.

Lowry heard the twinkle of ice hitting glass. Ah, the familiar sound of another glass of Scotch whiskey on the rocks.

Duff snorted. "I can't run afoul of the management down here."

"You're the elected representative of the people. You're the one who needs to step up and solve this issue, Duff."

Lowry edged closer to the living room, the pain in her face easing with the cold pack and medicine.

"If you don't, then I'll do it, but it will make you look like a paid crony of management. That wouldn't look very good come next election, Duff." Then Nick's voice dropped to a whisper. "I don't want those convicts around Lowry."

Duff exhaled. "Okay, but let me discuss this with the management, and maybe the threat of contacting the UN will be enough to get the convicts out of here. Frankly, I don't like them any more than you do."

"We'll give you twenty-four hours, but after that, *I'm* getting in touch with the UN." Nick walked back toward the front door. "I'm hiding out somewhere since I don't trust the management, but be assured that we'll be watching." The sound of his footsteps stopped momentarily, and his voice rose. "Duff, I want those convicts on a ship out of here by the end of the week."

# CHAPTER 19

The next morning, Lowry sat in the reception area of the newly constructed Department of Justice building, waiting for her meeting with Elliott Halder, the Attorney General of the United States.

An odd—and in this instance, welcome—distraction was the spectacle of Halder's secretary, a character study in curiousness. The receptionist nervously looked in a small mirror, patting her heavily made-up face with oil-absorbing tissues.

The secretary noticed Lowry observing her. "Oh, I just can't keep the oil off my face!"

She finished fussing with her make-up and then arranged the photos on her desk. A spasm darted across her face as she turned to Lowry, picking up a photo of a young man in camo with an assault rifle.

"This was my boy, Henry—he was killed in the war." She pointed to the small dog beside him in the photo. "Dexter is dead, too." With her mouth pinched into a brittle smile, she placed the photo back down on her desk, her hand lingering on the frame. Then her face brightened as she flipped her hair back with her hand. "I don't like little dogs. Do you?"

Lowry started when the receptionist's phone buzzed, closing the curtains on the show.

"Yes, sir, I'll tell her, sir." The receptionist motioned to Lowry. "He's ready for you."

They walked down the long corridor, and Lowry kept her distance from the receptionist as if her peculiarity might be contagious. The woman opened the door and ushered Lowry in to a well-appointed corner office.

Elliot Halder looked up and said, "Thanks, Sheila." He tilted his head. "And please, no interruptions."

"Yes, sir, and you're most welcome, Mr. Halder!" Sheila turned on her heel and swept past Lowry with her head thrown back and her eyelids blinking rapidly, saying, "It was certainly nice meeting you, Ms. Walker." She strode dramatically out of the room, and Lowry breathed a bit easier, but then she pivoted toward Mr. Halder.

He rose to greet her, dressed in an impeccable but severe suit—he was a man who exuded confidence, but it was edged in arrogance. "Good morning, Ms. Walker. Welcome to D.C." With a smile on his face but not in his eyes, he shook her hand. "I trust you had a pleasant flight?"

Nodding, Lowry gazed around the spacious office. It was beautiful, adorned with huge windows that lit the mahogany paneling with bountiful sunlight. His desk looked to be an antique and was probably worth a fortune.

He observed her gazing at the desk. "I see you've noticed the desk; it was brought from the old offices and is over two hundred years old. It's irreplaceable. But, please, have a seat." He waved Lowry toward a chair, and she sank into the leather armchair—facing one of the most powerful men in the world.

They studied each other. Halder was a handsome man in his late forties with intense dark eyes under tightly curled salt-and-pepper hair, which was clipped close to his head. His face was finely chiseled, but with a terminal backward tilt and a slight projection to his chin, his eyes persistently looked down—the hallmark of someone who talks at the person they're addressing rather than to them.

His eyes remained locked on hers, like a boxer sizing up an opponent. He pursed his lips, and his mouth twitched into a smile. "Ms. Walker, you appear to be an intelligent woman."

"And you appear to be a perceptive man," she parried.

He laughed lightly, but his smile faded quickly. "All right, let's get to why we called you in today, Ms. Walker."

"Please, call me Lowry."

"Okay." He folded his hands on the desk and then leaned forward. "Oh, before we get started, you should know that I have spoken with your father."

She tilted her head, but swallowed hard. "So I've heard."

"Your father also seems to have intelligence, as well as a political career ahead of him. Perhaps we can help him to succeed in that career. Amerada does a lot of investing around the world, and Antarctica is one of our lands of interest."

Lowry kept her eyes calm as her stomach churned at the taint of depravity. *Convenient that Dad didn't mention a possible quid pro quo dangling out there.*

Inwardly shuddering, she pushed herself deeper into the chair to be as far from him as she could. As if facing a poisonous snake, she had to keep her wits about her.

She had researched a bit on Mr. Halder's background— he was intelligent, but with a weakness for power. He appeared to be a person who was born a cold seed and then had become a cold, manipulative man. His *modus operandi* was a quiet thrust of a political dagger into his enemy's gut with an equally silent disposal—no muss, no fuss.

The silence was developing a life of its own when Halder said in a clipped voice, "You seem to be someone who keeps their cards close to the vest."

"I find it's healthier."

His lips were tight as he drummed his fingers on the beautiful desk. "Let's go over your deposition with the other attorney on the case."

Halder stood up, and she rose to follow him. He opened a door near a large picture window and smiled as he motioned her to continue into the next room. She passed the window, hesitating as her eyes followed a flock of birds soaring across the blue sky. *If only I was that third bird on the left.*

She turned from the window and entered the small conference room, gasping at the sight of Gerwin sitting at the table with his signature smirk pasted on his face. Woodenly, she sat at the table across from Gerwin, and then Halder sat next to her. She shifted in the hard wooden chair as they leaned in toward her.

Halder cleared his throat. "Lowry, I've gone over your deposition that you gave to Mr. Gerwin on the space station right after the event. The reason we wanted to meet with you today is so that you can understand our position and how your impending testimony might impact our case."

He leaned back in his chair. "Ever since the melting and the subsequent combining of America and Canada into Amerada, the Eskimo tribes have felt threatened, since the treaties they had with Canada are in the process of being rewritten by our legislature. A particular leader of an Inuit group, Mr. Jean-Luc Kimalu, has been threatening the US with action for years, and we think this attack on the space station is their first calling card."

Lowry looked uneasily from one man to the other. "I've told you all I know already, so what is it you are wanting from me?"

Gerwin broke in, staring at her as he spoke. "Ms. Walker, the case against Mr. Jean-Luc Kimalu could hinge on your testimony. We must be certain before you go on that stand precisely what is going to be coming out of your mouth." Like an irate dog, his lip twitched, and his eyes bored into hers. "Do you understand me?"

Lowry felt her blood pressure rise. Picking someone she hated to persuade her wasn't the best tactic. Her eyes matched Gerwin's in a duel to the death.

"It sounds to me that you want me to say exactly what you want and not deviate from the party line."

Halder tapped his finger on the table. Then he sat back with an ominous smile and spoke with a cogent tone. "Lowry, we finally have a case against a terrorist Eskimo group that has been giving the United States of Amerada fits for years. They have been throwing up roadblocks for our people to have a home, people who lost everything when the ice melted."

Lowry grimaced. *Maybe these two are among the most powerful men in the world, but they aren't reading me very well.* She snapped, "When I was five, my mother and I had to leave our home due to the rising water, but we didn't have to steal someone else's land to survive."

She looked at Gerwin and then back to Halder. *Here goes nothing.*

With a smooth voice, she said, "You are aware that my uncle found evidence, when he searched the site of the OPALS transmission, that the space station may have been attacked by a South American tribe protesting a power plant being built in their tribal lands, and not the Inuits. What about pursuing those leads?"

Halder cocked his head back further, and the angle of his eyes stabbing arrogantly down at her became deadly. "Your uncle did tell us that story, and if they were viable leads, we would chase them down."

With a slight shake of her head, Lowry asked, "Why do you say they are not viable?"

Gerwin slammed his fist onto the table, shouting, "We're not the ones being interrogated here!"

Lowry turned to Gerwin and dismissed him with a long blink of her eyes. She shifted her eyes back to Halder.

Halder's eyes glistened as he met her gaze. He raised his hand to stop Gerwin from continuing. "Now, Mr. Gerwin, Lowry is a thinking human, so we just have to explain the facts to her."

A fleeting smile crossed Halder's mouth before he continued smoothly. "We have a solid motive for the Inuit tribes to involve themselves with the shutdown of the space station." His face became rigid, and with the end of his index finger striking the table, he said harshly, "The US cannot tolerate terrorism in the homeland, whether they strike on the land or on the space station, and mark my words, Lowry, we will bring them to justice with your help or without. And if it is *without* your help, you may find your future just a little more difficult, my young friend. Do you understand the penalty for aiding and abetting a crime?"

He stood up and walked over to the large window in the conference room. He gazed out over the city, his handsome profile highlighted against the bright sky.

"And your uncle, of course, is under the same scrutiny."

Lowry retorted, "My uncle had nothing to do with this, and there's no way to prove he did."

Halder pivoted toward her. He stood motionless, staring at her with callous eyes, like someone accelerating toward a squirrel in the road. Then, with his lips clamped into a fixed smile, he approached her chair with deliberate steps and leaned over her shoulder, placing his hand on the table. He began to speak, and Lowry flinched against his breath caressing her cheek. "You see, Lowry, life just isn't fair. The settlers are moving into the land to the north, just like the European settlers did when this continent was first colonized."

His voice dropped to a whisper, and the hair rose on the back of Lowry's neck. "It's as simple as this: the people of Amerada want that land, and the people will get it." He smiled down at her with teeth perfect and white. "And there's not a rat's-ass thing you or I can do about it. It's the human way."

Halder stood up, tapping his chin as if analyzing a problem. "And what about you, Lowry? Isn't it odd that *you* received this supposed 'transmission' that shut the power off to the space station?" He turned and walked to the end of the table, continuing in his velvet voice, "You've recently been divorced. In many of these difficult situations, people harbor ideas of suicide, and unfortunately, some poor souls might wish to create a spectacle of it." He gazed at her, lifting his hand into the air. "What higher drama would there be than to bring down a hundred people on the space station with you?"

Abruptly, he bent toward her with his mouth taut. "Perhaps we might contact your ex-husband and get a statement from him. Frank, I believe, is his name?"

Lowry pinched her lips together; obviously, her father had filled them in very well. But she had faced demons in her life with courage—she could never bow to this vile man and allow him to manipulate her with his devious tactics. The hardships she had endured had unbound her from the fear of loss, and with that freedom, power was springing forth.

She bit the inside of her lip, meeting his stare with one of her own. She coolly replied, "I've done some studying of your methods in dealing with the Eskimo tribes in the Arctic regions. You've managed an incredible campaign of tying up treaty renewals so that illegal homesteading can flourish without consequence. You point the finger at Congress and shrug that there is nothing legally you can do to stop the stealing of Eskimo lands." Squinting at him, her nose twitched. "The smell of corruption oozes out of you."

Halder's mouth bent into the shape of a smile. "Politics is a dance of subtle corruptions hidden behind a veil of humility. A palm greased here, a good deed done there—all in balance."

She gazed at him. "Mr. Halder, perhaps you have Borgian ancestry?"

"Ah, you're a student of history."

She replied lightly, "I find it helpful to survive."

Halder's lips were as thin as a razor. "Yes, to survive."

No one spoke for several minutes; the tension palpable as no one yielded their position.

Then Lowry spoke softly to Mr. Halder. "Do you ride horses, sir?"

His eyebrows furrowed, and then he blinked. "What?"

"Do you know anything about horses?"

"Not a thing."

Lowry gazed from Halder to Gerwin as they stared back, momentarily frozen into their respective roles—the intimidating confidence of Halder and the self-important pig eyes of Gerwin. But despite their arrogance and power, these were little men—on top for an instant in time, with the next kingmaker waiting in the wings. History would be the judge of them.

Her face was placid as she spoke. "The survival instinct of each horse within the herd requires it to discern the hierarchy of the group. The first time you ride a horse, they will determine who is going to dominate whom, and the rider prevails with a combination of intelligence and tenacity. If you win their trust and respect, you can have a great partnership. But if not . . . you find yourself eating dirt."

Lowry got up and shot them each a look. "Enjoy the dirt, gentlemen." She walked around the table toward the door and said, "I'll see you in the courtroom."

# CHAPTER 20

The attorney for the defense had a small office several blocks away from the courthouse—nothing like the Department of Justice's stunning edifice. Lowry walked up the stairway, found the offices, and opened the door to a small reception area. No one was there to greet her, but she heard a phone ringing and a woman's voice answering the phone from a back office area.

After a minute, a female voice called out from the other room. "Hello?"

In a loud voice, Lowry replied, "Yes, I'm Lowry Walker, here to meet with Ms. Chavez on the case against the Inuit?"

A woman walked into the reception area, smiled, and shook Lowry's hand. "That would be me, Anita Chavez. Thanks for coming, Ms. Walker."

"Please, call me Lowry."

Chavez cocked her head. "I'll apologize in advance for a bit of chaos around the office. Our secretary is out today; her kids are sick. So, of course, the phones won't stop ringing." She waved Lowry to follow her back to her office. "Lowry, would you like some coffee or something to drink? I can grab something for you—"

"No, I'm fine, thanks."

"Okay, let's go back to my office," said Chavez. Lowry followed her into a small office with a window overlooking an alleyway.

"Please be seated."

Lowry gazed at the indigenous artwork gracing the walls and shelves.

Chavez waved to the artifacts. "We work for pennies here, but the gifts we receive outweigh any compensation." She folded her hands. "Lowry, I'm a public defender who specializes as an advocate for indigenous people in the States. As mentioned, the pay sucks, but I sleep well at night." Chavez's phone buzzed, and she glanced at the caller ID. "Sorry—let me catch this call, and then I'll turn it off."

Ms. Chavez was obviously bright and dedicated to her causes, but it also appeared that she was extremely overworked. Lowry wondered about her capabilities of sparring with someone as razor-sharp and unscrupulous as Halder. But honestly, she was probably all that the defendant had money to pay for.

Chavez pulled up the file for the defendant, Mr. Kimalu, and then opened Lowry's deposition.

Lowry raised her finger and said, "Ms. Chavez, before we get started—I know you're the one who called me to testify at the trial—but I want you to know that the Attorney General asked to review the deposition with me as well. I met with them yesterday."

Chavez sat back in her chair, blinking as she scrutinized Lowry's face. "How did that go?"

"Honestly, if you want to know the truth, I believe that the government just wants to prosecute your client in order to shut up the Inuit tribe so they'll stop making trouble for the settlers who want to take their land."

Chavez looked at her quizzically and then said with a smile, "Well, I think you've summed that up pretty nicely." But then her face turned serious, and she drummed her fingers on the desk. "Unfortunately, there is a good chance that they will succeed in their plans."

Lowry spoke in a hushed tone. "There is another possible set of suspects that I'm assuming you haven't heard about, since the government doesn't want any hint of another group being responsible for the station shutdown."

Chavez held up her hand for Lowry to stop. She turned to her computer and started some music playing in the background to cover their conversation. Turning back to Lowry, she nodded. "Just in case of prying ears. Go on."

"The only thing we really know is that the message came from Antarctica, which you are aware of, but after investigating the area where the signal was transmitted, my uncle Nick discovered some evidence that a Colombian tribe may have sent the signal as a part of a protest over a power plant that is planned to be built within their tribal lands."

Chavez pursed her lips. "Well, I haven't heard that story or any other possible suspects who may be involved, but can you tell me what the evidence is?"

"My uncle found a blow dart near the transmission location. He knew of a Colombian miner at the mining station, and went to ask about the dart, but he had moved out. In the miner's room, Nick discovered a 1998 newspaper clipping of a threatened mass suicide of the tribe if their land was desecrated. This year marks the hundred-year anniversary of the protest."

With a grimace, Chavez replied, "Hmm, that's the only evidence? Sounds pretty circumstantial."

Lowry sighed, nodding her head. "I'm afraid so."

Chavez knitted her brow, with a finger on her lips. "But still, worth throwing doubt of my client's guilt if there is even a hint of other possible perpetrators, so I appreciate you telling me this." Her eyes searched Lowry's face. "What is the prosecution's attitude toward you testifying? If you are hostile to their case, it sounds like they would just as soon you weren't on the witness stand."

Lowry shrugged. "Only a few threats of 'aiding and abetting' and how our futures may be 'troubled' if I testify to the possibility of other suspects."

Chavez paused, and then she spoke softly. "You know, Lowry, it's quite true that they could make things difficult for you, so if you don't feel comfortable with me asking the question as to whether you believe there may be other suspects, I need to know that now."

"I can't deny that I'm worried." Lowry exhaled. "But I couldn't live with myself if I didn't testify that there may be other suspects and let your client go to jail for something that I don't know that he did." She looked at Chavez. "If you ask me the question, I'll answer it truthfully. What can they really do to me that's worse than living with a lie?"

Chavez sighed deeply. "The Attorney General has an agenda, and anyone who gets in his way is apt to get run over, and I'll warn you, that may not just be a figure of speech. He'll want to mitigate every risk that might upset his agenda, and he isn't above buying a federal judge here, stacking a jury there, to make sure of an outcome." Chavez narrowed her eyes at Lowry. "At the moment, you're a risk to him winning the case."

Chavez leaned back, her face drawn and weary. "It seems that we are living through the same thing that happened with the opening of the Old West in America, but now it's the opening of the North. What I'm afraid of is that the Eskimo tribes are just going to be collateral damage, and there is nothing anyone can do to stop it."

"Oddly, Mr. Halder said the same thing."

Chavez blinked. "Frightening." She stood up. "Thank you for coming in today, Lowry, and telling me what your uncle found, but I'll have to think about what is best for Jean-Luc and our case." Then she looked intently at Lowry. "But remember, Halder isn't someone to cross. You'd better watch your back, my friend."

*　　*　　*

Lowry left Chavez's office, descended the stairs to the sidewalk, and walked toward the corner to wait for a Robocab. Her heart thumped a staccato as she realized a black car was shadowing her. She walked faster, and the car accelerated.

*Is Chavez right?*

Lowry started running, but the vehicle sped up and passed her, coming to a halt in front of her.

The passenger window opened, and Edward yelled to her. "What's wrong, Lowry?"

Lowry grimaced at him, exhaling in relief. "You scared me, Edward. I thought someone was following me."

"I was on my way back to the Justice building but caught sight of you—do you need a ride?"

"I'm supposed to catch a Robocab at the corner."

"I can take you back to your hotel." Edward peered at her with a doleful look on his face. "Look, I'd like an opportunity to say I'm sorry. Is that okay?"

Lowry shrugged. "I guess." She got into the car but sat staring forward with pinched lips. "It's the Marriott on Wisconsin Avenue, if you know where that is."

He nodded and said to the car, "Marriott on Wisconsin."

Lowry cocked her head. "We're not quite up to the current technology with auto-vehicles in Antarctica."

"The insurance companies mandated them here. This car is a federal version, so the driver has some control."

They started back to her hotel. Edward glanced at Lowry and said, "I really am sorry about the other day, Lowry—sometimes my passions take me places I shouldn't go."

Lowry looked at Edward and noticed a raised bruise on his head. Chuckling, she said, "Looks like I beaned you pretty good."

"Ha, ha," he said, brushing his hair over the bump.

"Well, you know the saying: 'An apple a day keeps the hard-on away.'"

Theatrically, Edward grasped his chest as if a dagger had gone into his heart. "You struck me to the core."

They both laughed, and then Edward touched her arm briefly. An awkward silence fell between them. Lowry tilted her head away from him, pulling out her phone and checking her messages.

Edward cleared his throat. "Well, how do you like Ms. Chavez? Did she tell you that we went to Yale Law together?"

"No, she didn't."

"She's very intelligent." He turned to her. "I don't want you to be nervous about the trial, Lowry, and I hate to say anything against Mr. Halder, but I warn you that he can be an asshole sometimes."

*"Sometimes?"*

With a wig-wag of his head, Edward murmured, "Okay, most of the time." Then he raised an eyebrow. "Even if he's as hard as nails—everyone has a backstory, Lowry, including me."

He stared ahead and then exhaled. "I met Mr. Halder through an internship, and he helped me out of a jam during my senior year at Yale." Edward glanced at her. "I don't want to go into details, but let's just say it involved the police. He was able to get the conviction off my record, or I would have been toast trying to get a position at a law firm." With a slight shake of his head, he continued. "He's not all bad, Lowry."

Pursing her lips, she said softly, "But he also has you by the collar, Edward." Lowry looked at him. "Did you ever consider that perhaps he saved you for his own reasons?"

"What difference does it make? He saved me—that's what counts."

"Halder has an agenda, and that's what counts with him." She tilted her head. "What *is* Halder's backstory?"

He shrugged. "The only thing I've ever heard is that he was adopted after being abandoned by his birth parents." He tilted his head at her. "Halder and I both had a rough start in life, but we turned it around."

"Edward, selling your soul to the devil isn't 'turning it around.'"

His lips twisted, and then he exhaled. "I did what I felt I had to do to survive."

They turned onto Wisconsin Avenue, a few blocks from the hotel.

Edward rubbed his jaw, and with a smile, he snapped his fingers. "Say, I can help you if you want to practice your testimony. You just tell me what questions you expect Chavez to throw at you, and I'll ask you, and then you can respond."

Lowry stared out the window, chewing the inside of her lip, amazed that he would think her so stupid as to fall for his subterfuge. Squinting, she shot him a look. "You were sent by Halder, weren't you?"

Edward reached his hand out to her. "I may be employed by Halder, but I'm just trying to help you—why would I trick you into disclosing your testimony?"

"'Cause you're an asshole slut."

"Okay, fine, never mind." The car stopped in front of the hotel. "We're here." With an amorous gaze and melting smile, he picked up her hand. "Hey, let's let bygones be bygones— have dinner with me tonight?" Edward bent down to kiss her fingers.

With a flicker of a smile, she extracted her hand, opened the door, and stepped onto the curb. "I need to be able to keep my food down, so no thanks, Edward." She slammed the door as he gestured for her to wait.

"Lowry!"

With a dismissive wave over her shoulder, she strode into the hotel.

When Lowry reached her room, she called Ms. Chavez. "Ms. Chavez, I wasn't sure who to call . . . but I just thought you might want to know that Edward picked me up near your office and gave me a ride back to my hotel."

"Lowry, wait a moment—let me call you back on a different line."

The phone rang, and Lowry answered, "Ms. Chavez?"

"Yes, I wanted to be sure we were talking on a private line. Go ahead."

"I'm pretty certain that Edward was trying to smoke out my testimony."

"I'm not surprised." Chavez paused. "Lowry, I'm going to send a car for you tomorrow morning; it will be parked in the back parking lot, so go out the rear entrance of the hotel. There will be a maroon car waiting for you with my husband, a police officer who happens to moonlight as a security guard."

"Wow, do you think that's necessary?"

"Maybe not, but sounds like they're sniffing around—let's make sure you're testifying tomorrow."

Billions of humans moved inland, like locusts laying waste to the land. Religious leaders cried out that this was the second great flood, calling all to repent.

Real estate values skyrocketed, and cropland disappeared. Regional wars and riots for food and land ensued as people fought for survival.

"Don't kill him; he's my only child!"

# CHAPTER 21

Lowry's alarm rang the next morning. She knocked her phone off the nightstand, sending it spiraling on the floor. Groping under the bed, she captured the phone and turned off the alarm. She rolled onto her back and stared up at the ceiling, realizing with a groan where she was—in a hotel in D.C.—and more to the point, this was the morning of her testimony.

Yawning, Lowry got out of bed and stumbled into the bathroom. She started a hot bath and moved back into the other room, pressing the button for coffee. She dully watched the cup fill as she sat on the edge of the bed with a robe wrapped over her shoulders. When the cappuccino was done, she returned to the bathroom, sipping the hot liquid.

Lowry placed the cup on the side of the tub and slid into the steaming water. She submerged herself, letting her body float in the warm water. In a few minutes, she sat up, smoothed back her wet hair, and drank the rest of her coffee. Then she closed her eyes, massaging her temples in an attempt to relax her mind. But nervous thoughts of the impending trial ricocheted inside her head.

Despite the quandary that her testimony might influence the outcome of the trial—for better or worse—the other side of her mind fought against the fear of the potential consequences hinted by Halder for her family. She sighed. Today was lose, lose, no matter what.

Lowry finished her bath and glanced at the clock. Her court appearance was at ten; she had to hurry. She jumped out, dried herself quickly with a towel, and blow-dried her hair. She dressed in the only suit she owned and looked in the mirror. *I guess I'm presentable.* Despite her shaking hands, she downed a second cup of coffee and half of a scone before her stomach revolted.

She swept the crumbs from her clothes and brushed her teeth mechanically. Exhaling, she shot another look into the mirror, pointing at the pale face staring back. *You can do this.* She murmured to herself, "This is just like debate class." She grimaced—hadn't she gotten a D in that class?

Lowry grabbed her bag, opened the door, and glanced along the hallway before she scooted for the back stairway. She flew down the stairs and cautiously looked out of the glass doors to the parking lot behind the hotel. A maroon vehicle was sitting near the curb, and it flashed its lights at her. She opened the hotel door and walked to the car.

A man waved to her, got out, and opened the back door for her. "Lowry Walker, I assume?"

Lowry nodded as she crawled into the back seat.

"Arnold Chavez at your service." He closed the door behind her, walked to the front of the car, and got in. He said to the car, "Federal Courthouse." The car moved off, and he turned to Lowry with a grin. "It will be over soon, and don't worry. I've heard rumor that my wife is a decent lawyer."

The car started off, locking the doors as they moved onto the avenue. At the next intersection, the car veered to the right.

"What the heck?" Mr. Chavez said, pushing a button. In a clear voice, he repeated, "Federal Courthouse," but the car continued down the road away from their destination. With furrowed brows, he turned to Lowry. "Something is wrong with the auto-car." He chewed his lip. "I'm calling my wife." Mr. Chavez punched in his wife's number, but an error message came up, saying his call couldn't go out, and his phone went dead.

The car sped along the road, traveling from the expensive neighborhood surrounding the new D.C. center through a transitional neighborhood, and exited at a sign for Rock Creek Park. They drove along an inlet with seagulls flying overhead and passed into a woodland area. Deeper into the park, the trees became sparse, and they entered a ramshackle shantytown.

Lowry blinked in astonishment at the thrown-together shelters built from scrap boards and plywood and topped with old corrugated metal roofs. They passed a hut sporting a car windshield for an awning over the door. She had read about the thousands of people forced from their homes, fleeing the rising water like rats. Makeshift slums rose from the debris of wrecked buildings that had washed up on the shoreline, filled with desperate people living desperate lives—fighting to survive in a world that had abandoned them.

The car came to a standstill in the middle of the slum. People shuffling on the matted grass stopped and stared at the vehicle. Lowry bit her lip, watching the children gape at her with their dirty faces and torn clothes. Smoke rose out of chimneys fashioned from old metal pipes, and clothes hung on lines strung in the trees. A mother was cooking a small animal over a fire. Lowry felt nauseous at the sight of dead seagulls hung on the rooflines of their shacks. The odors of humanity permeated the camp, mingled with the pungent smell of fear.

Minutes ticked by as Mr. Chavez, cursing, tried to get the car to start. Lowry swallowed hard as men circled them like mongrel dogs. More joined, tightening the ring around the car. With furtive looks, they sized up the risk–return of attacking the occupants.

Mr. Chavez pulled a gun out of his coat pocket. "I don't want to use this unless I have to." He watched the men edge closer. "Lowry, if they breach the car, run toward the west," he said, pointing out the window to the left.

Lowry moaned. "My god, what's happening?" She swept her eyes over the men in tattered clothing surrounding the vehicle, who were murmuring as they gathered the nerve to attack. Gaunt faces with tragic, sad eyes drifted around the car, revealing not only hunger but also the fear of hunger. What would it be like to not know where the next meal would come from? And all due to an unforgiving ocean that had destroyed their lives.

She squinted at a face in the back of the crowd that reminded her of one of the miners on Antarctica who had been injured and unable to work—no money to ship out and no money for food. The mining community had helped his family, but she remembered the shame on his face as he shuffled down the streets. Her heart turned from abject terror to sympathy.

*These poor people.*

She chewed her lip and drew money out of her purse. She opened the window, and the stench of the place seeped inside.

"What are you doing, Lowry?" yelled Mr. Chavez.

Lowry smiled and handed a bill to a man nearest her window. He gazed at the money, and then, with a little smile, he nodded. She gave another to the next man, and so on, until she had nothing else to give. The faces in the crowd around them softened.

Gesturing with her hand, she said to Mr. Chavez, "Let's give them the rest of our money."

He hesitated but then handed her his wallet. She handed more money out, waving two of the children over to the car to give them the last two dollars. The kids asked her where she was from, their eyes growing wide when she told them Antarctica. Waving goodbye, she closed the window. At that instant, her phone rang, but no number came up on the screen.

Bewildered, she answered. "Hello?"

"Good morning, Lowry." Elliot Halder's face appeared on the screen, and he asked in a velvety, cold voice, "Having a nice ride?"

Lowry kept her face passive and replied carefully, "It's a beautiful park, Mr. Halder."

He blinked and was silent as he digested her words. Then, his icy smile surfaced. "That shantytown is a little taste of what life might be like if Jean-Luc gets off because of your testimony."

"I guess you've never seen the mining station on Antarctica, Mr. Halder."

A man in filthy clothes started banging on the window and holding out his hand. Lowry shrugged and shook her head. Latecomers to the party approached the car, but these men were not the down-and-out—they were mean to the bone. The leader of the gang shouted and kicked the man beside her window to the ground. Groaning, he crawled away, and the gang members surrounded the car.

Mr. Chavez said quietly, "This looks like a criminal gang. They probably run the shantytown." He looked at Lowry and handed her the gun. "Save yourself, Lowry."

The men grasped the car and rocked it back and forth. Lowry gasped as she was thrown from side to side, and she braced herself with her hands.

Mr. Chavez yelled at the men, "We gave you all of our money!"

The gun fell to the floor, and the phone, with Halder's grinning face on the screen, slid back and forth across the seat. In the midst of the uproar around the car, Lowry heard Halder say, "Isn't this fun?"

Lowry screamed as a bat smashed through the side window, shards of glass showering over her. A dirty hand reached in, but she whacked it with her water bottle. Mr. Chavez grabbed the man's arm and wrenched it across the front seat, bringing the weight of his body down onto it until the bone cracked. Shrieking, the man jerked his busted arm out of the car and rolled on the ground. With a yell, another man rushed at the broken window. Lowry groped the floorboard in front of her to find the gun.

Abruptly, the car started and accelerated forward, bumping one of the men off the car and slammed him into the dirt. The car made a sudden U-turn and picked up speed as it re-approached the group. The men shouted and leapt away from the car barreling down on them. A gauntlet of bottles and rocks peppered the car as they zoomed past.

Breathing hard, Lowry stared out the window as they left the park, returning to the road back to the central D.C. area.

Mr. Chavez reached back and patted her arm. "Are you okay, Lowry?"

Halder's face stared up at her from the seat of the car. With an arrogant smirk, he said, "I hope our little chat was productive. See you soon." Then he hung up, and the screen turned dark.

Lowry breathed a sigh of relief. They were headed back in the direction they had come from. With trembling hands, she gave the gun back to Mr. Chavez.

He put the gun back into his coat. "I guess we just witnessed the power of the federal government. Let's hope we really get you there this time."

Lowry nodded silently, clenching her hands on the seat as they drove through the streets. She heard seagulls cawing and gazed out of the window at a flock flying over the car toward the coast. "Why hasn't the government provided help to those people in the shantytown?"

Mr. Chavez sighed. "The merging of the governments of Canada and America has been a nightmare. Coupled with the sheer number of displaced humans, there's not enough money to cover the poor souls falling through the cracks."

They pulled up in front of the federal courthouse, and he said, "I'll wait here until you get inside."

Lowry opened the door but paused, looking back at Mr. Chavez. "Thank you for trying your best to protect me."

Mr. Chavez nodded, and Lowry got out of the car and climbed up the marble steps. At the massive doors, she turned to wave at him and, with a deep breath, entered the building. She passed through the metal detector, and a security guard motioned her forward to be checked in. Once she was signed in, she was directed to the waiting room adjacent to the courtroom where the trial was being held. Her legs shook as she sank down onto one of the chairs.

Ms. Chavez came into the room, her face deathly white. "My husband just told me what happened. I know Elliot, and I can't believe he did this." She put her hands on Lowry's shoulders. "If you don't want me to go into the line of questioning on possible other suspects, I wouldn't blame you, Lowry."

Lowry looked down at the floor but then lifted her eyes to Ms. Chavez. "If I don't tell the truth as I know it, I just couldn't live with myself."

Ms. Chavez pushed a strand of Lowry's hair back in place. "Okay. Try to relax. You'll be called in a bit. You have time to freshen up; the bathroom is just down the hall to the left." She patted her shoulder. "I'll see you in a few minutes."

Lowry walked into the bathroom and washed her face. She smoothed her hair back with her wet hands and straightened her suit in front of the mirror. A piece of glass from the broken car window slipped from her clothes and pinged on the floor. Staring down at the chip of shattered glass, she felt woozy and leaned onto the counter. Images of the angry faces at the camp swirled in her mind. Her body trembled, and tears streamed down her face, falling onto the floor beside the translucent chip.

Kneeling down, she exhaled and breathed in slowly to clear her head. Lowry picked up the window fragment and rolled it between her fingers, feeling the rough edges. Holding it up to the light, she peered into the hazy glass as if it were a crystal ball. What would be her future if Halder aimed his malice at her?

She stood up and gazed into the mirror at her ashen face; did she have the courage to testify? Her mother's voice came into her head: *"Lowry, be who you are, and don't be afraid of anyone— except God."* Closing her eyes, she murmured, "Momma, please help me be courageous today."

Sighing, Lowry dropped the glass fragment into her pocket and wiped her tears away. On unsteady legs, she returned to the waiting area and sat down on the hard wooden chair. She sipped some water and leaned back, rubbing her temples. Lowry flinched as the door opened abruptly and the bailiff appeared.

"Ms. Walker?"

"Yes."

He motioned her to follow. They crossed the hallway and entered the packed courtroom.

# CHAPTER 22

All eyes were on Lowry as she walked toward the witness stand, but she only had eyes for the defendant. He was a defiant young Inuit dressed in an ill-fitting suit. She felt sorry for him, sitting bolt upright behind the defense table. Lowry could see the anxiety in his pinched face.

Chavez motioned for Lowry to proceed to the front of the courtroom, and then she turned and spoke to the judge. "The defense would like to bring our next witness, Lowry Walker, to the stand, Your Honor."

Lowry moved to the witness stand and was sworn in.

Chavez came toward her. "Good morning, Ms. Walker."

Lowry nodded, breathing deeply to calm her staccato heartbeat.

"Now, Ms. Walker, let's recap your background. You have an undergraduate degree in geophysics from the University of Texas?"

Lowry replied, "Yes."

"You are currently a graduate student working on your doctorate in geophysics, and this satellite imaging project on the space station is a part of the data collection for your dissertation; is that correct?"

"Yes."

"And you actually lived on Antarctica as a child. Is that correct?"

"I spent my early years in the States, and then I moved to Antarctica when I was twelve years old."

Chavez turned to face the jury as she asked Lowry, "Are you are aware of any evidence that my client, Mr. Kimalu, had anything whatsoever to do with the laser message you received, which supposedly shut down power briefly on the space station?"

"No, as far as I know, there is no connection between the message I received through the satellite onto my computer and any group in the Arctic region."

Chavez turned to the jury. "As a matter of fact, my client has an alibi that confirms he was nowhere near Antarctica when this event happened."

She turned back to the witness stand. "Ms. Walker, do you have any idea who might have sent this message and why?"

Gerwin jumped up and shouted, "OBJECTION! Counsel is leading the witness into a line of questioning that is superfluous to this case!"

The judge said, "Overruled. Counsel can ask the witness her belief as to other possible suspects in pursuit of justice for her client." She nodded to Chavez. "Please continue with your line of questioning."

Chavez nodded to Lowry. "Please answer the question."

Lowry faced her with an odd mix of relief and fear. She glanced at the prosecution table—Halder's head was tilted back, his calculating eyes shifting from the witness stand to the jury—and then at Gerwin, who was hunched forward like a bulldog, glowering at her from under his heavy eyebrows. She was asked the question and could answer truthfully. If she ended up in a shantytown, perhaps she might be dirty on the outside, but she'd be clean on the inside. And who knows? With proper cooking, seagull might be delicious.

Lowry focused on Chavez's face, and a strange calm settled over her. She took a deep breath. "My uncle is a volunteer police officer at the mining station and searched the area from where the signal emanated. He found a campfire with a dart buried in the coals, which, by the way it was constructed, appeared to be from a Colombian tribe."

Gerwin tilted his head back with a slight angle toward the jury box and snickered. Lowry knew he was attempting to show, for the jury's sake, the prosecution's contempt of the idea that a South American tribe could hatch this scheme.

The judge reprimanded him. "Please, quiet in the courtroom."

"Yes, Your Honor," he said, smoothing his mustache over his sardonic grin.

Lowry continued. "My uncle also found evidence that this Colombian tribe is objecting to a power plant being proposed within their lands. They've had a history of public protests, and the shutdown of the space station may have been a way to make their point."

Chavez nodded. "And what was the other instance of protests?"

Gerwin jumped up from his chair. "*Objection!*"

"Is this relevant, Ms. Chavez?" asked the judge.

"If there is evidence of Colombians perpetrating this shutdown along with a history of protests from a specific Colombian tribe, then I believe it is relevant, Your Honor."

Arching her brow, the judge said, "I'll let you finish this line of questioning, but we need to move on." She turned to Gerwin. "Overruled."

With a nod from Chavez, Lowry resumed her testimony. "This particular Colombian tribe threatened mass suicide in 1998 when a petroleum company wanted to drill for oil within the tribal lands. They successfully stopped the intrusion onto their domain." Lowry stared at Chavez. "The number 1998 flashed on my screen just before the power went out."

Mr. Gerwin's face soured at the murmuring voices in the courtroom.

Thank you, Ms. Walker," Chavez said, and then she turned to the judge. "I have no more questions for this witness, Your Honor."

Lowry glanced at Jean-Luc, whose eyes studied her with curiosity.

Gerwin smiled at the judge. "May I cross-examine this witness, please?"

The judge nodded. "Yes."

Lowry's beloved Mr. Gerwin wiped the sweat from his face as he reviewed his notes. His chair squeaked as he rose, and then he approached the front of the courtroom, nodding to the judge as he passed the bench. His nose twitched as he paused in front of witness stand, staring grimly at Lowry.

Lowry bit the inside of her lip but kept her face expressionless under his glare. Her left hand tingled as she clutched the arm of the seat. With her right hand, she reached into her pocket, pressing her fingers against the sharp edges of the glass fragment, a token of her fear—and the path beyond it.

With a smirk on his face, Gerwin sighed disdainfully. "Now, Ms. Walker, let's start at the beginning. You stated that you were the 'accidental' recipient of the message, which supposedly was sent to shut down the space station; is that true?"

"Yes, that's true."

"And you have stated that, in your opinion, this was due to the fact that you were acquiring satellite imagery of the surface of Antarctica at that exact time and place *and* that the perpetrators had advance notice in order to plan this attack on the station."

"Yes."

"And this was from a remote portion of Antarctica?"

"Well, all of Antarctica is remote, but the signal came from an area away from the main station, yes."

Grinning, he faced the jury. "Thank you for clarifying."

Then his smile faded as he swung back to her. "Ms. Walker, there is no real way to confirm that the message even came from Antarctica, is there?"

"I had a narrow, high-definition receiver band on."

"But there is no way to totally corroborate that the signal didn't come from, say, the Arctic instead of the Antarctic."

"It would be pleasant to think God might send me a personal message, but I don't believe that either. No, sir, the message came from Antarctica. There are no other physical possibilities. Light waves bounce only certain ways."

Gerwin tapped his lip with his finger. "Ms. Walker, assuming what you say is true, is it possible that this Eskimo group sent a drone to Antarctica to send the laser message that knocked the power out to the space station, in order to hide their involvement?"

"That I cannot say, but if a group wanted to take credit for it, I'm not sure why they would try to go to that extreme to hide their involvement."

"Just answer the question, Ms. Walker; do not speculate on reasons why they may or may not do it."

The judge nodded and said, "Yes, please keep your answers brief and specific."

Lowry shrugged. "I can't say one way or another about a drone being the conveyance of the OPALS message."

He pointed his finger at her. "Following up on the question of claiming responsibility for the attack, in order to further some political statement, don't you think it odd that the Colombian tribe didn't take credit, if indeed they were the perpetrators?"

Lowry pursued her lips. "No group has officially claimed responsibility."

With his finger on his chin, Gerwin paced toward the jury box and then pivoted back to the witness stand. "Let's try another line of questioning." Gerwin faced her with a twitch to his mustache. "Your Uncle Nick had trained with the Eskimos prior to his going to Antarctica, didn't he?"

Lowry blinked in shock. She looked at Edward sitting behind the prosecution table. He glanced at her briefly but then dropped his head as if reading his tablet. Obviously, he had passed the information gathered during his bedroom interrogation to Halder.

Chalk up another betrayal for Edward.

"Ms. Walker?"

She turned back to face Gerwin. "Yes, it is true that he had some brief training with an Eskimo tribe in Alaska as a part of the required instruction the mining company provided before he shipped out to Antarctica, but that was years ago."

"Let the record state that Mr. Walker has maintained those contacts over the years."

"For God's sake, Christmas and birthday cards don't constitute a conspiracy!"

The judge shook her head at Lowry. "Ms. Walker, please keep your comments to yourself—this is a court of law."

Sitting back in the chair, Lowry chewed the inside of her cheek. *Your Honor, that's the real question—is this a court of law?*

Gerwin spun slowly around as he continued his assault. "Let's move on to the 'possibility' of another group being the perpetrators in the attack on the space station," he said with an incredulous look on his face. "Now, Ms. Walker, you're telling us that you think some Colombian bush people traveled through the Amazonian jungle, crossed the entire continent of South America, navigated to Antarctica in a dugout canoe, set up a laser signaling device, sent up a signal to the space station, and then calmly blow-darted a bird, had lunch, and moseyed on home?" He glanced toward the witness stand, raising his eyebrows.

Laughter erupted from the courtroom, and Lowry glanced at the jurors' smiling faces.

With lips pinched, she gazed into Gerwin's mocking eyes but was determined to not rise to his bait. She replied calmly, "I know it sounds crazy, except that one of the miners at the station was from Colombia. He fled right after the event but left a newspaper article, seemingly for the authorities to find." She shook her head. "It just seems too coincidental to not have legs to it."

Gerwin chuckled. "Well, at least you acknowledge that it sounds crazy." With a sympathetic nod, he said softly, "Perhaps you might consider some R&R. You've had a tough few months with your divorce and all." He turned to the judge. "No more questions for this witness."

Lowry clenched the arm of the witness chair, watching Gerwin move back to the prosecution table. *Where is a bolt of lightning when you need one?*

Chavez shook her head as the judge looked over to her.

The judge called out, "Witness dismissed."

Stewing, Lowry moved out of the witness stand toward the gallery. She stared daggers at Gerwin as she passed the prosecution table. He sneered back at her, but Halder focused on his tablet, disregarding her completely.

Lowry made her way to the gallery, ignoring the looks tossed her way from the spectators—some sympathetic, some amused, but all salivating for the main event. Seeing an empty seat near the prosecution table, she squeezed past an older couple and plopped down. With trembling hands, she gulped down some water and exhaled as she leaned back in the seat. But the show was just beginning. Lowry's rattled nerves flinched when Chavez called out, "I would like to call my next witness, the defendant, Jean-Luc Kimalu, to the stand."

The gallery buzzed as he approached the witness stand.

The judge pounded the gavel. "Silence in the courtroom!"

Jean-Luc was sworn in and sat in the chair, perusing the court with fierce brown eyes. He had a square face with high cheekbones and a wide mouth, topped with an unruly shock of black hair. He held his head high, but Lowry bit her lip at the sight of him gripping the arms of the witness chair just as she had done.

Chavez walked in front of the stand. "Mr. Kimalu, can you tell the court a little about yourself?"

"I'm half-Inuit and half French-Canadian. I was raised in my village but then went to the university at Quebec, where I received a law degree. Then I returned to the Inuit tribes to help them with the overwhelming legal issues caused by the invasion of the squatters."

Chavez turned to him and asked sharply, "Mr. Kimalu, were you involved in the transmission which disrupted power to the space station on the date in question?"

"No, *absolutely not*," he said, flashing an insolent look at the prosecution.

"Can you tell the court where you were when this shutdown of the space station occurred?"

"I was at a meeting of the Inuit council discussing the latest political maneuver of the United States to disenfranchise my people of their land. I have statements of the tribe elders to back me up."

"Yes, and we have filed those statements with the authorities."

She turned on her heel. "Mr. Kimalu, do you know Nick Walker, or have you heard of him?"

"No, I do not know him, and I had not heard of him prior to this case. I'm aware there is an Aleut tribe who has a training facility for companies and governments to help people prepare for harsh expeditions into cold climates, but the Inuits do not conduct that type of instruction. Therefore, there would be no reason for him to have contacted our tribe to do any advance training for Antarctica."

Chavez faced the jury. "It sounds as if there is *no* evidence that connects you with the power shutdown of the space station at all."

"OBJECTION!" screamed Halder, pointing at the judge.

Chatter in the gallery rose to a crescendo until the judge banged the gravel.

"Sustained. Please focus your remarks on the testimony being given and not your opinions, counselor."

"Yes, Your Honor. My client would like to make a statement in his defense."

The judge nodded to Jean-Luc. "You may proceed."

Jean-Luc exhaled and turned to the jury. "I want you to know that I am *not guilty* of this crime. All I have done is help my people keep the rights to their land. This land is our heritage, and the Inuit tribes have lived on the land for thousands of years. It is only recently, when land in the south was engulfed in water and ours warmed, that it became desirable to you. And the government does nothing to protect us and our rights. They just turn a blind eye to what is happening with the invaders from the south."

Angrily, he waved toward the prosecution table. "The truth is that the United States of Amerada wants to steal our territory. They are using this incident with the space station to paint us black in order to justify their illicit acts. Some say they are encouraging the squatters to take our land so the displaced people can have property and the government can collect more taxes."

He paused and then reached out to the jury with his hand. "Taking our land is paramount to taking our lives. We appeal to your humanity. Don't let this mockery of charges brought by the Ameradan government succeed." Jean-Luc finished speaking and leaned back in the chair.

The courtroom was silent as Chavez spoke to the judge. "No further questions, your honor."

Halder twisted his cufflinks as he reviewed his notes. He focused his eyes on Jean-Luc and rose abruptly, the legs of his chair shrieking against the floor. He buttoned his coat, and with his lips bared into a grin, he approached the witness stand.

He nodded to Jean-Luc, acknowledging him in a smooth voice. "Good morning, Mr. Kimalu." He pivoted away from Jean-Luc and took a few steps toward the jury box. "I am submitting several pieces of evidence, which alone seem circumstantial but *together* show motive and a reasonable connection to the attack on the ISS."

He paced in front of the jury, gesturing with his hand. "I'm very glad that Ms. Walker stated that the fingerprint on the virus sent through the satellite was the year 1998." He pivoted and grabbed the railing in front of the jury. "Obviously, this was a very active year for indigenous peoples." A smile crossed his face. "We have discovered that in 1998, the Canadian government 'apologized' to one-point-three million of the Eskimo peoples for abuses against them, but many factions of the tribes were never satisfied." He gestured with his index finger. "Now the treaties with the tribes are being renegotiated, and the leaders throw that agreement up as a part of their protest against the United States government." A smile grazed his face. "In 2098, it's a perfect occasion to use the hundredth-year anniversary to launch a protest." He turned to the judge. "I'd like to submit a copy of a *New York Times* article to the court."

Chavez shook her head. "Objection to this material being put forth as evidence. This is absolute circumstantial material and in no way an indictment of my client."

Halder cocked his head toward Lowry. "As Ms. Walker acknowledged, neither group has claimed responsibility—your so-called 'evidence' connecting a Colombian tribe is circumstantial . . . at *best*, Ms. Chavez." He turned back to the judge. "We are aware as to the sparsity of evidence, and as I've said, this information is just a leg to the stool . . ." Halder pivoted back to the jury, his voice raised. "But the fact remains that someone attacked the space station, threatening lives of citizens from around the world." He pounded his fist into his other hand. "We have to build the case on what we know and who has *motive*."

The judge nodded, but with a raised eyebrow. "You can submit the article, but please build the rest of the stool, Mr. Halder."

Halder nodded to the judge. "Secondly, I'd like to submit a video of an interview Mr. Kimalu gave following a conference of tribal members and congressional leaders." Halder swept his eyes across the members of the jury. "In this video, Mr. Kimalu is clearly angry in his tone discussing the now-defunct agreement of 1998, which was signed with the former government of Canada." He pointed his finger in the air. "But more important is his mention of the International Space Station"—he leaned toward the jury—"in a menacing tone."

"Objection!" Chavez shouted.

"Sustained." The judge narrowed her eyes at Halder. "That is your subjective opinion, Mr. Halder."

With a thin smile, Halder tilted his head. "I'd like to play the video now and let the jury decide for themselves." He nodded to Edward to begin the clip.

The video came up on the monitor facing the courtroom. A reporter had a microphone in front of Jean-Luc. "Mr. Kimalu, can you tell us the status of the treaty negotiations with the government of Amerada? We've heard they've been delayed once again."

The camera zoomed in on Jean-Luc's face, his brow furrowed and lips tight. "Delay *is* their negotiation tactic while trespassers invade our reservation and steal our land. The Ameradan government has spat on the agreement and the apology of outrages that the Canadian government signed in 1998. The United States Congress has thrown it into the trash and wants to start over but conveniently never finds the time to complete the treaties."

Jabbing his finger at the camera, Jean-Luc shouted, "We must have sovereignty in order to stop the squatters from occupying land which has been tribal territory for thousands of years." Angrily, he waved at the sky. "The Ameradan government has time to put the new International Space Station into orbit but can't find an opportunity to finalize our treaty terms—it's despicable, and frankly, it smells of complicity with the advocates of a land grab." Then he stormed past the reporter.

Halder gestured to the screen. "Mr. Kimalu seems to be an angry and desperate man, in my opinion." He shrugged. "It is for you to decide whether his words could also be construed as a threat."

Ms. Chavez leapt to her feet. "*Objection*—there is nothing that Mr. Kimalu states in the interview that could be construed as a direct threat against the ISS."

"Overruled; Mr. Halder did not explicitly say whether it was a threat or not, Ms. Chavez." The judge nodded to Halder. "Please continue, Mr. Halder."

Halder turned on his heel and faced Jean-Luc. "I'd like to ask you a question, Mr. Kimalu: were there any other witnesses besides the tribal leaders to corroborate your alibi that you weren't transmitting a message to shut down the space station?"

Jean-Luc's eyes narrowed. "No, it was strictly Inuits at the council meeting since we were discussing legal means to stop the intrusion of squatters on our land."

Halder pursed his lips and shrugged. "I guess it might be considered a conflict of interest for them to say you were not at the meeting, wouldn't it?"

Jean-Luc's mouth twitched. "Are you accusing all of them of lying that I was present at the meeting that day?"

Halder smiled and looked at the jury. "This is the third leg of our case: does Mr. Kimalu have an ironclad alibi?" He pivoted back toward Jean-Luc. "The problem I have is I don't know who else would have the motive to shut down the power to the station as a political statement." He put up his hand to stop Jean-Luc's angry response. "Not a question, my boy, just an observation."

Ms. Chavez rose half out of her chair. "Objection!"

"Sustained." The judge stared at Halder. "Please watch your tone during your line of questioning, counselor."

"Yes, Your Honor, and no further questions at this time."

With his jaw set, Jean-Luc stood up and was escorted back to his seat behind the defense table. Chavez touched his arm and murmured something to him, but he stared straight ahead.

Then Chavez looked down at her notes and spoke to the judge. "I would like to call my last witness, Mr. Akiak Sataa, to the stand. Your Honor, Mr. Sataa only speaks Inuktun, so with your permission, I have a young woman as a translator for him during his testimony."

The judge replied, "Yes, that's allowed, but she must give a literal word-for-word translation and must also be sworn in."

From the back of the courtroom, Sataa shuffled to the witness stand. He had deep-set brown eyes in a weathered face framed by brilliant white hair, which reached to his shoulders.

182

He peered intensely into the clerk's face as she asked, "Do you swear to tell the truth and nothing but the truth?"

Sataa turned to the translator, who repeated the clerk's words to him in Inuktun, and he nodded his head. After they were sworn in, the old shaman sat in the witness stand with the young Inuit woman standing next him.

Chavez approached the witness stand, nodding at him. "Mr. Sataa, thank you for coming today; we are honored to have a distinguished leader of the Inuit tribe here today. I'd like you to describe in your own words what has been occurring on your tribal lands since the squatters have been invading."

"Objection! She's leading the witness," boomed Halder.

"Sustained. Please keep your phrasing as unbiased as possible, Ms. Chavez."

"Yes, Your Honor."

Chavez turned back to Sataa. "I'll rephrase the question. What has been the reaction of your people to the recent events with Ameradans from the south coming into your tribal lands?"

He spoke softly, and the translator repeated in English to the court: "Mr. Sataa told me that the dog people coming to their land are like a flock of geese coming back in the spring. They fly around, make lots of noise, and defecate everywhere."

The courtroom exploded with laughter. After the mirth had subsided, Chavez asked her, "The dog people?"

The translator said, "Our people believe that some of the Eskimo people migrated to the south and became the ancestors to the white people." She smiled. "They were called the dog children because they were the hairy children."

Chavez grinned and gestured to her. "Please tell Mr. Sataa to continue."

Sataa spoke until he nodded to the translator. She turned to the court with a serious look on her face. "The dog people, unlike the geese, do not leave—they bring their big trucks and build houses closer and closer to our villages and into our hunting lands. The animals flee before the loud music, the lights of the cars, and the big TV screens. The squatters buy what little food, medicines, and dry goods there are in the stores, which are not easily restocked. Our children are afraid, and several have been hit by drunks in cars. They trespass on our ancestors' land, where we have lived for thousands of years. The invaders are destroying our way of life."

Chavez nodded and then asked, "Mr. Sataa, for the record, were you at the meeting in question on the day the space station was shut down?"

The translator spoke softly to Sataa and then replied, "Yes."

Chavez tilted her head. "Was the defendant, Mr. Kimalu, also at this meeting?"

Through the translator, Sataa said, "Yes."

Chavez pursed her lips. "Mr. Sataa, do you have any knowledge of any involvement of the defendant, Jean-Luc Kimalu, in the transmission of the message in question to the space station?"

After Sataa answered, the translator said, "No."

Chavez said, "Thank you, Mr. Sataa." She turned to Halder. "Your witness."

Halder looked up from his notes and sauntered to the witness stand. "Good morning, Mr. Sataa."

Expressionless, Sataa cocked his head as Halder advanced.

Halder tilted his head back, looking at Sataa with an arrogant gaze. "Mr. Sataa, rest assured that the government does not condone the homesteaders, but we have no way to stop them at this point until the treaties are re-ratified. However, the case at hand is whether some members of your tribe were involved in the attack on the space station perpetrated to bring attention to the Eskimos' current situation. But first, I'd like to ask a few questions so that we understand your background and position in your tribe."

Halder looked down at his notes and smiled briefly. "Mr. Sataa, you are a shaman of the tribe?"

The interpreter said, "Yes, but in English, that might be better translated as a leader in the tribe."

Halder turned to the judge and said, "Your Honor, the translator is not allowed to put her own spin on the witness' words. I would like the record to state that 'shaman' is not just a 'leader' but is defined as a spiritual leader, an intermediary for the tribe to the spirit world."

The judge agreed. "Yes, I would agree that the translator must translate exactly and not alter or expand the translation." She turned to the translator. "Do you agree with Mr. Halder's definition of shaman for the court?"

The translator spoke with Mr. Sataa, and then said, "For the record, we'd like to state that a shaman is both a leader of the people and a spiritual leader."

Halder nodded. "Mr. Sataa, I believe you are considered an honored shaman in the tribe, correct?"

Sataa nodded his head.

"And Mr. Sataa, just to clarify, do you know what the space station is?"

Through the translator, he replied, "I have heard that it is like a large bird that circles the Earth."

"Yes, that is a good analogy. Do you know why the radicals in your tribe would want to cut the power on the station?"

Chavez yelled, "Objection! Leading the witness, Your Honor."

"Sustained."

Halder faced Sataa. "Do you have knowledge of a plan to interrupt the power to the space station for political reasons?"

Sataa listened carefully to the interpreter and then spoke angrily in his native language.

The interpreter looked at him, but he waved his hand for her to translate what he had said. "He says the government must be lying when they say that Jean-Luc Kimalu or any of the Eskimo tribes were involved in anything to do with the space station. I never heard anyone ever speak of the space station except you." She hesitated, glanced at the judge, and then continued with her translation, "Perhaps it is you, the government, who was involved in the attack on the space

185

station in order to accuse our young men so that we can't fight you."

Halder held his hand up and cleared his throat. "The government does not bring false charges for frivolous reasons, Mr. Sataa."

Sataa gazed upward and, as if in a trance, started rocking slightly in the witness chair. He began to chant with his hands, gesturing to the sky. Mesmerized, everyone waited, staring at this man as if he were a messenger from heaven—or hell.

He finished speaking and nodded to the translator. She blinked as she studied Sataa's face. He nodded again, gesturing with his hand for her to translate what he had said. She turned to the hushed courtroom and took a deep breath. Straightening her shoulders, she gazed across the expectant room.

Then her voice rang out. "In the history of the world, there has been an epic battle between tribes in balance with the Earth and tribes out of balance with the Earth. The tribes out of balance have spent generations migrating and conquering others, as if they are afraid that if they stop moving, they may die. They conquer many civilizations, not for need of food, but for need of power. Power is a storm that blows the trees but does not last." She faced Halder, staring directly at him. "Tell us—when will you lose your power to blow?"

The courtroom was deathly quiet, and even Halder appeared to be at a loss for words.

He looked at the judge. "No further questions for this witness, Your Honor." Halder retreated behind the prosecution table.

Lowry was seated just behind them and overheard Gerwin quietly ask Halder, "Why didn't you go after him?"

In a hushed voice, he replied, "It's easy to make a liar look like a fool, but attacking a simple, honest man just makes *you* look like a fool, Mr. Gerwin."

The judge announced, "If there is no objection, the prosecution and the defense will have their closing arguments after lunch. Court will take a lunch break and return at one p.m."

Both lawyers nodded, and the courtroom slowly cleared. Jean-Luc was ushered out past the witness stand, and the jury filed out. Chavez walked toward the rear exit, caught up with Lowry, and asked, "Want to grab a bite to eat?"

\* \* \*

They strolled to a restaurant near the courthouse and sat in a booth near the back. The Robowaiter brought their lunch, but Lowry gazed at her bowl of soup and crackers, trying to decide whether she could keep it down or not.

Chavez looked at her with a smile. "You did very well, Lowry. We just have the closing arguments now, and if too many aren't on the payroll, the jury will either believe them or us."

Sipping her soup, Lowry shrugged. "At least my testimony is over," she murmured. She felt a gurgling in her belly and laid her spoon down for a moment so her stomach could wrestle the bisque into submission. Staring vacantly into the bowl, she reached up to smooth her knitted brow.

Chavez tilted her head toward a table on the far side of the restaurant. "Check out the Walrus and the Carpenter to your left—the booth near the window."

Lowry stole a glance at Gerwin and Halder sitting across from each other with a tray of raw oysters between them. Gerwin raised an oyster to his mouth, swallowing it whole with the juice spilling onto his mustache. Halder demurely lifted one to his mouth and cocked his head back, sucking the hapless oyster down in a flash.

With a twinkle in her eye, Chavez lifted her fork and recited:

> *"The time has come," the Walrus said,*
> *"To talk of many things:*
> *Of shoes—and ships—and sealing-wax—*
> *Of cabbages—and kings—*
> *And why the sea is boiling hot—*

*And whether pigs have wings."*

Lowry quipped, "Assholes on the half-shell, please," and then began to laugh and could not stop. The strain of the last days crumbled her into a giggling schoolgirl. She dropped her head into her hands, and her shoulders shook, jiggling the table, the bisque quivering in its bowl. Tears rolled down her cheeks until she finally was able to stop. Gasping for air, she wiped her eyes with her napkin. "I needed that laugh."

Chavez smiled and touched Lowry's hand. "It's been a rough day." She glanced at the time and swept her Mcard over the bill. "We'd better scoot—I need to get back in there for the finale."

They walked back into the courtroom, and Lowry found a seat close to the jury box. The court clerk announced the return of the judge. After the court was in session, Halder stood up and asked the judge if he could proceed with his closing statement. She nodded, and he approached the jury box.

"Good afternoon," he said with a smile. Halder pointed into the air as he paced up and down in front of them. "This is one of the first major e-terrorist cases that has come to trial in the US, and I want you to realize the historical significance of this. Unfortunately, we may not have as much testimony and evidence as we would like due to the difficulties of gathering forensic data in this situation."

He pivoted back and stood in front of the jury box. "But, my friends, we have a solid motive, and that is the key to this case! Think about this carefully: who else would want to attack the space station with nearly one hundred lives aboard?" He pointed his index finger into the air. "One: we have a sophisticated virus beamed up to the ISS flashing the year 1998."

Halder's face was incredulous as he gestured with his hands. "Could this be the work of a primitive group hidden deep in the jungles of Colombia?" He pivoted again and put two fingers up. "Two: we have agreements which have become

188

stalled in Congress." He grinned. "We all know how Congress works—or not." The jury laughed, and when he had them mesmerized, he turned to face them again, now with three fingers in the air. "And three: we have a questionable alibi and possible ties from an Eskimo tribe to the same man in Antarctica who found the 'evidence' of a Colombian connection."

He leaned onto the rail in front of the jury, and his voice softened. "And what if they are not satisfied with a power outage? How do we prevent more attacks? By standing by helplessly while our family, friends, and neighbors are circling around the Earth, trusting us to do the right thing? Or do we do what is *right*, my friends, to protect the United States of Amerada?" He paused dramatically and then turned and nodded to the defense with a scornful glance at Chavez.

Chavez strode over to the jury and gazed across the faces of the jurors. She pursed her lips, shaking her finger in the air. "There is not one shred of evidence that ties my client, Mr. Kimalu, with this case." She waved toward the prosecution table. "The prosecution's connection of my client and this event is completely without merit!" She paced before the jury box. "And I will say for the record that there appears to be a conflict of interest on the part of the United States. And indeed, I believe it is a 'convenience' to connect the Inuits with this case in order to further erode the rights of the Eskimo peoples."

She stopped and gripped the rail. "Mr. Halder talks about doing what is right, but it is the government of the United States of Amerada who should be on trial today—on trial for allowing people to squat on lands within the Eskimo reservations. In some extraordinary cases, the government has condemned homes and forced evacuations on Eskimo lands! All to further advance the homesteading tendencies of Ameradans pushing into the North as the waters rise in the coastal areas farther south."

Pointing to Jean-Luc sitting stone-faced behind the defense table, Chavez said in a clear voice, "Without real evidence, you *cannot* convict my client, Mr. Kimalu; it would be a travesty of justice. The United States was built on the rule of law, not the rule of the strong."

Then she turned to the judge. "Thank you, Your Honor."

The judge said loudly, "This court is adjourned, and the verdict of the jury will be read after they complete their deliberations." The boom of the gavel echoed through the courtroom as the judge ended the trial.

The crowd filtered out, but Lowry sat numbly, observing the actors in the play. The prosecution was huddled around their table while Chavez packed her briefcase. Sataa passed Lowry and went over to the defendant, placing his hand on Jean-Luc's shoulder. The bailiff stood to the side, waiting to escort Jean-Luc back to his holding cell. Jean-Luc stood and turned to Sataa, and they clasped each other's arms. Frozen for a few seconds, their profiles bespoke their wretchedness of being caught in a system not of their own making.

Lowry's shoulders slumped at the ludicrous tragedy of it all.

# CHAPTER 23

Dazed, Lowry stumbled from the courtroom and collapsed against the wall of the corridor. Her hand trembling, she touched her cheek and drew her fingers down her face, as if to reassure herself that she was a human being and not just a marionette in the surreal drama that had played out in the courtroom. An old saying throbbed into her mind: *When corruption has its thumb on the scale, justice rarely has a chance to triumph.*

Edward came out of the courtroom and passed her with a glance, and then he stopped in mid-stride just beyond her. She studied a smudge on the wall, hoping he would keep going, but he turned, taking a step toward her. She felt his hesitancy as he rocked back and forth on his feet, but she refused to look at him.

Finally, he leaned against the wall facing her, clearing his throat, while his fingers drummed against his legs. Biting his lip, he muttered. "I'm sorry, Lowry, but I had no choice."

A white-hot anger rose in her, flushing out the muddle in her head. Lowry jerked her head up, and with a glare, she snapped, "Edward, you made love to me and then used my family's personal information in a court case to sway a jury." She jabbed her finger at him. "In life, you have to make the choice to be a man or someone's bitch—you chose to be Halder's bitch."

Gazing down at his shoes, Edward sighed. "You're right." Then he shot her a glance, his clear blue eyes edged with despair. "But to paraphrase an old saying, I'd guess I'd rather be a live bitch than a dead lion."

Blinking, Lowry studied him. He was still handsome and impeccably dressed, but the man who stood before her knew his soul was owned lock, stock, and barrel by Halder, yet he had willingly accepted his fate and the chains which accompanied his choice. Perfect on the outside—all that remained was this shell of a human being, a beautiful puppet for Halder's theater.

Halder and Gerwin strolled out of the courtroom but paused near where Lowry and Edward faced each other. Edward glanced up at Halder's face and then back down at his shoes, like a guilty cur.

Waving Gerwin on, Halder stepped toward them with a sliver of a smile, punctuated by a cock of his head. "Edward, I need you to catch up to Gerwin."

An almost imperceptible spasm of pain rolled across Edward's face. The muscles in his neck twitched as he swallowed hard. Nodding to Halder, he said, "Yes, sir."

Then he turned back, meeting Lowry's eyes with sad smile. He bent his head toward her, whispering, "Bye, Lowry." He reached out and gripped her hand, squeezing it gently as if asking for forgiveness. Without a glance to Halder, Edward pivoted stiffly and walked toward Gerwin, who waited for him at the end of the corridor.

Lowry chewed the inside of her mouth, watching Edward stroll down the hall toward Gerwin until her view became obscured by Halder's smug face leaning against the wall in the same spot Edward had vacated. With his head flung back, Halder stared down his nose at her. Pushing her nails into her palms, Lowry gazed coolly back at him, but her heartbeat matched the tempo of the *click, click* of wingtip shoes as Edward walked down the long corridor.

A court clerk led a family past Edward and down the hallway toward them. Halder's demeanor changed as they approached, and he smiled to them. Then his smile faded into a smirk as he turned back to Lowry, murmuring, "Your testimony was most helpful today."

After the group had passed, his brow furrowed, and he hissed under his breath, "I'm not one to waste energy on grudges, so just like Jean-Luc, your fate hangs on the verdict— if he's found guilty, you are free, but if he's found innocent"— a razor-edge smile flashed over his face—"my dear, you'll wish you were never born." Halder blinked, pausing to let his words sink in, and then continued smoothly. "And if you or Nick brings any new information on the Colombian absurdity, you may well land back in court. My suggestion is to let it go." He pressed closer to her, bringing his penetrating gaze to bear, trying to dominate her spirit like he had done to Edward, by the sheer will of his personality.

Lowry thought back to Edward's pitiful gaze, and she struggled to not spit into Halder's face. She did not know Halder's history. Perhaps this man went through hell when he was young, but no one had the right to own another human being—even if, by some misguided path, they acquiesced to that slavery.

She rode out a wave of rage, shoving it back down her throat. Giving in to her fury would only give him control. Clenching her hands, she breathed deep and met his gaze, smiling into his stony eyes. She said softly, "If you bring us to court, we might have another opportunity to flesh out alternative theories, possibly ruining your case against the Inuits."

Halder threw his head back with a practiced laugh and then said, "Lowry, you are just delightful!" He continued with a slight shake of his head. "You are the opposite of my good friend Edward: too honest to be bought and too stubborn to be useful for a man such as me."

Lowry could smell his musky cologne as he edged closer down the wall toward her. Nausea rose in her stomach, but she forced herself to stand her ground and not step backward.

"You are like Joan of Arc"—Halder's voice dropped to a deadly whisper—"and may well end up like her." Shaking his head, he whispered gleefully, "Would you like fries with that stake?"

His lips slowly dropped into a jagged sneer, and they glared at each other, neither willing to concede the battle of wills, until Chavez came out of the courtroom and approached them with a frown on her face.

Tilting her head, Chavez asked Halder, "I hope you're not harassing a witness?"

The icy mask on Halder's face broke into a grin as he shook his head. "Me? That would be illegal, Ms. Chavez."

Chavez rolled her eyes. "Since when has that stopped you?"

Halder narrowed his eyes as he pivoted toward her. "I wouldn't be too loose with your words, Ms. Chavez. You may find yourself drowning in them."

"I have a good pair of water wings, Halder." Then, with a jabbing finger, Chavez launched into a verbal assault. "Halder, you spend way too much time railroading innocents instead of protecting the people of this country. Perhaps instead of stealing native lands, your government could do something useful and reclaim poor neighborhoods in inner cities." Waving her arms, she continued passionately. "You could use tax incentives to build assembly and distribution plants, utilizing vast acres of abandoned properties and employing those desperately needing jobs."

Chavez pantomimed with her hand as if she held a sword. "Halder, you could be a modern King Arthur with his Excalibur in a world where might serves the people—a hero creating an economic renaissance out of urban blight."

Halder rubbed his chin and raised an eyebrow. "If successful, it might be the ticket to the presidency." Smiling, he raised his index finger. "Except my sword would be dubbed 'Eminent Domain.'" With a nod, he said, "Good idea, Chavez, and if it doesn't work, I'll find some convenient scapegoat to blame for the failure—perhaps you? I would love to pop your water wings." With a curt salute, he turned on his heel and walked down the hall.

Shaking her head, Chavez sighed. "Heaven help us if he gets the presidency."

Halder disappeared around the corner, and Lowry exhaled. "Now that he's gone, I can breathe." She sniffed the air and said dramatically, *"But the wizard's scent remained . . . ."* Lowry turned back to Chavez. "Edward mentioned that Halder had a tough beginning before he was adopted. Or maybe he rose from the dead."

"I could honestly believe he's a vampire." Chavez exhaled and then pursed her lips. "Halder keeps his past to himself, but the rumor is that he was abandoned by his parents and homeless for months as a child before he was picked up by Child Protective Services. Eventually, after multiple foster homes, they placed him in a good family, but no doubt that early experience hardened him."

With raised eyebrows and a wobble of her head, Chavez said, "Whatever his past, he's a bona fide sociopath." She gazed at Lowry. "It's sad—Halder has a brilliant mind and is well-educated, but he uses his talents to further himself with no qualms about right or wrong."

Chavez's face softened, and she placed her hand on Lowry's shoulder. "Despite what you've been through today, and I know it's hard to believe, the assholes don't always win." With a sigh, she continued. "I keep reminding myself that no matter the current score, there is a balance to life, and we must focus on the big picture. Evil eventually runs out of steam."

"I'm not sure about that last bit." Lowry chewed her lip. "I just wish that my testimony hadn't hurt more than it helped."

"The morsel of information on your uncle's connection with a tribe of Eskimos was unfortunate," Chavez replied, nodding her head.

"I had mentioned it to Edward, but just . . . ." Lowry raised an eyebrow with a shrug. "Uh, casually—not during the deposition." Brushing her hair back, she stuttered, "He was simply asking how my uncle and I came to be on Antarctica. Just an off-the-cuff conversation. I can't believe he used it in the trial."

Chavez sighed, touching Lowry's arm. "I can. My dear, at Yale, Edward was known as a mega-partier and ladies' man. He cleaned up his penchant for drugs once he was hired by the DOJ, but Halder designed a particular role for him, and Edward has become known as the Gigolo, Lowry. Halder sends him to ferret out seemingly innocuous information—by *any means necessary.*"

"Bastard," Lowry snapped, clenching her teeth as she stared at the floor. Then she glanced up and saw the impish twinkle in Chavez's eyes. Lowry's anger evaporated in the absurdity of it all, and slumping against the wall, she laughed until her sides hurt. In the midst of this maelstrom, being made a fool of by Edward was the least of her worries.

Exhaling, she wiped the tears from her eyes. Edward may have felt compelled to go to the dark side to survive, but betrayal creates its own noose, tightening its grip around the neck of those who partake of its power.

She glanced down the vacant hallway. *Poor bastard.*

# CHAPTER 24

Lowry shuffled into her room at the hotel. Emotionally drained, she changed out of her clothes and collapsed onto the bed. She wasn't a particularly religious person, but staring up at the ceiling, she floated a prayer to the heavens for Jean-Luc. She shuttered her mind away from the idea of blowback from Halder. She had done the will of her conscience, and that was all she could do.

Her eyes fluttered as the tension of the day fell away, but the swirling faces haunted her as she drifted into a restless sleep. She fell into a dream, a twisted version of the dancing monkeys fable that Adam had told in the Garden.

The curtain rose on a dark stage, and then a spotlight shone on a single figure standing at center stage dressed in a dazzling prince's regalia. The light moved upward to the prince's face, revealing Elliot Halder playing the role. He smiled and raised his arm to cue the start of the play. The lights and music rose as a horde of masked monkeys in fantastical costumes appeared from the wings of the stage, dancing and twirling to the delight of the faceless audience. The prince brandished his sword, saluting the crowd as the monkeys cavorted around the prince. When the music paused, the troupe bowed to the cheers emanating from the shadows.

In the midst of the acclaim, Adam leapt from the wings, scattering peanuts upon the stage, and the dream became a nightmare. The prince stepped back as the monkeys ripped their costumes away and tore off their masks, exposing the distorted faces of Gerwin and Edward. The prince laughed as the monkeys forgot their fine manners, racing to the peanuts strewn on the stage.

A spotlight beamed onto Adam, and a sinister melody rose in the hall. He waved his arms, and the peanuts lying on the stage morphed into tiny humans who leapt up and sprinted across the stage like mice. The savage monkeys chased the miniature people down, catching them in their hairy paws and devouring them whole.

Then the old shaman, Sataa, appeared beside her in the darkness. He spoke softly in his native language, but she could understand him. "The monkeys have not been taught how to be men but are only mad beasts who do not even respect themselves."

The crowd was hushed at the tiny humans' desperate cries but did nothing while the monkeys scrambled to catch them—brutally fighting amongst themselves over the last ones. The lights on the stage dimmed, and the monkeys gathered together, turning their greedy eyes toward Sataa and Lowry. Her heart beat a staccato at the look of hunger on their faces, and she grabbed Sataa's arm.

He turned, gazing at her bleakly. "Do not worry; they won't harm you. They have no interest in you."

Led by the prince, the troupe of monkeys slunk down the steps from the stage and crept to where Sataa and Lowry stood. Sataa pushed Lowry away from him as the prince and the monkeys gathered near them. The prince stared at Sataa with a sneer and snapped his fingers. The monkeys jostled each other as they encircled the old man, the shreds of fabric from their costumes shimmering in the dim light. Quietly, they began to whine, baring their gleaming, blood-striped teeth.

Sataa said in a resigned voice, "Ah, you are still hungry. You monkeys are never sated, are you?"

The prince smiled coldly. "I'm afraid not—their appetite is quite limitless."

"Prince, a day will come when it will be *you* they turn on to satisfy their cravings," Sataa murmured. "And you *and your offspring* will be no more on this Earth." In the dim light, he closed his eyes and began to shuffle his feet, chanting a tribal prayer.

The prince nodded to the monkeys. A drone rose from the hairy beasts, and they rocked back and forth around Sataa as if under a spell. With their steely eyes locked on their prey, the swaying became more intense, and the knot tightened.

Sataa tilted his head back, singing louder to shield his mind from the rising wails. He slowly spun in place, shadows and light shifting across his weathered face. He raised his hands to the heavens, his eyes tightly shut against his impending death.

Then the monkeys shrieked as one and attacked Sataa, leaping onto his head and back, forcing him to the ground. Sataa groaned as they ripped into his body with their sharp teeth and claws, shredding through the leather clothes, sending blood flying into the air. Monkey Gerwin bit into Sataa's skull as Monkey Edward's long teeth tore into his jugular, and the life of the gentle old man was gone, his body lying in a pool of blood. Screaming in victory, the monkeys dragged his dead body off into the darkness.

In her nightmare, Lowry stood frozen in place, nauseated with shock and abhorrence at the scene before her. A breath tickled the hair on the back of her neck, and she flinched.

Then Adam whispered in her ear, "Not all is how it appears, is it?"

Lowry jerked toward him, but as she turned, he disappeared into the darkness. She turned back, and the prince was also gone. Only an empty gloom remained.

What crime had Sataa committed to warrant this sentence of death? Was it simply the beliefs that he held? Even within her dream, she knew it was neither. Greed had harnessed the power of fear, which, like horses whipped into a frenzy, drove over the old man with no real malice but killed him as sure as a bullet to the heart.

Lowry awoke, terrified and shaking, her arms clutching the covers now twisted around her body. Gasping, she became aware of her surroundings and realized she was in her hotel room.

*Thank God, it was just a dream.*

Untangling herself from the sheets, she looked at the clock and realized she had slept through the night. Trembling, she got out of bed, went to the sink, and splashed water on her face, hoping to shake off her nightmare. Exhaling, she started the coffee and took a shower while it brewed. The hot water streamed over her, washing the residue of the nightmare from her mind as she scrubbed her hair. She stepped out feeling more normal, rubbed down with the towel, and pulled on a robe. She grabbed the coffee and sat on the bed, sipping from the steaming cup.

Lowry clicked on the television and found the morning news, but her jaw dropped when the newscaster said, "Breaking news just in: the jury in the Jean-Luc Kimalu trial has just returned with a final verdict. The head juror has informed the court that the jury finds Jean-Luc Kimalu guilty of sabotage and endangerment of the lives of all on board the International Space Station. Sentencing will follow after the judge completes her deliberations of the trial evidence."

In shock, Lowry slumped onto the edge of the bed, shaking her head. Staring at the TV, she whispered to herself, "My god, that poor soul." Halder must have put in a special order for a fast guilty verdict.

Lowry mechanically dressed as the news continued but turned it off, fuming at the defamatory statements spun against Jean-Luc as icing on the verdict. In the silence of the room, images from her nightmare resurfaced in her mind, and she paced around the bed, shaking her head. Without thinking, she grabbed her purse and left the room, running down the stairs and out a side door of the hotel. She had to escape and try to clear her head, to make sense of the nonsensical.

With no destination in mind, she randomly headed toward Wisconsin Boulevard, the acrid smell of the city filling her nostrils. As she walked to the corner, the blaring horns and clamor of construction assaulted her ears. The light turned green, and she shuffled across the street in the midst of a throng of people, moving together like a centipede crawling across a rock.

Once across the street, Lowry stopped as she caught her reflection in the mirrored façade of the glass building, her brunette hair blowing in the wind of the skyscraper canyon. She looked up through the towering edifices at a plane ripping through a patch of blue sky, leaving a scar of ice crystals behind. People rushed around her, but she stood still, like a stone in a river, disoriented in the chaos of civilization.

Someone jostled her forward, and she wandered down the sidewalk aimlessly, reflecting on her humanness and her empathy for the Inuits. Like them, she was deeply connected to the natural world and had lived in the wilderness of a polar region, where humans were minor actors in the play of life.

Vaguely, Lowry looked up at the street signs, realizing she was walking toward the Federal Courthouse district. An intense urge hit her—she wanted to talk to Jean-Luc, to express her sorrow and to find out his side of the story. Catching a cab, she went to the federal jail where he was being held. Stepping out of the Robocab, she stared at the forbidding façade and then took a deep breath and went inside.

The security officers scrutinized her as she pushed through the heavy doors, but she steadied herself and went to the front desk to ask if she could see Jean-Luc. She signed her name and waited on a bench until a guard signaled her to follow him. They went through a security door and headed down a hall. As they walked along, she inwardly shuddered at the incessant echo of the clacking of their shoes.

They came to another set of heavy doors, and the guard opened the door, leading the way into the cellblock. Shivering in the icy glow of the lights, she waited for the guard to reclose the door. She swallowed hard at the stares of the furtive faces of the men in the cells as they walked down the corridor until the guard stopped in front of one of the cells. Lowry chewed her lip, and her steps slowed as she approached Jean-Luc's cell.

The cell was filtered in anemic sunlight from the small, mesh-covered window. The guard stepped back, and a sigh escaped from Lowry as the vestiges of the nightmare faded away. Sataa was alive, sitting cross-legged outside the cell, facing Jean-Luc. In his native tongue, Sataa was speaking softly to him, but Jean-Luc just stared vacantly at the cement floor, his face pensive and drained.

The guard set a chair for her outside the cell. "You can talk to him from here, and don't get too close to the bars."

At the guard's words, Jean-Luc turned toward them, flashing a dirty look at the guard and growling like a dog. The guard stepped back and stood at attention, watching them carefully. Lowry sat on the hard metal chair, clearing her throat in the awkward silence.

With a slight smile, she murmured, "Hello."

Jean-Luc furrowed his brow. "Why are you here?"

"I'm wondering that myself," she said, shrugging. "I guess I'm here because I don't think you're guilty."

Jean-Luc stared at her incredulously and then guffawed. "Since when does guilt have anything to do with a conviction?" His lip curled into a snarl. "This trial is merely a tool the United States government is using to pull the teeth out of our organization. They are systematically destroying the leaders who have held the homesteaders off our land. They've already bankrupted one of our other leaders by calling in his debts." He jabbed his thumb toward his chest. "I am just the second one on their hit list."

Lowry leaned forward. "Jean-Luc, I want to learn about your tribe."

He blinked and then snapped, "Another bleeding heart who acts like they give a shit?"

She gazed at him, shaking her head. "No, I was raised at the bottom of the world instead of the top, and I actually *do* give a shit."

He studied her, and then, with a resigned drop of his shoulders, he spoke. "My people have a rich heritage. Despite outside influences, we had been able to maintain many of the tribal rituals because we were so isolated before the melting of the ice."

Sighing, he gazed upwards, his head tilted. "I remember, as a small child, playing and dancing with the people in our village. It was a natural life filled with pride in the way of the ancestors—we hunted and worked together with such joy in our lives. The beauty of the land was extraordinary; the brilliant blue sea teemed with sea animals, and birds filled the skies. Our people were in balance with our world and took only what we needed from Mother Earth to live."

His face twisted, and he shot her an angry look. "But as the ocean started to move inland and the snow pack melted, our way of life began to change. The animals we depended upon left or died, their habitat disappearing as the ice melted away. However, we learned to adapt and hunt the caribou, which now stayed longer in our ranges, and other animals and birds began to appear, moving up from the south as the earth was exposed to the sun, and grass and low brush began to grow where only snow existed before. Our people changed some of the old ways but were still a cohesive tribe.

"Then, one day, my brother and I went hunting together, and a group of interlopers came over the hill in a four-wheeler, drunk out of their minds, and almost hit us. If my brother hadn't pulled me back, I would have been killed." He shook his head and scowled. "Ever since then, our tribe has fought to keep our land, but the government is stronger than we are and determined to steal our lands and our lives. Now, there are never-ending waves of people who keep coming for the land and the minerals in the earth. And many of these people who invade are not the cream of the crop, as it were, and in some cases are outright criminals who were forced by one means or another out of the south. It breaks the hearts of my people to see the land destroyed and our way of life disappear."

Despair enveloped his face. "History always repeats itself. The powerful take what they want and, in the process, destroy entire cultures. Then they have the audacity to feel sorry about it in a hundred years."

Lowry nodded sadly. "Like a flock of birds, once the fruit is plucked and eaten, I'm afraid they look for their next plunder."

Jean-Luc dropped his head in his hands, his face haggard and worn with battling a force greater than himself.

Sataa turned to Lowry and opened his mouth. She gasped at the sight of a strange animal object appearing on his tongue. Sataa reached up, pulling the small, carved creature out of his mouth, smiling as he held the thing up, turning it around so she could see it.

Jean-Luc looked up and explained to her, "He is the last practicing shaman of my tribe. What he has is a carved sea scorpion, which is his spirit helper, and it was passed down to him from generations of shamans."

Sataa began to speak softly, and Jean Luc translated for her. "My people believe that there is a spirit in the land. We still hold the Bladder Feast every year in my tribe to honor the spirits of the animals who were harvested the year before. I remember a quote from Aua, an Iglulik shaman:

"'The greatest peril of life lies in the fact that human food consists entirely of souls. All the creatures that we have to strike down and destroy in order to eat and make clothes for ourselves have souls, souls that do not perish with the body and that must therefore be pacified lest they should take revenge on us.'"

Jean-Luc spat out, "Modern humans have killed all souls. They don't even acknowledge that the Earth has a soul, so they crush life into asphalt wherever they can."

He looked at her dully as Sataa spoke again, and then he translated. "He says you are not like the others; you have an independent spirit." He stood and faced her, smiling sadly. "You remind him of the story of Sedna."

Lowry looked at Sataa and said to Jean-Luc, "Please, tell me the story."

Jean-Luc spoke softly as he told the story. "Sedna was a proud girl who refused to marry any of the suitors who were brought before her. And so she ran away with a seabird who promised her the good life. She discovered this was a lie and called to her father to rescue her. Her father took her away in a boat after killing the bird-husband, but the other birds followed. The birds created a giant storm, and her father threw Sedna overboard to save his own life. He cuts his fingers off in his despair over the loss of his child. Sedna went on to dwell in the sea and became the ruler of the sea mammals."

Entranced by the story, Lowry whispered, "Sedna of the sea."

A shout rang out from one of the other cells, and the guard ran back toward the scream, calling on his radio for backup. Shrieks echoed along the corridor, followed by shouts from the officers as they subdued the prisoner.

Lowry rose and stood facing Jean-Luc, who stood tall in front of her, his dark eyes flicking back and forth as he studied her. Here was a true champion of his people; a man who fought on regardless of self-sacrifice and nothing like the Franks or Edwards of the world. She opened her mouth, but no words came out. She cleared her throat. "Jean-Luc, this may sound strange . . . but I've never kissed a hero, and I'd like to."

Blinking in surprise, he stared at her, and then his face softened. He moved close to the bars, and Lowry stepped forward and met his lips between the bars—not a sensual kiss, but an acknowledgement of respect for each other.

Lowry flinched as the guard blew his whistle and yelled, "Step back, miss!"

They both stepped away from the bars, and she raised her hand to the guard. "Please, just a few more minutes, I promise."

The guard looked at her, pointing down the hall to where an inmate was being dragged out of his cell. "Lady, I already have one nut strapped into a straightjacket; I don't need another incident today." He glanced at his watch. "You have five more minutes, *if* you stay back from the bars."

Lowry nodded and looked back at Jean-Luc. "Jean-Luc, I'm so sorry. I wish I could have helped."

Jean-Luc's eyes had an eerie light as he smiled at her. "I believe you. Thank you for your effort at the trial, and I appreciate you coming here today. I want to hope that our tribal lands will be saved, but honestly, I don't believe it." He touched his lips with two fingers and motioned goodbye. "Lowry, you have a honest soul within you."

Sataa stretched his hand toward her and pressed a wadded up handkerchief into her hand. The guard glanced at them, so she quickly stuffed the handkerchief into her pocket. She waved to them as the guard cocked his head toward the exit. Walking back down the hall, she was indifferent to the staring eyes of the prisoners as they left the cell block.

After they signed her out, Lowry pushed through the heavy doors of the jail and stopped at the top of the steps, breathing in the fresh air. She opened the handkerchief and shook the contents into the palm of her hand, sucking in her breath at the sight of a pale finger. Examining it carefully, she realized it was a carving. "Sedna," she whispered, clutching the ivory finger.

# CHAPTER 25

Lowry urged the horse faster through a forest buried in fog. The cool air nipped at her face as they broke through the mist, racing to the top of the ridge. They stopped at the crest, above the dense clouds wedged like a cocoon in the valley below.

She breathed deeply the crisp air of a Virginia autumn, gazing at the sensuous curves of the ancient Blue Ridge Mountains dressed in shades of red, yellow, and maroon. Millions of years ago, the mountains had been as tall as the Alps, but erosion had worn away the tall peaks and filled the valleys below. This serene region was far from the coast, and though it had been the setting for one of the most violent periods for humanity, it had not been impacted by the Melt.

A red-tailed hawk drew Lowry's eye, and she followed her path across the sky. Two crows followed, harrying the raptor along its way. With the rays of the sun, the fog began to break in the valley below, revealing a beautiful red fox standing at the edge of the trees.

This was the first morning since the trial that she hadn't felt numb. She had come to her maternal grandparents' farm in western Virginia to rest for a week before returning to the space station. Shaken from the experience of the trial, she barely remembered her trip from D.C. Since her arrival, her grandparents had asked her little, and yet she could see the worry in their faces. Almost in desperation, she had ridden one of their horses into the rolling hills every day, struggling with her role in the Machiavellian theater in which she had been an unwitting actor and grappling with the helpless feeling that she could do nothing to aid the Inuit tribe.

Lowry turned her horse and started along the ridgeline, wanting to capture every nuance of the beauty surrounding her. A breeze kicked up, bringing the scent of the earth as it warmed in the sun. They walked over a trickle of water streaming out of a fissure in the rocks above.

A motion caught her eye, and she smiled at the sight of two huge greyhounds streaking up the valley toward her. The graceful dogs were poetry in motion sprinting across the curves of the land. She shielded her eyes against the sun, and in the distance behind the dogs, she saw two horses with riders slowly cantering toward her across the valley. She waved to her grandparents. They returned her wave, and she started down the face of the hillside to meet them.

They were lovely people who treated man and beast with the same joy and dignity. She couldn't help but grin as she approached them.

"We brought lunch!" her grandfather shouted.

"Thank goodness!" Lowry called back. "It's only been an hour or so since that huge breakfast."

They all laughed as they slowed to a walk, and she turned her horse to join them.

Her grandmother said, "We thought we would have lunch at our old fishing hole. Do you remember Bear Falls?"

Lowry chuckled. "How could I forget the place where I learned to swim?" She cocked her head. "But I do remember the time when I slipped on the rocks and fractured my arm."

"Oh, dear. I'd forgotten that incident—it was so long ago."

Lowry laughed. "No bad memories, Grandma. It's a lovely spot."

They moved to single file as they entered the forest, following a worn path down to the river and along the bank to the falls. Lowry recognized the rock formations ahead and bit her lip in excitement as she heard the rush of water over the rocks.

They picketed the horses and climbed up the huge rock balanced over the river. Lowry shielded her eyes from the bright sun on the exposed boulder. An errant breeze kicked up, and laughing, they struggled to spread out the blanket, which threatened to race away with the wind. Lowry grabbed several loose stones and placed them on each corner of the blanket to keep it from being carried off.

Lowry's grandmother set down the food hamper, and they sat cross-legged around it as she doled out the sandwiches and drinks. Through the thin coverlet, Lowry felt the warmth coming from the limestone rock underneath them.

As they got ready to eat, her grandfather said softly, "Let this food nurture our bodies as your teachings nurture our souls."

Her grandmother murmured, "Amen."

No one spoke as they started to eat, now hungry with the exertions of the morning.

Her grandfather pointed to a vine with fading blooms nestled under a rock near the water's edge. His face lit up as he said, "Look: there is some Man of the Earth vine still holding onto its blooms—a last gasp before winter."

Lowry stared at the white flowers with purple centers, beginning to wilt after the morning frost had bit their delicate petals. The memory of Elliot Halder and his devious games flooded back into her mind—so opposite of these sweet people.

She said bluntly, "Well, winter will soon kill any hope of flowers." She lay back on the face of the rock with the sharp cracks in the stone digging into her head.

Her grandmother asked her softly, "What's wrong, baby?"

"Just thinking of the evil side of humans and what it is that makes people value power over love."

Her grandmother shrugged, shaking her head. "I don't understand it myself. How can you allow yourself to damage your soul for a fleeting moment of dominance over another being? Nothing is worth that. You might as well thrust a dagger into your own heart as lie and cheat to hurt others."

Lowry turned onto her side, staring into the water rushing over the rocks. "Children are taught to love one another. Is it just another lie?" She sat up and waved her hand at the surrounding beauty. "To children, everything is a miracle— every tiny bud and insect. By adulthood, all that joy is burned out of us until none of the wonder of life remains." Her face was pinched as she cast a stone into the water. "No wonder God kicked us out of the Garden." The plunk of the rock echoed against the limestone walls.

Her grandmother was the first to break the silence. "Now, my dear, you mustn't become cynical." She scooted close, wrapping her arm around Lowry's waist. "Lowry, we know you've had a tough time, and if you don't want to return to the space station, we would understand and support you. And we could use some help around here anyway."

Her grandfather nodded. "We know how much you love this place."

Lowry stared grimly down at the churning water below them. "As much as I would love to stay, I cannot. I won't give them that satisfaction."

Her grandmother shook her head. "You're not used to dealing with people like you've had to deal with over the last several weeks." She patted Lowry's arm. "I'm afraid learning the dirty side of life is something we all have to go through at some point."

Lowry shrugged. "Well, I had to learn to deal with my father, so I guess he was good for something." Lowry threw another stone into the water. "I remember Dad downing a shot of whiskey and then joking that since the world was drowned, everyone might as well join in the party."

"What a *lovely* man," her grandmother snorted.

Her grandfather interjected, "I wish we had taken you after Margaret's death. It was something both your grandmother and I regret."

Her grandmother sighed, smoothing Lowry's hair. "Yes, we wanted to, but Duff insisted that you come with him, and we didn't know all of the circumstances."

"My father wasn't all bad. He loved me the best he could." Lowry sighed. "I guess that's as much as one can expect from any human being."

Her grandfather grimaced. "I know he's your father, but honestly, I never liked Duff. He courted Margaret with his big smile and smooth talk, but I felt there was something not quite square with him." He shrugged. "Margaret was stubborn and didn't want to listen to us."

"Your grandpa's right. Once he had the ring on her finger, the personality he had carefully manufactured slipped away." Her grandmother stared down into the pool below. "Margaret never told us much, and there was always some excuse keeping him away when you and your mother visited the farm. Frankly, she seemed happier once he shipped out to Antarctica."

Her grandmother laid her head on Lowry's shoulder. "You were the light in her life." She glanced at her husband with a sad smile. "Our Margaret loved you so much—when you came into the room, her eyes lit up." Her lips trembled. "When we visited her grave last week, it was a shock to realize it's been ten years since her death."

Her grandfather's face was grim as he flicked a red leaf over the falls. "I still think about the Girl Scout leader's decision to take all their phones away so they would 'go off the grid' and enjoy nature. How could she have been so irresponsible and not be warned about the turn of the storm?"

Her grandmother placed her hand on his shoulder. "She has to live with her torment, just as we have to live with Margaret's death." She turned to Lowry. "At the funeral, the Girl Scout leader told us that Margaret had tried to convince her to have at least one phone with a weather alert active, but she had insisted that she had checked the weather and everything was clear."

Lowry's shoulders crumpled, and with her head bowed from the strain of the last weeks, she wept like a child. "Mom was my champion—always there when I needed her. I can never forget that she sacrificed her life to save mine."

Her grandmother held her close, stroking her hair, as Lowry's sobs echoed around the stone facades. When her tears abated, she slumped in exhaustion, leaning against her grandmother's shoulder.

Handing her a tissue, her grandfather cleared his throat. "We must look forward and not dwell on the past."

They sat listening to the water rushing over the rocks until the sun was high in the sky and the stone beneath them had become uncomfortably warm. They stood and gathered the blankets and trash while birds darted over the water, catching the midday insects.

They silently climbed down the rocks, and when they reached the horses, her grandfather waved his hand toward the rolling pastures in the distance. "I hope this place will remain in the family. It's in a conservation easement, so the land can't be broken up into parcels. Just let us know if you have an interest in it."

"I thought my cousin was taking the farm."

"Yes, I think so, but the future is always uncertain."

Her grandmother asked, "Lowry, what are your plans after the space-station research project is completed?"

She shrugged. "We're almost completed with this initial data collection, and then I have to compile all the new data with the seismic data we already have. My final dissertation will be a report detailing the soil and aquifers of Antarctica in case the UN decides to open the continent to homesteaders." She sighed, staring up into the blue sky. "After my degree is finished, I'm not sure—it's possible that I may one day return to Antarctica."

They remounted and started back to the farm, quietly meandering along the trails. The day had warmed, but a pleasant breeze accompanied them across the fields. Lowry pointed out a hole near an outcrop of rocks. "What's that?"

Her grandmother looked at the opening in the ground. "It's a fox den, and that one has been there for years." She swept her hand toward the horizon. "Your mother used to fox-hunt with the local club, and our farm is one of their fixtures." With a smile, she shook her head. "But they don't really hunt the foxes, they just chase them."

Her grandfather smiled. "We rode at the back, but your mother was so brave on Cooper, her thoroughbred gelding, jumping five-foot fences, careening up and down steep slopes—it was both terrifying and majestic to watch."

They reached the stables and dismounted. Her grandfather stretched out his legs and gestured to the stables. "Your mother did such a lovely job on the barn plans—she believed in designing to the landscape."

They led the horses into the barn, untacked them, and sprayed off the sweat from the long ride, and then they put them in the stables with a flake of hay and a cool bucket of water.

Her grandmother came out of the tack room holding a small black helmet. She dusted the helmet off and said, "This was your first riding helmet. We bought it for you when you and your mom came for a visit—you were six years old." She blinked, trying to hold back her tears. "Do you remember your first riding lesson?"

Lowry shook her head. "Vaguely—I remember the pony, but not so much the lesson."

"Margaret put you on Minnie and led her around the ring with you in short stirrups in a tiny English saddle." She grinned. "You were smiling and singing until Minnie shied and you slipped off, hitting the ground. You cried a little, maybe more with humiliation than hurt. Then your mother asked if you wanted to get back on, and you nodded your head, so back up you went."

"Now I remember. Minnie could be nasty." Lowry took the helmet and caressed the sun-faded felt. "My mom was a strong woman, but not domineering." Lowry raised her eyebrow. "But she could have a temper." A smile drifted across her face. "Most of all, she wanted to teach me something dear to her—to love this crazy thing called life." She handed the helmet back to her grandmother. "Uncle Nick was the one who got me the horses when I moved to Antarctica. I would have been a different person without horses in my life."

"Can I get some of that life experience over here?" her grandfather said, cleaning one of the stalls.

Laughing, Lowry walked over and took the rake from him. "I'll finish the stall, Grandpa."

He leaned on the stall door as she cleaned the stall. "I don't know if you remember, but when you were a little girl, you used to stay with the animals for hours, learning to read what was in their minds. That's a rare characteristic, and it takes a caring personality, perception, and frankly, respect. The person who respects an animal respects themselves." Beaming, he rolled the wheelbarrow out of the stall. "Nothing like caring for an animal to make you at peace with the world."

Grandma yelled, "Here comes the Philosopher King with his load of manure!"

Lowry grinned. "You and Grandma are such wonderful, hardworking, and loving people. You both have such pride in work and love of life without the annoying arrogance."

Her grandmother smiled. "We've worked all of our lives, your grandpa and I, whether in our teaching careers or here at the farm. And we still have such a joy in learning." She looked lovingly at him. "It's made us centered and happy."

Her grandfather dumped the wheelbarrow and then returned, nodding. "We make choices in our lives, Lowry. We can strive to become honorable people or, as some do, use our gifts to manipulate those around us to further ourselves. The path to happiness is simple, but the road to hell is complex and harrowing."

*     *     *

The sunset illuminated the gravestones on the hilltop with a soft golden light. Within the family cemetery, surrounded by centuries of her family, Lowry stood in front of her mother's grave, finally strong enough to face her. Her hands shaking, she laid a bouquet of autumn wild flowers in front of Margaret's stone.

"Momma, I've failed to live up to your hopes and dreams." The words opened wounds she had held back for months, and tears streamed down her face, blurring her vision of Margaret's name on the gravestone.

A failed marriage. Lowry had been ignorant in her choice of husband and had tried to make it work, but it takes willingness on both sides. She caressed the smooth granite headstone. Her mother had also experienced the disease of an abusive relationship. To protect Lowry, she had hidden their marital troubles—not difficult since she, not baby Lowry, had been the lightning rod for Duff's anger. When Duff lost his job, he floated around the States until Nick found him the job in Antarctica, so he was absent for years until he took custody of her after her mother's death.

Uncle Nick had been the one who had told Lowry of the history of abuse by their father and how it had affected Duff. She had thought herself untouched by it all since she hadn't lived solely with her father until adolescence, but his mercurial and violent personality had affected her more than she had realized. She shook her head. *Shit rolls downhill.* Perhaps that was why she had been vulnerable to Frank's abuse.

Lowry knelt on the grass, and sighing, she thought back to the moral battle with the unscrupulous Halder. Did she skew the verdict of Jean-Luc with her testimony, especially her offhand remark about Nick's connection with an Eskimo training facility? Edward's probing reconnaissance mission had borne fruit with an innocuous comment twisted into damning evidence.

Under Halder's direction, the actors were manipulated by any means, whether wittingly, for a payout, or unwittingly by ignorance. Edward was a mere player, required to read his appointed lines. Lowry hadn't been aware she was even a part of the cast, and they both had played her like a fool. Halder would eventually be taken out by a more powerful manipulator with their own script, but for now, he had control of the curtain.

Was the play over? Would all the actors just fade away as the lights go down? Perhaps years down the road, the truth, whatever it was, would emerge, but it would be too late for the Eskimo tribes. Their tribal lands would be filled with apartment complexes, strip malls, and parking lots. The Halders would win because they direct the performances on the world stage.

She slumped onto the ground, smoothing her brow with her fingers, and gazed at the mountains around her, painted with vibrant hues as the rays of the sun bent over the horizon. *What was that saying—the dead get the best views?* With college and her insane life, it had been years since she had been able to visit her mother's grave. Lowry reached out and traced her mother's name with her finger to elicit her mother's strength and wisdom. "Momma, please help me find peace."

Lowry would return to the ISS tomorrow afternoon. This was her last night on Earth. She shifted positions and felt a poke in her side. Pulling out the finger of Sedna, she stared at it in the fading light.

*　　*　　*

Lowry awoke that night and lifted her head, listening in the darkness. Was that her mother's voice saying "Lowry"? Tears came into her eyes—just memories. She exhaled and lay her head back down on the warm pillow, wishing it were her mother's shoulder.

Fluffing the pillow, her hand touched the letter she had tucked beneath it. Her grandmother had given it to her after dinner, her voice thin as she said, "This was the last letter she sent—Margaret was sentimental and loved sending old-fashioned letters. We saved this for you to have."

Hugging her grandmother, she clutched the letter and slipped away to her room. When she was alone, Lowry climbed into bed and turned on the table lamp next to her. She caressed

er pants. S
ded the tent,

ndparents and
he sighed at the
t was her mother

river's rising!"
th them like a
ther shouted.
g nearer, and
he tent like a
mmie, jerking

*the delight of my life an*
*to watch her blossom into*
*her during the difficult times,*
*e truly become a better person*

"Get up the
the slippery

of the night. Tears seeped
oss of her mother hit her
rom her too early, leaving
l. Lowry stared up at the
she had seen her mother.

ssure of the
ylon fabric
head was
rial, but her
to free her
arled poles

\*

shing river
ldozer. An
nd Lowry
now up to
d them as

shouted in the darkness.
her eyes, and yawning, she
up, squinting as the flashlight
Mommy?"
one warned us there is a flash
ok the leg of Kimmie, the girl

heard frogs croaking in the
raining." She'd been looking
camping trip in the Hill Country
the older girls in the troop had
vas her turn.

flow and
dy water,
's ankle.
nally, the

eir gear, stuffing it into a bag.
upon us. It made an unexpected
nt of rain just west of us. We have
ters are barreling down on us." Her
eping bags as Lowry and Kimmie

ed away
current
s of the

ky with
arrival.

her tennis shoes and then yawned.
a cold dampness touching her leg.

217

wn, she felt water soaking h
"Water!" A stream of water inv;
around the flap.

yell ripped through the night. "Run—the
The floor of the tent bubbled up undernea
and grasping under a sheet. "Go, girls!" her m
In the darkness, they heard a rushing sound comi
then a wall of water slammed into the side of t
charging beast. Margaret grabbed Lowry and Ki
them toward the tent opening.

Kimmie scooted out, and Margaret shouted,
bank as fast as you can!" Kimmie scrambled up
bank.

Amid the deafening roar of the river, the pr
water increased, collapsing the tent, and the
wrapped around them like cellophane. Lowry'
covered, and she flayed under the shroud of mate
mother peeled it away. She lifted Lowry, attempting
from the remnants of the tent, but one of the s
trapped Lowry's leg.

Shouts came to them from the bank, but the r
muted their words. Another surge hit them like a bu
enormous weight of water shoved them forward,
felt the pole tighten around her ankle. The river was
Lowry's waist, and the muddy waters rushed aroun
her mother struggled to free her.

Her mother shouted, "Turn your leg into the
point your toe." Then she reached under the mud
trying to peel the twisted metal from around Lowr
Lowry felt her mother's nails scraping her skin, and f
pole slipped away, freeing her leg.

Heaving her up into her arms, her mother stripp
the rest of the clinging fabric from her body. The
accelerated, and the tent stakes broke away. The remai
tent disappeared under the frothy waters.

The leading edge of the storm raced across the
flashes of lightning and ominous thunder heralding its

Lowry wrapped her arms and legs around her mother, struggling toward the riverbank. The core of the storm arrived, and rain poured down on top of them.

"Up here, this way!" A flashlight beamed across the seething water.

Lowry faced upstream, and the light flashing across the river revealed a wall of water descending upon them. "Mommy, another wave of water is going to hit us!"

Her mother twisted her head around and shouted, "No!" Then she lunged toward the shore. "Lowry, you have to get to the bank!"

Seconds later, a towering mass of water slammed into them, knocking them over, and then whirled them under the surface of the raging river. Lowry's legs were ripped from her mother's hips, but she clasped her mother's neck as they were tossed in the current. Churning water covered her head, forcing its way into her nose, and she couldn't breathe. She sucked water into her lungs until the current pushed her upward and she broke through the surface into the air. Coughing, she felt rain pouring into her face, but she still gripped her mother like a millstone around her neck. Lowry rode piggyback as they raced downriver, her mother fighting to keep her head above the surface.

In the blackness, they hit something solid, and her mother clutched the broken limbs of a massive tree trunk, which had ripped out of the earth and now plummeted downriver in the swift water. Her mother clung to the slippery trunk as the roiling river swept them along, spinning and dipping to the mad tempo of the river like a wild carnival ride.

The trunk slammed into another object. Her mother grunted with the impact, and Lowry slipped forward. Lightning ripped across the sky, and the flash of light revealed that they were snagged on a huge upright tree not yet torn out of the earth by the insane river. Margaret reached back, pulling Lowry over her head toward the branches of the oak tree. "Climb up, Lowry, as high as you can."

Crawling over her mother's back, she balanced on the log for a second and then leapt into the tree. The rain buffeted her as she clambered up into the rough branches of the oak, climbing up until she felt a solid branch high in the tree. She clutched the wet limbs, looking down into the darkness for her mother. "Mommy, come on!"

Lightning flashed, and Lowry saw her mother kneeling on the log, stretching her arms toward the oak tree. But before she could leap, a fresh pulse of water hit the end of the log, twisting it away from the oak, and plunged it back into the surging river. Screaming, her mother flipped off the log, and then there was only the sound of the raging waters.

Lowry screamed into the darkness, "Mommy!"

She listened to the roar of the river, trembling at the sound of splintering wood surrounding her. Another round of lightning flashed over the churning river, revealing broken trees rolling in the foam . . . but nothing else.

Drenched, Lowry shivered, tears mixing with the rain on her face. "Mommy?"

$*$  $*$  $*$

Two days later, a couple walking their dog along the river discovered her mother's body jammed against one of the cement pilings of a washed-out bridge. A news photo showed her pale body wrapped in a shroud of sticks and plastic grocery bags.

With no other family members nearby, Lowry was deemed old enough to identify the body. She arrived at the morgue, gagging as she passed a stairwell with the nauseating smell of formaldehyde wafting from the floor below. A kind police officer escorted Lowry into her office, gently keeping her hand on Lowry's shoulder. "Lowry, this will only take a minute. I'm going to show you some photos. Just tell me if you know this woman or not."

The officer pulled out a set of photographs and placed them side by side on the table in front of Lowry. Taken from the front and profile, stark images of her mother's deathly white face lay in front of her. Blinking in disbelief, she nodded and reached out to touch the face of the woman who had given her life and then saved her from death. She dropped her head into her hands and began to sob. Her mother was gone.

*    *    *

During the funeral, Lowry felt like a china doll—one break in her façade and she would fall to pieces. Duff had returned from Antarctica for the funeral, and even though she sat in the pew of the funeral home with her maternal grandparents on one side and her father on the other, Lowry could feel the distance between them. Lowry stared ahead as the choir sang hymns, but all she heard were the last words her mother had said to her: *Climb as high as you can.*

The service ended, and her grandmother turned to her, tears flowing down her cheeks. "Lowry, I want you to know what your mother once told us." She squeezed Lowry's hand. "You were her sunrise and her sunset."

Lowry stood in the receiving line with a vacant smile on her face, her grandmother holding her hand as friends and family greeted her with compassion, but she also felt a thread of pity in their glances. Her insides were balled up with the uncertainty of her future.

When the funeral ended, Duff put his arm around Lowry and brusquely told her grandparents, "Lowry will be coming to live with me. I have everything arranged."

When violence is woven into the fabric of life, particularly around an impressionable child, those strands of abuse become deeply imbedded and the pattern familiar; the tears never completely heal. Who holds the blame? The only remedy is to break the pattern—to be the mother or father who examines the past, understands the cause, and is determined to not repeat the cycle.

Nick zipped up his jacket as the cool night air nestled around him. He sank back into the chair, his head buzzing as he stared up into the brilliant night sky.

From a dim corner of Nick's mind, a line from an old poem emerged: *From birth, we humans gather wounds . . . and are forever scarred.*

Finishing his whiskey, Nick stared into the glass, rolling the remnants of liquid around the bottom of the tumbler. Liquor had been the escape from the pain of living for his father, and then his brother, but he had been spared the curse of alcoholism. He rarely indulged, but he was thoroughly human, and other vices had haunted him over his life: envy, sorrow, and deceit, to name a few.

Like a child with a spyglass, Nick brought the bottom of the glass to his eye and gazed upward, turning it like a kaleidoscope with the stars swirling against the black sky through the crystalline base. A sad smile flitted across his face. His savior in life had come in the form of a grieving twelve-year-old girl who had just lost her mother in a tragic flash flood.

*       *       *

Nick waited on the dock. A damp, frigid wind sliced into his face, and he pulled up the hood of his coat. A horn blasted, and he turned to the bay, shielding his eyes from the sun as the ship bearing his brother and niece eased into the dock.

Nick turned back to gaze at the ramshackle port town of huts and warehouses looking like they'd fallen out of the sky and landed haphazardly on the ground. It was not much different than when he'd arrived on his first voyage to the envelope addressed to her grandparents and then carefully pulled out the letter. Unfolding it, she sighed at the sight of her mother's lovely handwriting, but it was her mother's words that took her breath away:

*Lowry is ten years old today—she's the delight of my life and the center of my universe. It is a joy and privilege to watch her blossom into a unique person. I cheer her triumphs and hold her during the difficult times, filling her with love until she overflows. I have truly become a better person because of her.*

An owl hooted in the emptiness of the night. Tears seeped down the sides of her face as the loss of her mother hit her once again. A mother's love swept from her too early, leaving a void which could never be filled. Lowry stared up at the ceiling, remembering the last night she had seen her mother.

*       *       *

"Lowry, wake up!" her mother shouted in the darkness. Twelve-year-old Lowry rubbed her eyes, and yawning, she stretched out her arms. She sat up, squinting as the flashlight blinded her. "What's happening, Mommy?"

"Hurry, get dressed. Someone warned us there is a flash flood upriver." Her mother shook the leg of Kimmie, the girl sleeping next to Lowry.

Lowry listened but only heard frogs croaking in the distance. "But it's not even raining." She'd been looking forward to the big Girl Scout camping trip in the Hill Country near Austin for a year. All of the older girls in the troop had raved about it, and finally, it was her turn.

He mother grabbed their gear, stuffing it into a bag. "Lowry, the storm is almost upon us. It made an unexpected hook, dumping a huge amount of rain just west of us. We have to get out of here—floodwaters are barreling down on us." Her mother bundled up the sleeping bags as Lowry and Kimmie found their shoes.

Lowry finished tying her tennis shoes and then yawned. She flinched away from a cold dampness touching her leg.

Reaching down, she felt water soaking her pants. She screamed, "Water!" A stream of water invaded the tent, seeping around the flap.

A yell ripped through the night. "Run—the river's rising!"

The floor of the tent bubbled up underneath them like a hand grasping under a sheet. "Go, girls!" her mother shouted. In the darkness, they heard a rushing sound coming nearer, and then a wall of water slammed into the side of the tent like a charging beast. Margaret grabbed Lowry and Kimmie, jerking them toward the tent opening.

Kimmie scooted out, and Margaret shouted, "Get up the bank as fast as you can!" Kimmie scrambled up the slippery bank.

Amid the deafening roar of the river, the pressure of the water increased, collapsing the tent, and the nylon fabric wrapped around them like cellophane. Lowry's head was covered, and she flayed under the shroud of material, but her mother peeled it away. She lifted Lowry, attempting to free her from the remnants of the tent, but one of the snarled poles trapped Lowry's leg.

Shouts came to them from the bank, but the rushing river muted their words. Another surge hit them like a bulldozer. An enormous weight of water shoved them forward, and Lowry felt the pole tighten around her ankle. The river was now up to Lowry's waist, and the muddy waters rushed around them as her mother struggled to free her.

Her mother shouted, "Turn your leg into the flow and point your toe." Then she reached under the muddy water, trying to peel the twisted metal from around Lowry's ankle. Lowry felt her mother's nails scraping her skin, and finally, the pole slipped away, freeing her leg.

Heaving her up into her arms, her mother stripped away the rest of the clinging fabric from her body. The current accelerated, and the tent stakes broke away. The remains of the tent disappeared under the frothy waters.

The leading edge of the storm raced across the sky with flashes of lightning and ominous thunder heralding its arrival.

Lowry wrapped her arms and legs around her mother, struggling toward the riverbank. The core of the storm arrived, and rain poured down on top of them.

"Up here, this way!" A flashlight beamed across the seething water.

Lowry faced upstream, and the light flashing across the river revealed a wall of water descending upon them. "Mommy, another wave of water is going to hit us!"

Her mother twisted her head around and shouted, "No!" Then she lunged toward the shore. "Lowry, you have to get to the bank!"

Seconds later, a towering mass of water slammed into them, knocking them over, and then whirled them under the surface of the raging river. Lowry's legs were ripped from her mother's hips, but she clasped her mother's neck as they were tossed in the current. Churning water covered her head, forcing its way into her nose, and she couldn't breathe. She sucked water into her lungs until the current pushed her upward and she broke through the surface into the air. Coughing, she felt rain pouring into her face, but she still gripped her mother like a millstone around her neck. Lowry rode piggyback as they raced downriver, her mother fighting to keep her head above the surface.

In the blackness, they hit something solid, and her mother clutched the broken limbs of a massive tree trunk, which had ripped out of the earth and now plummeted downriver in the swift water. Her mother clung to the slippery trunk as the roiling river swept them along, spinning and dipping to the mad tempo of the river like a wild carnival ride.

The trunk slammed into another object. Her mother grunted with the impact, and Lowry slipped forward. Lightning ripped across the sky, and the flash of light revealed that they were snagged on a huge upright tree not yet torn out of the earth by the insane river. Margaret reached back, pulling Lowry over her head toward the branches of the oak tree. "Climb up, Lowry, as high as you can."

Crawling over her mother's back, she balanced on the log for a second and then leapt into the tree. The rain buffeted her as she clambered up into the rough branches of the oak, climbing up until she felt a solid branch high in the tree. She clutched the wet limbs, looking down into the darkness for her mother. "Mommy, come on!"

Lightning flashed, and Lowry saw her mother kneeling on the log, stretching her arms toward the oak tree. But before she could leap, a fresh pulse of water hit the end of the log, twisting it away from the oak, and plunged it back into the surging river. Screaming, her mother flipped off the log, and then there was only the sound of the raging waters.

Lowry screamed into the darkness, "Mommy!"

She listened to the roar of the river, trembling at the sound of splintering wood surrounding her. Another round of lightning flashed over the churning river, revealing broken trees rolling in the foam . . . but nothing else.

Drenched, Lowry shivered, tears mixing with the rain on her face. "Mommy?"

\*　　\*　　\*

Two days later, a couple walking their dog along the river discovered her mother's body jammed against one of the cement pilings of a washed-out bridge. A news photo showed her pale body wrapped in a shroud of sticks and plastic grocery bags.

With no other family members nearby, Lowry was deemed old enough to identify the body. She arrived at the morgue, gagging as she passed a stairwell with the nauseating smell of formaldehyde wafting from the floor below. A kind police officer escorted Lowry into her office, gently keeping her hand on Lowry's shoulder. "Lowry, this will only take a minute. I'm going to show you some photos. Just tell me if you know this woman or not."

The officer pulled out a set of photographs and placed them side by side on the table in front of Lowry. Taken from the front and profile, stark images of her mother's deathly white face lay in front of her. Blinking in disbelief, she nodded and reached out to touch the face of the woman who had given her life and then saved her from death. She dropped her head into her hands and began to sob. Her mother was gone.

*       *       *

During the funeral, Lowry felt like a china doll—one break in her façade and she would fall to pieces. Duff had returned from Antarctica for the funeral, and even though she sat in the pew of the funeral home with her maternal grandparents on one side and her father on the other, Lowry could feel the distance between them. Lowry stared ahead as the choir sang hymns, but all she heard were the last words her mother had said to her: *Climb as high as you can.*

The service ended, and her grandmother turned to her, tears flowing down her cheeks. "Lowry, I want you to know what your mother once told us." She squeezed Lowry's hand. "You were her sunrise and her sunset."

Lowry stood in the receiving line with a vacant smile on her face, her grandmother holding her hand as friends and family greeted her with compassion, but she also felt a thread of pity in their glances. Her insides were balled up with the uncertainty of her future.

When the funeral ended, Duff put his arm around Lowry and brusquely told her grandparents, "Lowry will be coming to live with me. I have everything arranged."

# CHAPTER 26

Nick sat on a folding chair in the yard with the ice tinkling in the glass as he twirled his scotch. He sipped the smooth whiskey, letting it linger in his mouth for a second before he swallowed. The warmth of the liquor spread down his shoulders, and he relaxed into the chair, gazing at the dazzling southern constellations from the best seat in the house.

A pinpoint of light caught his eye zipping across the heavens—the ISS on her polar orbit. Lowry should be arriving back at the space station any time now. He followed the resolute light across the arc of the heavens until the ISS disappeared over the horizon. He blew a kiss at the empty sky.

"Come home safe, Lowry-girl."

He exhaled, shaking his head. Now that the trial had ended, Nick hoped the intrigue with the space-station shutdown was over. The investigators had left Antarctica, but not before scrubbing any evidence on the Colombians they found, even penetrating his cloud account and the professor's to ferret out and wipe all of the photos he had taken. Without enough proof to bring any Colombians to trial, there was no hope of overturning the Inuit's conviction through legal avenues.

Since Jean-Luc's verdict, news reports obligingly slanted the story of the trial the way the Ameradan government wanted, thereby crucifying the entire tribe on a digital cross.

Nick shook his head, thinking of his conversation earlier in the day with Duff, who still had contacts at the DOJ. The news hadn't been released to the public, but a junior attorney on the prosecution team had perished that morning in a bizarre car accident. *Had Lowry met Edward Douglas during the proceedings?*

With his index finger, Nick stirred the ice around in his glass, and then stuck his finger in his mouth, sucking the whiskey off his skin.

Duff had come out smelling like a rose for his role in supporting the prosecution. Rumor was that his war chest for his next election was overflowing, that even his gambling debts were settled. Perverted justice at its finest . . . .

His brother wasn't all bad, but the violence of their childhood had dented him, and parts of his psyche had never recovered. And alcohol had drowned any chance for Duff to rise above his past. Addictive to the core, he was a man-child whose weaknesses made him vulnerable to the vices around him—vices that spiders like Halder delighted in exploiting. The Duffs of the world were just a means to an end.

The momentary happiness of the whiskey left him as memories of the past flooded into his mind.

He closed his eyes, clenching the arm of the chair. No stories of pats on the back for two boys growing up in Scotland. More likely punches in the face from a father who turned violent when he was drunk—and most nights, he was drunk. As the oldest, Duff was his primary target, though Nick had felt the blows at times. Nick knew his mother had protected him more, perhaps because he was younger. Or maybe she had deemed Duff the sacrificial lamb and tried to protect at least one child.

But violence sprays shrapnel farther than its intended victim. They had all been branded by the brutality, just as their father had been branded by his father. Their mother was too terrified to leave him, though Nick knew she had considered it. Then a miracle saved them. Their father died in a fiery, drunken car crash, but the psychological damage had already occurred.

When violence is woven into the fabric of life, particularly around an impressionable child, those strands of abuse become deeply imbedded and the pattern familiar; the tears never completely heal. Who holds the blame? The only remedy is to break the pattern—to be the mother or father who examines the past, understands the cause, and is determined to not repeat the cycle.

Nick zipped up his jacket as the cool night air nestled around him. He sank back into the chair, his head buzzing as he stared up into the brilliant night sky.

From a dim corner of Nick's mind, a line from an old poem emerged: *From birth, we humans gather wounds . . . and are forever scarred.*

Finishing his whiskey, Nick stared into the glass, rolling the remnants of liquid around the bottom of the tumbler. Liquor had been the escape from the pain of living for his father, and then his brother, but he had been spared the curse of alcoholism. He rarely indulged, but he was thoroughly human, and other vices had haunted him over his life: envy, sorrow, and deceit, to name a few.

Like a child with a spyglass, Nick brought the bottom of the glass to his eye and gazed upward, turning it like a kaleidoscope with the stars swirling against the black sky through the crystalline base. A sad smile flitted across his face. His savior in life had come in the form of a grieving twelve-year-old girl who had just lost her mother in a tragic flash flood.

*       *       *

Nick waited on the dock. A damp, frigid wind sliced into his face, and he pulled up the hood of his coat. A horn blasted, and he turned to the bay, shielding his eyes from the sun as the ship bearing his brother and niece eased into the dock.

Nick turned back to gaze at the ramshackle port town of huts and warehouses looking like they'd fallen out of the sky and landed haphazardly on the ground. It was not much different than when he'd arrived on his first voyage to

Antarctica. That day had been gray and overcast. He was fresh off the turnip truck, a young man just out of college. He chuckled, remembering the first words spoken to him as he debarked from the ship.

"Move on, buster," one of the crew members had yelled, maneuvering a hover pallet down the ramp. Nice start to the adventure of a lifetime . . . .

The ship maneuvered into the dock, and he turned to scan the deck of the ship for his niece, Lowry. He shook his head. Poor kid had just lost her mother, and her father was bringing her to a mining camp in the middle of nowhere. The crew readied the ship for debarking, and Nick caught sight of her on the deck, face pale, grasping the rail as she gazed out at the desolate town.

"Lowry!" He waved to her, smiling.

Lowry broke into a fragile smile and waved back. "Uncle Nicky!"

Duff appeared by her side and waved, then he trundled a cart overloaded with Lowry's bags down the ramp. She ran past him and leapt into Nick's open arms at the end of the ramp.

Nick held her close as they stood together on the dock, and he whispered softly, "I'm so sorry about your mom." He placed his hand on her head. "I wish I could have come to her funeral."

Shivering, Lowry buried her face under his chin. In a brittle voice, she whispered, "I miss her."

"I know, sweetie." He stroked her hair, and she peered up at him, her lips quivering. He smoothed away the tear escaping down her cheek. "She loved you very much."

Lowry laid her head on his shoulder, and Nick felt her tremble, and then she burst into tears. As she clutched him, spasms of grief wracked her as the floodgates of her sorrow opened. Tears poured down her face as she sobbed uncontrollably. Holding her close, he could feel the moisture of her tears soaking through his shirt. Nick rocked her back and forth, biting his lip, struggling to keep himself from breaking down.

"You're okay," he whispered.

Lowry was calming as Duff reached them with the cart, despair written on his bleak face. But as he stopped beside them, he squinted at Nick with a peculiar darkness.

Lowry glanced at Duff but then turned back and dropped her head onto Nick's chest with a heavy sigh. Nick sensed a distance between Lowry and Duff. He'd never excelled at marriage, nor parenting, but Nick hoped that Duff had gained some maturity and would rise to the occasion.

Duff dropped the bags on the dock and pushed the empty cart to the side. A gash of a smile momentarily appeared, but hostility flashed in his eyes. "A little help, *brother.*"

Nick studied him quizzically. *Is he dealing with grief . . . or could he actually be jealous?* Nick loosened an arm from around Lowry and dug a tissue from his pocket. He handed it to her, and she blew her nose. Exhaling, she gazed up at him, swaying with exhaustion, but a shadow of a smile flickered on her face.

Nick patted her shoulder and then picked up a couple of the bags. He turned to Duff. "I found a wonderful house just outside of town." He put his arm around Lowry's shoulder with a smile. "And Lowry, it has a barn and *horses.*"

Lowry's puffy eyes widened, and her mouth dropped open. Color came back into her cheeks, and she broke into a smile. "Horses?"

Duff's eyebrow twitched as he stared at Nick. "Horses?"

Nick gestured to Lowry. "Let's keep going. The crew will be unloading shipments right behind us." Lowry turned and walked across the dock in front of them.

Nick shot a sideways glance at Duff. "I'll fund the horses," he said under his breath.

"Damn right." Duff's eyes narrowed. "You're just buttering her up."

Out of the side of his mouth, Nick whispered, "Lowry just lost her mother, and she doesn't know anyone here. She needs companionship, Duff, and not just two grouchy men."

They loaded the bags onto the hovercar and then moved past the piles of ore, warehouses filled with mining machinery, and scattered houses. They passed a small, cement-block school, and Nick pointed to it.

"There's your new school, Lowry."

She blinked and nodded her head, studying the bare exterior.

Duff smiled at her. "It may not look like much, but it's a good school, Lowry. I want the best for my little girl." He shrugged. "Of course, we may have to add in a few online classes."

They continued down a gravel road to a farm on the edge of town. The small farmhouse was set into the lee side of a hill, surrounded by several acres of pasture and a few scrub trees.

They got out of the hover, and Lowry gaped at the sight of horses grazing in the pasture. An old man hobbled out toward them. "Hello!"

"Hi, Thor." Nick gestured to Lowry. "This is Duff's daughter, Lowry."

Lowry stuck out her hand. "Nice to meet you, Thor."

Thor shook her hand and then stuck his thumb out toward the barn. "I was getting ready to feed the horses. Do you want to help me?"

Lowry's eyes lit up. "Sure."

Nick followed Lowry and Thor to the barn while Duff walked around the house. The horses trotted up to the gate near the barn, and Thor pointed out each horse and its name to Lowry. When the horses reached the gate to the corral, Thor reached across the fence, running his hand over the long fuzzy coat of one of the horses.

"They stay pretty furry most of the year but will start shedding soon. I'll show you how to groom them."

"My grandparents have horses, so I know a little." Lowry petted and scratched their backs while he filled the flat feeders with grain. He opened the corral gate, letting the small herd in to eat dinner.

Lowry sat on the fence while the horses fussed with each other, vying for the grain. "Do they always push each other around like that?"

"Yes, horses have a herd hierarchy, and the top one bosses the others, and so it goes down to the bottom horse." He winked at Lowry. "Just like people do."

After they finished the grain, Thor opened the gate, and the horses wandered back into the pasture.

Duff joined the group walking from the barn to the cottage, and Thor waved toward the hillside at the back of the house.

"I blasted into that hill and built half the house in there to save on heating." He gazed at the little house and gestured with his hands. "I built all of this myself."

Thor reminisced while they walked through the simple house and then led them onto a sunny screened-in porch with a swing. He pointed to a cistern and the small garden just beginning to grow on the sunny side of the property. Behind the garden was a chicken coop with a dozen hens pecking the ground for insects.

"I've got tomatoes, cucumbers, and broccoli coming up, and the chickens lay a good amount of eggs. I even sell my extras in town." He sighed. "But now my health is . . . well, the doctor tells me I need to take it easy."

Lowry looked up at him. "We'll take care of everything; don't worry."

Nick nodded. "You have a wonderful farm here, Thor." He turned and placed his hand on Lowry's shoulder. "Thor will be leaving for home in a few months, but he's going to teach us how to care of the horses, and I found a lady that can give you some riding lessons, Lowry."

Duff muttered under his breath to Nick, "Which you're also paying for, I assume."

"My mom taught me to ride a little." Lowry watched the horses grazing in the pasture and then looked up at her father. "Dad, can we get a dog?"

Her father beamed and threw his arm around her shoulders, pulling her to him. "Sure, Lowry—a farm girl must have a dog." Duff steered her toward the hover. "We'd better get back to town and settle in before dinner."

Thor walked with them, and Nick smiled with a wave. "We'll finalize the papers and set a closing date."

Lowry climbed into the hover while Duff put his hand on Thor's shoulder. "Don't worry about a thing, Thor. Just let us know when you're moving, and then we'll schedule our move." He smiled broadly, patting Thor on the back. "And the elections are coming up. Don't forget to vote for me before you ship out!"

Chaos encroached with the rising seas, deeply eroding the tenets of civilization and washing away the foundation of human society . . .

# CHAPTER 27

The Garden was quiet. The artificial lights dimmed into twilight, and the forest shifted from day to night creatures.

Adam glided down the path. Stopping for a moment, he cocked his head to listen. He smiled at the sound of faint barking and moved toward it. As the barking became clearer, he squatted down, slowly pulling a fern branch out of his line of sight. He saw the rog barking as it struggled to loosen itself from the overgrown vines in the berry patch.

He froze like a stone. His eyes alone moved as he studied the creature, the "skin" ripped off in places, revealing the metal beneath. Bile came to his throat as he thought of these people who considered themselves gods, so pompous as to attempt to create an animal.

Anger brought an ancient chant into his mind. To the beat of the sound in his brain, he slowly lifted the blowgun to his lips. Poppy looked up at the sight of a human, her tail wagging feebly in the grasp of the vines.

Poppy squealed as the first stainless steel dart entered her body. She struggled violently to no avail, and the second dart drove itself into her inner workings. Buzzing sparks discharged from the motherboard as the metal shaft crossed her circuitry. The final dart entered one of her artificial eyes, and she slowly lay down with lubricant oozing like blood upon the ground.

Adam looked around carefully and then slowly got up and went over to the body, standing over the rog for a second. He bent and, with a sharp blade, methodically untangled it from the grasping vines, ripping more of the artificial skin away from the metal. He freed it and threw the body over his shoulder, trotting back to his hut.

He entered the dark hut, placing the limp rog on the dirt floor, and then, using the large knife, he began to dissect Poppy. He opened the main body cavity, looking with wonder at the still-pulsing electronics, and then spat in disgust. Impulsively, he grabbed the rog and threw it into the small fire that burned in the center of the hut.

Adam smiled as the lights popped and the metal slowly collapsed in the flames.

# CHAPTER 28

The shuttle slowed, approaching the dock at the ISS. Lowry glanced back at the Earth through the tiny window, wondering if her grandmother had found her mother's letter on the bed with her note.

*Please keep this until I return from the ISS.*

A small thump signaled that the shuttle had docked, and the interior lights brightened. Lowry unsnapped her seatbelt. A thin smile veiled her inner turmoil as she debarked with the other passengers. She recalled her first arrival to the space station, when she had been anxious but excited for a new adventure. It felt like she had aged since then, the weight of the world bowing her shoulders as the revelation of how things "really work" in life sunk in.

The passengers drifted into the pod, and Lowry held onto the straps, staring out the window as they moved to the outer ring, the artificial gravity inexorably pulling them down. The doors opened, and she left the pod, walking in stony silence down the corridor to her quarters. She sidled past the cafeteria, averting her face from the diners, and continued down the hall. But before she could get around the bend, a crowd of people spilled out of the cafeteria, running up and surrounding her.

"You were on the news!" someone shouted.

The throng pulled her back into the dining area, and they replayed the newscast of her testimony. Lowry gaped at the video of her performance at the trial and her inadvertent role in the conviction of Jean-Luc. The newscast jumped to the reading of the guilty verdict with a close-up of Jean-Luc's pale, defiant face, but Lowry saw the internal pain in his eyes.

Lowry couldn't speak, and in reality, there was nothing she could say. She forced her lips to curl into a smile as she waved to the group of well-wishers, and then she headed back down the hall to her cabin.

"Lowry, wait."

Lowry glanced back at Zoë running up to her.

Zoë bounded in front of her, grabbing her arm. "Lowry, I'm truly sorry. I don't know what got into me."

Lowry chewed her lip, still tasting Zoë's betrayal. "I know *what* got into you, but *why* is the real question."

"Ha, ha." Zoë exhaled, and staring at the floor, she shook her head. Then she raised her eyes, which were brimming with tears. "Lowry, please forgive me. I don't want this to destroy our friendship."

Lowry sighed. "Zoë, Edward was sent up here to gather information for the prosecution to use against the Inuit tribe— *by any means necessary.* And frankly, I'm sure he enjoyed his work." She pointed at her. "When he interviewed you, did he ask you anything more than about your involvement with the file that came through the satellite?"

Zoë knitted her brow. "He said he wanted to 'interview' me, and yes, we discussed the encrypted file." She shook her head, looking at the ground. "But that day you were leaving, he wanted to walk in the Garden, and he asked me about my background. We were sitting under the apple tree, and he touched my prosthetic . . . then his hand moved upward." She bit her lip. "Lowry, it's been a long time since a man made love to me."

Lowry glanced down at the hard plastic shank peeking from under Zoë's pant leg. Her relationship with Edward had been a fantasy at best. She was vulnerable and he had taken advantage of her. Was there any difference in what Zoë had gone through?

Lowry closed her eyes and brushed her fingers against her brow, trying to smooth away her disquiet. Then she opened her eyes and looked into Zoë's worried face. With a little smile, she said, "Honestly, Zoë, he had no reason to entrap you like he did me. He's a ladies' man, and you're a catch."

She placed her hand on Zoë's shoulder. "I'm just pissed that the prosecution team dreamed up a seduction scheme for Edward to manipulate me and ferret out details to help convict the Inuit."

With raised eyebrows, Zoë looked at her. "You're not mad at me?"

Lowry shook her head. "Nah—end of story." She waved and walked down the hall. "Let's have dinner later, Zoë."

Lowry continued to her cabin, and once inside, she dropped her bag onto the bed. She shuffled to the tiny window in her cabin and stared out at the empty dark sky, no Earth in view to give her solace. Feeling trapped, she paced around the room as the stress of the last several weeks whirled in her head.

The monitor in her room lit up with a blue light.

"Lowry, I heard you were back," Bob said softly.

Lowry sighed. "Hi, Bob."

"You don't sound happy—are you all right?"

Running her fingers through her hair, she shook her head. "No, Bob, I'm not all right." She whispered, "I'm sick"—she rubbed her hand across her forehead—"from overexposure to the wretched side of the human beast."

"But humans are fundamentally good . . . aren't they?"

Growling, she burst out of the door and found herself walking toward the Garden.

Lowry surged through the last sliding door and breathed in the moist atmosphere enveloping her. The tension slowly faded as she strolled along the path to the rocky shoreline of the freshwater lake.

The sound of birds filled the air over the still water. She sat on a rock hanging over the water, gazing down at her reflection, the scars beneath the surface hidden in a pretty young face.

She picked up a stone, firing it into her image shimmering on the surface. "Take that, fool!"

The water rippled out from the impact, and now, with the mirrored surface broken, Lowry saw the plants, fish, and insects beneath the surface, locked in a never-ending battle of life in a simple pool of water. A knot of tadpoles feasted on a dead minnow, bumping it back and forth on the surface as other minnows fed on the algae nearby.

An acceptance of death.

Lowry sighed. An acceptance of death, even if that death is of the image you have of yourself. The whimsy that everything will be wonderful, when reality is screaming something else. At some point in your life, you have to wake up and smell the charred flesh as the delusions in your mind are burned away. To really live, there must be an acceptance of truth, no matter how bitter and humbling it might be. The ads promise sparkling white teeth, but once they're knocked out, it really doesn't matter anymore.

Lowry rubbed her temples. There was no returning to a fool's paradise once the bubble had burst. The wax figure you have conjured up melts into a pool of uncertainty, oozing between your toes. Perhaps you might gaze down, aghast, as you look at the remains of who you thought you were. If you're lucky, you stumble away before someone shoves you into reality. If you're not so lucky, you remain frozen at that spot, gazing down, ever-wishing the image would reassemble itself. *This growing-up crap is for the birds.*

The tadpoles had picked the minnow down to the skeleton. Lowry reached down past the tadpoles and retrieved the stone she had so violently thrown into the water. She stared at the small white rock in her hand and then clutched it in her palm. A tiny perturbation can make big ripples.

She turned and ran down a path as fast as she could, like a child after a ball. Then, out of breath, she stopped and sat down in the soft grass. Sighing, she lay down and stared up at the domed sky. *Who are human beings? Are we animal, vegetable, or mineral?* She brushed the sweet grass. *We no longer know.*

Lowry reached into her pocket and brought the carved finger out. Holding it above her face, she stared at the delicate object, wondering how old it was. She imagined an old man or woman lovingly carving the talisman, perhaps sitting near a fire. The ivory had yellowed with age, and there were tiny cracks running along its length—it had to be ancient.

The sound of footsteps caught her attention, and Adam came into view, lurching down the path with a walking stick in his hand and bungee cargo nets over his shoulder. He stopped at the sight of her and then walked slowly to where she lay. "You're back," he said. "I thought perhaps you'd be gone longer."

"I just returned." Lowry sighed. "I don't know how much you know about it, but the trial of the supposed attacker of the ISS was a farce." She gazed at Sedna's finger. "I tried to help the Inuit, Jean-Luc, but . . . he was found guilty."

Adam shook his head. "No surprise. He was an indigenous person—did you think he would get a fair trial?" He pointed to the carved finger. "Where did you get that? It looks like an amulet."

Lowry sat up. "The shaman of the Inuit tribe gave it to me after I testified." With the ivory finger in the palm of her hand, she extended her arm toward him. "He said I reminded him of Sedna, a woman from one of their ancient tales." She sighed. "He's an incredible man."

He furrowed his brow. "A shaman gave it to you as a gift?" Adam shifted the bungees on his shoulder. "I have to go," he said brusquely and stepped back toward the path, but then he stopped. Puzzled, Lowry watched his head shifting back and forth, as if he were arguing with himself.

*Adam is an odd bird.*

Then he turned to her with a peculiar look on his face. Grimacing, he came back to her side, and holding the bungees and stick in one hand, he reached out to her with the other. "Come, I want to show you something."

Lowry blinked in confusion but took his hand, and he pulled her up. He cocked his head for her to follow and then scurried toward the berry bushes. She stepped forward but then froze. He turned to her and waved for her to follow, but she stood still until he disappeared into the brush.

*Why do I feel like Alice following the White Rabbit?* She looked down at the talisman in her hand; when she had taken the step toward Adam, it had shifted in her palm and now pointed to where he had vanished. "Here we go," she mumbled as curiosity overcame her. She slipped the ivory finger into her pocket and ran after him.

Lowry caught up to him as the path narrowed into a warren of creeping vines. She stopped, studying the maze of berry briars with reluctance.

"Come on, Lowry," Adam grunted, gesturing her to follow.

He crept into the darkness of the tangled brush, and within steps, she could barely see him. Her heart thudded as she stooped over, following him into the shadows. The path faded to an animal trail as they crawled under massive briars with the smell of moist earth hitting her nostrils. She became tangled in the grasping appendages of the bushes and tore them from her clothes. Adam had gone ahead, and she could no longer see him. Fearing she was lost in this bizarre labyrinth, she crawled faster and then knocked into a garden spider's web. The web covered her head and face, and shuddering with a shriek, she swept it away.

Adam crawled back to her and smiled. "Almost there."

Past the briars, the trail broadened, and they could walk upright. They came upon a small meadow. Lowry shook herself, brushing off the twigs and stickers, relieved to be out of Adam's secret jungle.

A bark hut stood in the center of the clearing with a web of woven twine stretched from the top of the hut to several of the tall bushes surrounding the edge of the clearing. Lowry sucked in her breath with a shiver. Dead chickens and rabbits hung from the rope like laundry.

Adam stood patiently while she perused his domain, but then he motioned her to come to the hut. She edged toward the entrance and crawled through the tiny door. A small fire smoldered in the fire ring, and she sat cross-legged near it. Adam entered behind her and dropped the cargo netting on the floor of the hut. He placed his carved walking stick against the walls of the hut, near the entrance, next to a sack filled with . . . darts. Lowry's heart beat a staccato. It wasn't a walking stick; it was a blowgun, and the darts were eerily similar to the one Uncle Nick had found.

He sat across from her, took a stick, and stirred the fire. Flames leapt up, and in the flickering light, Lowry was able to see the primitive abode with handmade tools and cooking utensils neatly arranged in the tiny space. The flames crackled, and her eyes were drawn to a glittering object hung on a hook above the fire. She gasped. It was Poppy—at least what was left of her. Her undamaged eye glowed in the reflection of the flame, and Lowry trembled in disgust.

*What has Adam done to Poppy?* She glanced at Adam. *And what might he do to me?*

Adam turned away for a second. Lowry lunged for the door, scrambling across the dusty floor. He leapt after her and grabbed her leg in mid-leap. She hit the ground midway out of the hut and screamed at the top of her lungs, but he jerked her backward, her fingers scratching a trail in the dirt floor. Flailing her arms, she tried to find something to grab, but hit the blowgun, knocking it, along with the sack of darts, to the ground, spilling the deadly barbs around them.

Adam sucked in his breath as a dart hit the top of his head, but he didn't let go, yanking her back from the entrance, his strength belying his small stature. Lowry clutched a dart and twisted around, trying to stab him. He grabbed her arm with a violent wrench, peeled the dart out of her hand, and threw it into the depths of the hut.

Adam clutched her arms, and she could not move.

"Don't leave! I won't hurt you!" he gasped, trying to catch his breath.

Lowry shouted, "Let me go!" She twisted her body, trying to break his hold on her.

He said calmly, but without releasing her, "Please, you mustn't leave." He looked into her face and repeated softly, "I know this is all strange to you, but *I will not harm you.*"

She studied his eyes as he stared into her face. *He seems sincere.* She nodded, and he released his grip, motioning her to come back to the center of the hut. Abruptly, he pushed her down to the floor against the center pole and grabbed one of the bungee nets with his other hand.

Lowry screamed, kicking out at him, but he dodged her foot, continuing to wind the net around her and the pole. Her arms now trapped, Lowry snaked her head as his arm came around and sunk her teeth into his hand. Adam grunted but did not release his grip on her. He pulled the net tight with one hand, holding it taut with his foot. He pulled her hair back until she released her teeth from his skin. He grabbed the netting with his good hand, wrapping the end of the net around her legs, and then fell back onto the packed dirt floor.

Adam lay panting, studying her face. "I'm sorry if I hurt you, Lowry."

Trussed like a pig for roasting, she spit at him and then slumped against the pole.

A slight grin passed over his face, but then he looked at his hand where the skin was torn and bloody from Lowry's bite. He wrapped a bandage over his hand and checked his watch. He scratched in the dirt, uncovering D rings buried in the ground, and snapped the ends of the cargo net to the rings.

He puttered around the hut, pouring water on the fire and covering it with dirt, and then he walked back into the corner of the hut and picked up another cargo net.

Lowry snarled, "Let me go, Adam!"

He returned and squatted in front of her with a gentle smile. "I know you don't understand as yet, but I am trying to save your life."

Adam sat down with his back to hers, and Lowry felt his shoulders move as he calmly lashed himself to the pole just as he had done to her. He attached the ends of the net to the same

D rings. Then, in silence, they faced the opposite walls of the hut.

Lowry said hoarsely, "You are the contact inside the space station."

She closed her eyes as he replied, "Yes. And, as I believe the expression goes, the second shoe is about to drop."

Swallowing hard, she opened her eyes, staring vacantly at the rough bark walls as the reality of what was happening sunk into her mind. "Adam, why?"

Adam shifted his body and then whispered, "I come from the A'wa tribe in Colombia, where the native peoples move to the song of the jungle, and the pulse of life is born of blood, not electricity."

She cringed as his body swayed back and forth behind her.

"We work maybe two or three hours a day, and that work consists of hunting, tending the cultivated plants or gathering wild foodstuffs, preparing the food, and caring for the children—all the things you squeeze into a couple of hours. Ironically, what we do every day is what the modern world does as leisure activities."

She felt his shoulders move as he sighed, and then he continued wistfully.

"In the tribe, one spends a great deal of time preparing for ceremonies and dancing. Life began this way. Humans evolved in small groups. In the jungles of South America, families spend most of their waking time together, not spending the day away from one another with strangers instead of a real family. Strangers—who could expect strangers to be a family?"

His voice became hard. "Humans must demand an end to the insane technological stampede before all that came before is crushed and forgotten. It is said, 'The land is like the Garden of Eden before them, but after them a desolate wilderness, and nothing escapes them.'"

He twisted his head toward her and whispered, "Lowry, you are the only one who understands what I am talking about."

"Adam, you are right in spirit. God knows that modern life is out of balance. But violence is not the answer." Then she asked quietly, "What are you afraid of, Adam?"

She felt him tense up against her back. "Why do you say I'm afraid?"

"Fear is the seed of anger. It is what compels the human beast to do horrendous acts. Courage is simply not letting fear win."

He sneered. "What do you know of fear? Have you seen your family starving because the land that had been yours for thousands of years is stolen from you? All the animals and fruit you ate to survive—gone? Fear and anger come from an empty belly . . . and an empty heart."

Silence enveloped the hut except for the rise and fall of Adam's breath.

Then he said softly, "My tribe was a happy place when I was a child. Singing filled the air, and wonderful food filled my belly. But during a flood, our village was washed away, and I was separated from the tribe. I wandered for days until I was found by a doctor. She spoke of the wonders of the modern world, so I followed her out and went to school in the States—that was my undoing. I never could return to the ways of the tribe after that." His voice quivered. "Today marks twenty-five years since I was ripped from my home. You see, Lowry, my anger blossoms from the death of my life as I knew it."

"Adam, destroying all of these innocent lives aboard will not change the world. Surely, neither your family nor the tribe would want this."

"Who said they are innocent?"

Lowry's head sagged back, and she grimaced at the sight of Poppy's mangled body hanging just above her head.

Adam's voice became harsh. "Everyone on board is guilty! Guilty of putting their techno-god ahead of Mother Earth, and for that, they shall *die*."

Lowry felt his shoulders slump as he continued. "My tribe does not know anything about this, and the other two involved only wanted to make a protest statement by momentarily shutting down the station."

He shifted under the net. "What they didn't know was that the OPAL message I created not only had the temporary shutdown file but also contained a virus allowing me access into the main computer. Once the temporary file had run its program, it destroyed itself—only the kernel virus program remained, buried in the system like a tick imbedded in the skin, waiting patiently for me to instruct it to begin the final stage. When the security people ran a full scan, they didn't bother to check a simpleton's personal files, or they would have found the file which mated with the kernel to give me control of all the power systems."

He leaned his head back toward her, and she flinched as his hair brushed against her neck.

He whispered, "I called it, 'A Spider Sat Beside Her.' Do you like the name?"

Involuntarily, Lowry shivered and swallowed the bile that backed up into her throat. She now fully realized Adam's madness.

Then her legs shook, not from fear, but from the ground beneath her.

"Adam, what is happening?"

"I have become a burning ash on the wind to incinerate this false world."

"My god, what have you done?"

"Your religion speaks of the destruction of false idols. This golden calf of the modern age will be thrown to Earth just as Lucifer himself was thrown down due to his arrogance for thinking himself equal to God."

She snarled, "You may take us down for your own reasons, but the US government is accusing the Inuit Eskimos of the attack in order to steal their lands."

"The US *wanted* the attack to be from the Inuits. It fit their agenda, and if not this, they would have found some other excuse to disenfranchise them."

The shaking became worse, and Lowry felt the boom of explosions from underneath her and then, like a final death knell, the faint sound of crumpling metal. One final shudder, and then a deathly silence enveloped them. No sound of birds, no wind in the trees.

Adam whispered so quietly Lowry could barely hear him. "You see, Lowry, the governments of the world are not on the side of the creatures of the world, including the native peoples; they are on the side of power, wielding it for their good and not for the good of the Earth." He sighed heavily. "The only protest they hear is an attack on their control, and technology is one of their weapons. That is why I'm taking down the ISS. It represents the highest form of their supremacy."

"Adam, I know it is maddening, but the system does eventually work."

Adam leaned back, and Lowry flinched against the rigidity of his shoulders. "For whom, Lowry?"

Lowry stared into the dimness of the hut. The root of civilization is fairness and respect for the individual—even a mule will kick at the traces with an unjust master holding the reins.

The bungee webbing pressed around her as she bobbed slightly upward. Her heart throbbed as she realized the station must no longer be rotating. Poppy's head lifted, and her legs began to float—a zombie marionette, awakening from the dead.

The netting vibrated with the reverberation of new explosions. Cocking her head, Lowry listened for more, but only an eerie silence followed. Then a trace of artificial gravity eased her body back to the ground, loosening the grip of her cocoon. A motion over her head startled her, and she watched Poppy's torn body wilt back into its death pose once again.

A stillness descended upon them like the quiet before a storm. A flock of confused chickens passed near the hut, clucking their disapproval over this mad state of affairs.

Lowry flinched as the webbing slowly tightened with the G-force of acceleration. Her lips trembled as she asked, "Please tell me, Adam. What is happening?"

"I have programmed the station to shoot itself like a comet directly into the Earth's atmosphere. We are just beginning to feel the acceleration into the outer layers." His voice softened as he said, "I know you are not the same as the others on board, and I am truly sorry, Lowry, but there is no going back now."

She looked up at the roof of the hut and exhaled a little prayer. *Please don't let this be my end.*

The vibration became worse, and the ground tilted. Poppy fell from her hook, and her head detached itself from her body, bouncing into Lowry's lap. Poppy's melancholy eye stared up at Lowry. Shivering, she twisted her body to the side, throwing the rog's head off. The head rolled across the slanted floor until the metal edges snagged in the cargo netting.

Abruptly, the station's center of gravity changed. The ground beneath them tilted beyond the angle of repose, and the shell of the hut flipped over, tearing away from its ties. The hut lurched down the steep slope with the remains of Poppy's mangled body chasing behind it. Lowry groaned as the netting holding her to the steel pole dug into her skin.

Now they were exposed to the chaos of the Garden gone mad. Brush and trees swayed insanely on the edge of the clearing, and the deafening screams of terrified creatures filled the air. Like a ship sinking in a storm, the station listed further to its side, and the cargo net tightened its grip on Lowry's body as the turmoil accelerated.

They heard rushing water in the distance, and they were surrounded by a myriad of animals racing through the clearing. The lakes had been thrown out of their banks and now drained down the slope, and a wall of water headed toward the clearing.

Adam cried, "Hold on, Lowry!" as the water came toward them.

The newly formed river struck them, lifting them up as far as the netting would let them rise. Adam and Lowry held their mouths above the churning water filled with squirming fish and mud. The water moved over their heads, and Lowry couldn't breathe.

The river shifted with the twisting space station and drained away from them. Gasping, Lowry shook the muddy water out of her eyes, staring at animals caught in the raging flood, their heads bobbing up and down as they struggled to keep their heads above the water. The station continued to spiral, and the mad river carried the helpless animals out of sight.

Screeching birds filled the air, circling high above their heads, afraid to land on any semi-stationary object. A rabbit leapt along the muddy ground until the twisting space station bounced him into the air, and in the shifting gravity field, he soared in slow motion over the trees like a superhero.

A lightening of the sky drew her eye to the ceiling of the space station garden. They were entering the atmosphere.

"God help us," she whispered under her breath.

The clear skin of the roof glowed yellow, and smoke rushed across the transparent glass as the edge of the station burned away in the friction of the atmosphere. Lowry's eyes were transfixed on the dome above her head. The lights dimmed, flashed once, and then died, and she and Adam were enveloped in darkness except for the bizarre dawn breaking outside the skylight windows. They heard a grating sound, and a huge metal piece flashed by the window, followed by a crumpled arm of the space station.

They were beginning to break up.

The animals were deathly quiet now. The only sounds were the eerie groans of metal stressing beyond its specs. Drifting on a breeze, the nauseating scent of blood hit Lowry's consciousness. She shuddered at the smell of death from all of the innocent creatures destroyed as the station plummeted to Earth.

The sky lightened further, and shreds of metal raked the surface of the dome, scarring the glass. Then a human body slammed into the dome and bounced off the window, disappearing as the station sped downward.

Adam looked up at the noise.

Lowry hissed at him, "That should make you happy." More bodies flashed past the glass, blood streaming from the exploded faces.

She wondered what was happening to the rest of the station. It was strange; the Garden was a self-contained sphere, and they still had air, though at any moment, a large piece of metal could puncture the roof. Decompression at this height would kill them. Lowry began to make out shapes around her; they were descending into the sunlight.

The station shook and then began to revolve in the dense atmosphere. Peeled like an orange by the friction, parts of the station flew by the dome. The station was disintegrating like a meteor.

The webbing bit into her limbs as the remnants of the station spun like a Whirl-a-Twirl ride at a carnival. Lowry's head was pressed down onto her chest, but then she heard a whirring sound and, with effort, twisted her head to look up. The roof panels heaved up and down like the chest of a runner. She chewed her lip. The fragile sphere of the Garden could not take much more.

Lowry pushed her head back against the pole. She was determined to see her end. North America and the ocean spun out of sight to be replaced by the dark blue of the sky, and then the continents reappeared in a few minutes. They moved across Africa, descending toward the Atlantic Ocean. The final crash to Earth was near.

Adam twisted his head toward her, screaming into her ear, "Hold on as tight as you can!"

A shrill whistle deafened them as the ISS tore through the atmosphere on its collision course. From the corner of her eye, Lowry saw the languid white crests on a still blue ocean rushing toward them. With a thundering splash, they plunged into the ocean waters, waves of sound and water reverberating outward as if a meteor had struck the Earth.

Chunks of debris and water rained down upon them while Adam and Lowry flailed like puppets on strings, helplessly beating each other and the pole that held them fast. The pole broke in two and she catapulted away from Adam. Her last vision was the muddy ground, covered with flattened blades of grass, accelerating into her face.

# CHAPTER 29

Lowry awoke with the side of her face smashed into the wet grass. She opened her eyes, slowly focusing on a butterfly folding and unfolding its wings as it sunned itself on the carved finger of Sedna. Lucent in the sunlight, the ivory talisman was stuck point-down into the soft ground in front of her face.

She felt blades of grass in her mouth, and when she shifted her face out of the muck, the butterfly flew away. As she twisted onto her back, pain shot through her body, and she closed her eyes, waiting out the waves of agony. Then she became conscious of the ground rocking gently beneath her.

Lowry smelled the saltiness of the air and gazed at the shattered dome above her. She *was* floating on the ocean. Miraculously, the Garden had survived the fall from heaven. "My god, we're on Earth!"

She pushed herself into a sitting position, crying out as she put pressure on her left arm. Looking at the odd angle of the arm, she knew it was broken. Head throbbing, she examined her bruised and battered body, taking deep breaths to clear her mind.

Once her pain subsided, Lowry looked around and realized she was several meters away from where the hut had stood. Glancing back to the ivory carving, she found it amazing that Sedna's finger was delicately poised in the mud and hadn't disappeared in the madness of the fall. With her relatively undamaged right hand, she plucked up the finger, cleaned the tip on her shirt, and then carefully placed it back into her pocket.

Lowry exhaled, not looking forward to moving, but she had to see how Adam had fared. Clenching her teeth against the pain, she wrenched herself onto her knees and crawled across the ground toward the now shattered pole, where pieces of the netting were strewn about like spaghetti. At the base of the metal pole, tangled in the shredded net, was Adam's motionless body, surrounded by a flock of seagulls glaring at her with their beady eyes.

"Adam, we made it!" Lowry shouted to him. Then her smile faded, and she touched his foot, which was half-buried in the muddy hole that was his fire ring. "Adam?" She reached out, grabbed his arm, and pulled him over—and then gasped. The steel pole had snapped, burying its jagged end into the side of his skull, scattering pieces of his brain across the ground.

Lowry shuddered at the horror before her and collapsed in a heap at the sight of his lifeless eyes staring into the intense blue sky of his beloved Earth. Perhaps in death, he was happy at last—a tortured soul with no place to call home.

The greedy seagulls hopped back to Adam, casually picking up bits of brain and flying away with their dinner. Gagging, she covered her mouth as another bird went after the fresh meat. She shouted, and picking up a stick, she threw it at him. The flock flew up and patiently waited in the bushes nearby.

Averting her eyes from the scene of death, she gazed at the once-bucolic garden, now devastated as if a hurricane had passed through it. Even though he was the cause, Adam would have been appalled, and she imagined him fussing about, raking and picking up the ubiquitous rubble. But instead, Adam's mangled body lay supine, and every so often, she had to toss a stick to keep the seagulls from feasting on his brains.

Lowry sat pondering her next step until thirst drove her to crawl through the debris where Adam's hut had been. She found a small bottle tied to a stake and drank thirstily. Her broken arm ached, and she twisted some of the snapped bungee netting into a sling to stabilize it. She eased down onto the matted grass, the pain of her injured body pulsing like an unwelcome companion.

The sunlight shifted on its path through the sky, and the glint of something metallic caught Lowry's eye. It was the head of Sevy's rog, Poppy, entangled in a pile of brush. She shook her head, reflecting on the friends she had lost in the crash of the space station—Sevy, Zoë, and even poor Adam.

All dead, and for what purpose? The misguided souls of the world—some like Sevy, who substitute technology for human relationships—worshipping a techno-god instead of having real friends and lovers. On the other end of the spectrum, there was Adam, who hated this worship, believing that technology was a weapon of the powerful, and who had brought down the space station from the sky, but to no avail. It would not change a thing.

Technology was not the enemy. It was merely a tool. But if it became friend or foe, isolating humans from one another, therein lay the danger. And all of these innocents, separate and lonely, were marks to be manipulated by the power brokers of the world, who knew how to play them for their own nefarious purposes.

Lowry started at the beat of a chopper hovering over the gaping hole in the dome. The rescue had come at last. Painfully, she stood up as two men rappelled their way through the hole in the dome. With her good arm, she waved at them excitedly as they landed on the ground.

They unstrapped from the rope, pulled out their guns, and ran toward her. Stunned, Lowry blinked at the resolute looks on their faces—they were hunting for blood. She stood very still as they approached her.

"Where is he?" one of the men yelled at her.

"Who?" she asked, puzzled that they seemed to know who they were after. "If you are looking for the gardener, Adam, I'm afraid you are too late. He did not survive the crash."

"Yes, the gardener."

The leader of the group told the other man to check out Adam's condition. The subordinate jogged over, kicking Adam's body flat onto his back. The leader pulled Lowry aside, positioning his body to shield her from what the other man was doing.

"I'm Captain Stevens. Are you hurt, miss?" She tried to see around him to observe the other man bending down, going through Adam's pockets.

"A broken arm and bruises, but nothing life-threatening." Lowry looked up at the captain. "You know he was the one who sabotaged the station, not Jean-Luc and the Inuits. Apparently, this all stemmed from a protest of the A'wa tribe in Colombia, but Adam took it too far." Again, she tried to look around the captain's body as Adam was being stuffed into a body bag. "I'm afraid poor Adam was out of his mind."

Captain Stevens looked at her obscurely. "No, miss, he was just the gardener."

Lowry felt a jolt in her gut. "Then why did you ask, 'Where is he?' when you first came down?"

The captain turned toward his lieutenant, who was walking back toward them with Adam, now in the body bag, thrown over his shoulder. The lieutenant nodded his head to the captain.

Captain Stevens turned to her and said, "You may be the only survivor. The medics are minutes away, and we have to go clear the way for them to land." He pointed to the hole above them through which he and the lieutenant had rappelled.

They jogged back to the rappelling lines.

Lowry shouted after them, "Why are you taking Adam's body with you?"

Her words were lost in the noise of the helicopter still hovering above the hole. They hooked themselves onto the ropes, with poor Adam's body still slung over the lieutenant's shoulder. They were pulled up through the hole, disappearing into the fuselage of the helicopter. Moments later, they used the skids of the helicopter to break a wider opening in the dome so the larger medical helicopter could land through the gap. Once they had finished expanding the hole, they flew away, the sound of the rotor blades fading into the distance.

Lowry turned back to where Adam's hut had stood. Tears blurred her vision as she stared at the broken steel shaft glistening in the sun. A monument to delusion. Only an arrogant fool believes attacking civilization accomplishes anything. Humans may glance up and momentarily mourn the dead, but they then return to living, devouring everything in their path with their mindless propagation.

The seabirds had returned, fighting over the remnants of Adam's scattered brains, but she didn't have the strength to shoo them away.

A warm breeze found its way from the ocean as she sank to the ground. The birds sang, and frogs began to croak as the brackish water returned to the lakes. Bees harvested nectar from blossoms on a honeysuckle vine draped across an uprooted shrub.

Lowry ran her fingers over the soft grass, which had been flattened during the flood, but now the tender blades lifted toward the heavens.

The final fall of Man might be the best thing that ever happened to the planet Earth.

## The End

# ACKNOWLEDGEMENTS

Writing a novel is a journey with a myriad of twists and turns, and hills and valleys, but I was lucky enough to find the way lined with friends, family, and supporters, so there are many to thank. My writer friends: Lisa Tracy, who believed in me and bestowed great feedback for this novel, Cristina Pinto-Bailey for her critique and author Sonja Yoerg, for her prodigious support. My editors for this novel, Elizabeth Buege and Jim Thomsen. My family, for supporting me during the long process of crafting these novels. Thanks to Kit Foster for the incredible cover design and Walter B. Myers for the fantastic flooded Earth imagery. Friend Stevie Bond for reading and supporting my writings. And a special thanks to all my reviewers and readers.

K.E. I
she gr
laced v
huge l
NASA
into he

Lannir
Stephe
MBA i

Lannin
multi-c
society
for the

She no
family.

Her de
**MELT**
*Birds* (1

CPSIA information can be obtained
at www.ICGtesting.com
Printed in the USA
LVHW041032070419
613259LV00001B/155